Hostile Aliens,
Hollywood and Today's News

Hostile Aliens, Hollywood and Today's News

1950s Science Fiction Films and 9/11

Melvin E. Matthews, Jr.

Algora Publishing
New York

ISBN-13: 978-0-87586-497-6 (trade paper)
ISBN-13: 978-0-87586-498-3 (hard cover)
ISBN-13: 978-0-87586-499-0 (ebook)

Library of Congress Cataloging-in-Publication Data —

Matthews, Melvin E., Jr.
    1950s science fiction films and 9/11: hostile aliens, Hollywood, and today's news /
Melvin E. Matthews, Jr.
        p. cm.
    Includes bibliographical references and index.
    ISBN 978-0-87586-497-6 (trade paper: alk. paper) — ISBN 978-0-87586-498-3 (hard
cover: alk. paper) — ISBN 978-0-87586-499-0 (ebook: alk. paper) 1. Science fiction films—
United States—History and criticism. I. Title.

    PN1995.9.S26M356 2007
    791.43'6150973—dc22

                        2006102140

Front Cover: From the 1986 remake of "Invaders from Mars" (director: Tobe Hooper)
Copyright: MGM. Credit: MGM/Photofest

Printed in the United States

To all dreamers and freedom-seeking people everywhere.

Table of Contents

Table of Illustrations

spaceship is stricken, they wanted nothing more than to repair their craft and be on their way. Credit: Universal International Pictures/Photofest.

Page 65   Exeter (Jeff Morrow, in white hair) protects Earth friends Rex Reason and Faith Domergue from the Metaluna mutant in *This Island Earth* (1955). Credit: Universal International Pictures/Photofest.

Page 73   The anxieties of the Cold War and the nuclear age produced fears that the world was about to be destroyed. Emblematic of these concerns was *When World Collide* (1951), in which Earth faces destruction, not from nuclear war, but from a passing planet. In this scene, New York's Times Square is inundated by flood waters unleashed by the passing planet. Credit: Photofest, Inc.

Page 76   In addition to doomsday fears, the international tensions of the '50s engendered a return to religion among Americans. In *The Next Voice You Hear* (1950), an average American family is reconnected to God when the latter speaks to mankind over the radio. Credit: MGM/Photofest.

Page 82   Forty-eight years before the attack on the World Trade Center, New York faced a nuclear age terror in *The Beast from 20,000 Fathoms* (1953), when a prehistoric rhedosaurus awakened by nuclear testing stormed through the city. Credit: Photofest.

Page 87   Giant ants that mutated due to radiation from the first test of the atomic bomb in 1945 emerge from their hiding place in the desert of New Mexico in Warner Bros.' *Them!* (1945). The success of this film inspired the wave of atomic mutation films of the '50s. Credit: Warner Bros./Photofest.

Page 89   Carrying the fight to the enemy: Having located the ants' sanctuary in the Los Angeles sewers, soldiers move in to destroy them at the conclusion of *Them!* Nearly fifty years later, real-life American soldiers would be sent to confront and destroy enemies in Afghanistan and Iraq. Credit: MGM/Photofest but most likely Warner Bros./Photofest.

Page 98   The ultimate nuclear age monster crashes through the electrical barrier setup to defend Tokyo in the Japanese production Gojira (1954), later released in America as *Godzilla: King of the Monsters* (1956). Inspired in part by a real-life nuclear accident, Godzilla personified the Japanese people's reaction to the use of the atomic bomb against them during World War II and was the only '50s monster to outlast the decade. Credit: Rialto/Photofest.

Page 100 & 101   *The Incredible Shrinking Man* (Grant Williams) (p. 100) battles for his life against a tarantula, while *The Amazing Colossal Man* (Glenn Langan) (p. 101) goes berserk in Los Vegas. Both men's plight resulted from exposure to radiation, demonstrating the vulnerability of everyone to the dangers of the nuclear age. Similarly, everyone feels vulnerable in the post-9/11 world. Credit: Universal Pictures/Photofest.

Page 114   Five years before the September 11 attack on the Pentagon, aliens zapped the White House in *Independence Day* (1996). Credit: 20th Century Fox/Photofest.

Page 118   Shortly after *Independence Day*, Washington was again buzzed by aliens in Tim Burton's *Mars Attacks!* (1996). Compare this scene with another alien landing at the Capitol in *Earth vs. the Flying Saucers* (1956). Credit: Warner Bros./Photofest.

Page 119   See above caption. Credit: Columbia Pictures/Photofest.

Page 121   Philip Kaufman's 1978 remake of *Invasion of the Body Snatchers* presented a more graphic depiction of the duplication process. Here the alien duplicate is actress Brooke Adams. Credit: United Artists/Photofest.

Page 124   Compared to the hostile alien invaders of the 1950s, the kindly *E.T.: The Extra-Terrestrial* (1982) charmed and united people during the economically troubled early 1980s, leading some to equate him with Jesus Christ. Credit: Universal Pictures/Photofest.

Page 130   As Y2K fears abounded on the eve of the 21st Century, doomsday fears once again became popular movie themes. Two 1998 releases dealt with the havoc unleashed by galactic threats crashing into the Earth. In *Deep Impact*, a comet crashes into the

INTRODUCTION

1950s Science Fiction Films and 9/11 is far more than a well-researched summary of science fiction films. Author Melvin E. Matthews, Jr. examines one of America's most popular film forms and provides a thoughtful interpretation that should tantalize not only fans of the science fiction genre but also sociologists, film historians, and politicians.

The most memorable sci-fi films of the fifties were primarily entertainment vehicles. The bigger the monster, the bigger the box office. However, Matthews has looked far beyond the films' gross receipts and found a fascinating sociological correlation between sci-fi and society.

In the 1950s, when I did *It Conquered the World*, the headlines were dominated by threats to America and to civilization — including the Cold War, the McCarthy hearings, and atomic development. Mankind's future was at stake and Matthews probes deeply to show how the sci-fi movies of our era reflected America's hysteria and how that hysteria is related to current world events.

Matthews's thesis is supported by astute observation and keen interpretation of our era's films, especially *Invasion of the Body Snatchers*, *It Came from Outer Space*, *The Day the Earth Stood Still*, and *The War of the Worlds*.

In addition, Matthews's two years of research has resulted in a bonanza for Sci-fiers. He describes in detail how film costume and special effects wizards designed and created virtually every significant sci-fi alien, monster, and mutant that audiences have so enjoyed — and feared.

Beverly Garland

AUTHOR'S INTRODUCTION

Historically, American terror films became popular entertainment during crisis moments. Undoubtedly, the classic horror films that made stars of Bela Lugosi and Boris Karloff became popular during the Great Depression because they provided an escape from the genuine horrors of economic suffering. The genre's popularity carried over into World War II. Similarly, science fiction was a Hollywood staple during the Cold War, when anxieties about Communist subversion and nuclear war gave rise to stories of extraterrestrials and radiation-sired mutations. Instead of directly facing up to the realities of Communism and nuclear war, Hollywood addressed these issues metaphorically: Alien invaders represented the Russians, while giant ants personified the Bomb, just as Godzilla embodied Hiroshima for the Japanese.

It can be said that the genesis of this book began against the backdrop of the Cold War when I was a first grader at Garden City Elementary School in Roanoke, Virginia, during the 1961-1962 school year. Civil defense and fallout shelters were hot issues at the time, and my classmates and I were marched into the school hallway as part of civil defense drills. One day, thinking I was supposed to miss the school bus home as part of a civil defense drill, I walked down Garden City Boulevard toward home. I would have walked all the way, too, if my teacher had not seen me, stopped, picked me up, and driven me home.

At the same time, one of the neighbors on our street, Tiny Thompson, was an on-air personality at the NBC affiliate station WSLS. On Saturday evening, Thompson hosted *Saturday Theater*, which featured recent science fiction films. Thompson had a gimmick: When hosting the show, he sat with a mynah bird perched on his shoulder. As a youngster, I was too scared to watch these films; I finally sat down and watched the giant ant classic *Them!* in its entirety. If memory serves me correctly, in 1964 Mom took me and a friend, Al Albany, downtown to the now vanished Jefferson Theater to see two horror films: *The Curse of the Living*

Corpse and *The Horror of Party Beach*, the latter a '50s style film combining elements of beach party, motorcycle, and mutation films. Even earlier, my parents took me to another now-defunct film establishment, the Riverside Drive-In, where I saw my first Godzilla film, *King Kong vs. Godzilla*. During these years, I assembled the classic Aurora movie monster model kits and had a copy of *Famous Monsters of Filmland* magazine.

The memories of that era faded over time. At the end of the 1960s, they began resurfacing. As a ninth grader, I saw a copy of *Life's* end-of-the-decade issue where one page featured a photograph of a family in their fallout shelter. By the time I saw the magazine, that image seemed faraway but then it came back to me. More memories returned when, as a sophomore in High School, I discovered a book in the school library, Frank Manchel's *Terrors of the Screen*, which included a brief mention about the science fiction films of the 1950s that Tiny Thompson had introduced on television during my early school years.

Out of all this emerged my interest in the '50s. For me, the movie monsters and civil defense symbolized a "placid" era that gave way to the chaotic, psychedelic '60s. In the 1980s I began writing a book about the late '50s and early '60s, but then put it aside to get a BA degree in History and Communications. My senior thesis in History dealt with the Cold War's impact on American cinema in the '50s. Once college was completed, I wrote two book-length manuscripts on the '50s, neither of which went anywhere.

Then came September 11.' An article in *Time* appearing shortly after the attacks caught my attention. It described how great historical events from World War I onward have shaped popular culture. This gave me the idea for a history of popular culture from World War I to the War on Terror. An editor I consulted suggested that, as my expertise was in pop culture, a history of the '50s could be tied to September 11, citing concerns over civil liberties that arose during both eras. Thus the book that emerged from that labor is now a reality.

Several people deserve acknowledgement for their contributions to this book: Beverly Garland, star of 41 feature films and nearly 700 television programs and a successful businesswoman, graciously provided comments on her participation in the motion picture *It Conquered the World*, as well as providing general comments; Mark Dellinger, an attorney, furnished advice without being greedy about his fee; Robyn Schon shared her business expertise in reviewing my contract; Chris Hartness, my computer repairman, helped me master the techniques of transferring WordPerfect documents to Microsoft Word; and Eleanor Levine helped edit the final manuscript. I also thank Algora Publishing for their work in preparing the book for publication; and the staff of Photofest for all their assistance in providing the photographs for the book.

Melvin E. Matthews, Jr.

PROLOGUE

"It was like a movie." Thus did media commentator and film critic Neal Gabler characterize the attacks on the World Trade Center in New York City and the Pentagon in Washington, DC, on September 11, 2001 and the public's reaction to those events. First there was an explosion and resulting fireball, followed by the collapse of the buildings, "the dazed and panicked victims," finally culminating in the President's speech promising action — all of which could have been drawn from a movie. Life again imitated art when the White House press secretary reported threats to the presidential plane, reminiscent of the movie *Air Force One*.

The plotters who planned the events of 9/11, in Gabler's view, had drawn from Hollywood images to create their "own real-life disaster movie," one greater than anything Hollywood could offer and surpassing even the 1995 Oklahoma City bombing. When the first of the Twin Towers was attacked, no camera could be expected to be present to record the event; hence the terrorists arranged for a second attack, after sufficient time had elapsed; that second impact would definitely be recorded and replayed from different angles for a good long while.

The planning of the operation seemed to be like a movie as well. One could visualize the perpetrators making their plans "in a series of quick parallel cuts," stowing knives in bags, then driving to the airports to board the planes; and then jumping from their seats to take over the planes and execute their deadly scheme.

It was at this point that the terrorists' movie ended. But, for Americans, this was Act I. This would be followed by Act II — the investigation and hunt for the perpetrators — and, finally, Act III — retribution and America triumphant.[1]

One scene, recorded as it actually happened during the tragedy of September 11, again illustrated the cinematic quality of the scenario. That morning, immediately after the World Trade Center had been hit, a team of video-journalists was

1 Neal Gabler, "This Time, The Scene Was Real," *The New York Times*, 16 Sept. 2001, 4-2.

dispatched into the streets of New York City to record, live, as the videocassette of their footage says, "the horror and human drama of the unfolding tragedy." At 10:28 a.m., the trade center's North Tower collapsed, unleashing a massive cloud of dust and debris that rolled down the streets. The cloud rolled by what appears to be a coffee shop where one of the videographers happened to be rolling her camera. She was hustled inside the shop, her camera still running. As she continued filming, the dust cloud rolled by the shop window, like a giant blob, shutting out the daylight. "The world just went black," a voice is heard over the scene saying, "and, at that point, everybody was scrambling to breathe. There was no daylight at all." Over all this, the videographer is heard hysterically conveying her thanks for being rescued.[2]

Looking at that scene could evoke a feeling of déja vu. After all, it had been a mere three years since the Big Apple had trembled under Godzilla's onslaught and, 45 years before that, the *Beast from 20,000 Fathoms* had wreaked havoc in the same city.

The years immediately preceding 9/11 were saturated with Hollywood images of disaster. Besides the aforementioned *Godzilla* (1998), aliens had zapped New York, Los Angeles, the White House, and the Capitol Building in *Independence Day* (1996), while asteroids and meteors slammed into Earth, creating havoc in New York in *Deep Impact* and *Armageddon* (both 1998).

Even earlier, during the 1950s (seen nostalgically as *Happy Days*), America had faced destruction from invading aliens (though occasionally some of these otherworldly visitors were benign) or atomic mutants — the latter the result of man's nuclear weapons testing. Martians sought to conquer Earth in George Pal's *The War of the Worlds* (1953); alien ships crashed into the Washington Monument and the Capitol Building in *Earth vs. the Flying Saucers* (1956); giant mutant ants emerged from the New Mexican deserts to menace Los Angeles in *Them!* (1954).

One film professor has noted that movies help determine how we view the world. In that sense, the science fiction films of the '50s, "with their depiction of alien attacks against the United States, helped encourage the spread of a paranoid style: a tendency to see conspiracies as the driving force behind political developments." He notes that scenes of urban destruction have been symbols for forces the public feared. In that sense, *Godzilla* symbolized Japan's unease over nuclear weapons, while *Invasion of the Body Snatchers* was a metaphor for what Americans perceived as communist brainwashing.[3]

Half a century separates the 1950s from the September 11 era. Comparing the two eras in a *New York Times* article shortly after the World Trade Center's demise, Patricia Leigh Brown found similarities and differences between them. Threats of doomsday in both eras attracted entrepreneurs: salesmen peddled fallout shelters door-to-door during the Cold War, while their September 11 counterparts sold gas masks and Cipro — the latter an antidote to anthrax (don't forget the

2 *America 911: We Will Never Forget*, prod. Michael Rosenbaum, Spectrum Films, Camera Planet.com, 2001.

3 Steven Mintz, "Addressing Tragedy in the Classroom," H-net, www2.h-net.msu.edu/ teaching/journals/sept11/mintz/teaching.html) 20 Oct. 2002.

anthrax scare that immediately followed 9/11). The Cold War-era Federal Civil Defense Administration promoted the publication of bogus newspaper front pages and entire issues of magazines depicting a fictitious post-doomsday world. Civil defense messages were targeted at specific groups. Bert the Turtle taught American children how to "Duck and Cover." Their mothers were told to supply their fallout shelters with canned foods and other survival items in the same way their grandmothers supplied their pantries, making nuclear war merely another household issue.

In the September 11 world, anxiety prevention counsel is no longer gender specific: an issue of *Men's Health* provided its readers with the "25 Best Ways" for men to protect their families, including "leveling with them" and avoiding obesity as "a fit man evacuates his family faster from a burning house." According to *Ladies' Home Journal* reader polls taken after the terrorist attacks, revenge fantasies had supplanted sexual dreams, with 26% of poll respondents saying they had them at least once daily.

Not to be left out, the newly created Office of Homeland Security planned to issue guidelines to help Americans prepare for possible domestic terrorist assaults. The State Department's online "Reward for Justice" program proclaimed that children of terrorists "often enroll in schools in the middle of the year and may leave prior to the end with little or no notice."

The similarities aside, a vast difference exists between the America of the early twenty-first century and that of half a century ago. Then, Cold War civil defense measures were meant to prepare Americans for nuclear attack, not for fighting a war. The September 11 attacks convinced Americans that the unimaginable notion of a direct assault on the United States itself was quite possible. Moreover, Americans' attitudes toward their government have changed radically during the last fifty years. In the 1950s Americans possessed unquestioning faith in what their government told them. After all, this was the era when everyone trusted Ike to look after them. There was a sense of national unity and consensus. Vietnam and Watergate shattered that unity, creating a sense of skepticism that prevails to this day. The anxieties of the Cold War/nuclear age prompted an upswing in American religiosity. The early 2000s have witnessed an erosion of Christianity from the American mainstream in favor of tolerance of other religions and a belief that it is politically correct to accept diverse faiths.

Despite the similarities and differences between the '50s and the September 11 age, one common thread links both eras: the American tendency to dismiss hysteria. During the '50s, most Americans weren't stampeding to build fallout shelters and, as Patricia Leigh Brown noted, shortly after 9/11, a sense of calm returned to American life: "Sales of *nouveau* shelters are on the wane, and having now stashed away drinking water and duct tape, Americans appear to be overcoming their jitters and, lured by bargain fares, are beginning to fly again. . . . And no one has proposed the contemporary equivalent of 'Bert the Turtle' — yet."[4]

Before the '50s, very few science fiction films came out of Hollywood. Those filmed in the 1930s were mainly British productions set thousands of years in the future, in a world where the inhabitants wore togas and said things like, "Our Brother, the Giver of Power, is yonder." One critic noted that people of the future wore Tudor attire, looking more like they lived in the past. Science fiction virtually disappeared from the screen during World War II. Then, "a few of the early postwar space movies," noted film historian Nora Sayre, "suggested a return to the frontier and a revival of the pioneer spirit among those who set off to explore the moon."[5]

The science fiction boom of the '50s owed its existence to several reasons: World War II and the advent of the atomic bomb; a change in the public's attitude toward scientists, which elevated such figures as Wernher von Braun and Albert Einstein to celebrity status; the Cold War between East and West, and Soviet and American competition in rocket technology; anxiety over nuclear war and paranoia over communist subversion; and the "flying saucer" scare. Consequently, '50s science fiction films were characterized by several themes: the atomic bomb and its consequences; the effects of atomic radiation; alien invasion and alien possession; and world destruction.[6]

Like war films, science fiction films depicted America confronting a crisis situation, requiring everyone to unite together to win — only this time, not just America but civilization itself is at stake. Compared with '30s horror films, '50s science fiction movies were more subdued both in atmosphere and in the acting — the latter illustrating '50s conformity. Washington and science became the saviors of America in science fiction. Science created the monster but also provided the means to eradicate it. Peter Biskind's *The Other* featured alien monsters threatening the center. The latter also distrusted utopianism as illustrated by advanced otherworldly civilizations that attacked Earth because they had despoiled their own home worlds.[7]

Many of the themes born of the Cold War also apply to the present War on Terrorism that began with September 11, 2001. As with the alien invaders, America is told that it faces an implacable enemy out to destroy our way of life, and any disunity, any questioning of ends or means, is painted as disloyalty. We once again turn to Washington for guidance and deliverance from the threat. The enemy, they say, seeks to replace our way of life with his own Islamic system. While times have changed, the threat remains just about the same.

---

4 Patricia Leigh Brown, "Armageddon Again: Fear in the 50's and Now," *The New York Times* 23 December 2001, 10.

5 Nora Sayre, *Running Time: Films of the Cold War* (New York: The Dial Press, 1982) 191-192.

6 John Brosnan, *Future Tense: The Cinema of Science Fiction* (New York: St. Martin's Press, 1978) 72-73.

7 Peter Biskind, *Seeing Is Believing: How Hollywood Taught Us to Stop Worrying and Love the Fifties* (New York: Pantheon Books, 1983) 102-104, 111-115.

CHAPTER 1. HOSTILE ALIENS: THE THING AND THE WAR OF THE WORLDS

"I first became aware of a movie called *The Thing* when I saw the original film," recalls film director John Carpenter. "It was 1952, and I would've been about four or five years old. I think I saw it in a re-release. It was one of those films where, as you watched it, it was so frightening, that my popcorn flew out of my hands. In other words, when they went up to the doorway and they had this Geiger counter, and they opened the door and he's [the Thing] right there, I went nuts. I went crazy."[1]

Carpenter was describing his reaction to the film that heralded the "monster-on-the-loose/invasion" movies of the 1950s: *The Thing (from Another World)*, produced by Howard Hawks and directed by Christian Nyby, with an uncredited assist from Hawks. A box office hit when initially released in 1951, it was re-released in 1954 and 1957, again scoring, and it still holds up today.[2]

The Thing and its ilk wouldn't have been possible without the "flying saucer" craze that began after World War II. In reality, "flying saucer" or UFO sightings were nothing new. The first such sightings reported in the United States dated back to the 1890s, when people in several states reported viewing "airships" that traveled from five to two hundred miles per hour, making odd noises; blue, red, and green lights; and people peering out the windows at those on the ground. The next time UFO sightings were reported was during World War II, when American pilots reported seeing them on bombing missions over Germany and

---

1 "John Carpenter's The Thing: Terror Takes Shape," *The Thing*, dir. John Carpenter, Universal Home Video, 1988.

2 Kenneth Von Gunden and Stuart H. Stock, *Twenty All-Time Great Science Fiction Films* (New York: Arlington House, 1982) 26-27.

Japan. A flood of UFO reports in Western European and Scandinavian countries followed this in the immediate postwar period.[3]

The modern flying saucer era began the afternoon of 24 June 1947, when Kenneth Arnold, a thirty-two-year-old Boise, Idaho, businessman, flying over Washington State's Cascade Mountains, experienced a blue-white flash he initially took to be an explosion. This was followed by another blue-white flash, which came from the north, ahead of Arnold's plane. In the far distance, he witnessed dazzling objects skimming the mountaintops at amazing speed. Arnold thought they were a squadron of new Air Force jet fighters. Though the distance was difficult to determine, Arnold believed they might be twenty miles away, nine of them flying in a tight sequence. Every few seconds two or three of the mysterious crafts would dip or bank slightly, reflecting sunlight from their mirror-like surfaces. Arnold judged their wingspan to be forty to fifty feet, and decided to assess their speed. The time on his panel clock, when the first craft zoomed past Mount Rainier, was exactly one minute to 3:00 p.m. The elapsed time, when the final one zoomed past the summit of Mount Adams, was one minute, forty-two seconds. Consulting his map, Arnold noted that the peaks were forty-seven miles apart. He deduced that the speed was 1,656 miles per hour, almost three times faster than any jet he knew of.

Touching down at Yakima around 4:00 p.m., Arnold told his story to Central Aircraft's manager Al Baxter, who, in turn, summoned a number of his pilots. One of them opined that what Arnold had seen might be a salvo of guided missiles from a contiguous test range. Yet they were not aware of any rockets that could bank and turn.

Taking off for Pendleton, Oregon, shortly afterward, Arnold was met by reporters. Despite some skeptical questions, Arnold held fast to his story. Asked to characterize what he'd seen, Arnold thought they resembled speedboats in rough water, or perhaps the tail of a Chinese kite blowing in the wind. He then said, "They flew like a saucer would if you skipped it across the water."

Within days of the Cascades affair, at least twenty other people all over the nation said they'd made similar sightings, some of which reportedly happened the same day Arnold saw his. Some were made earlier, some a day or so later. Just the same, the modern saucer era had begun.[4]

In all, there were seventy-nine reported sightings in 1947; from then until the end of the 1950s hundreds of sightings were reported yearly.[5] Fueling the flying saucer phenomenon was the publication in 1950 of an article in *True* magazine, "The Flying Saucers Are Real." Its author, retired Marine Corps Major Donald E. Keyhoe, asserted that the reason behind the Air Force's denial of UFO sightings was that it knew that they originated in outer space and was powerless to stop them. In the wake of Keyhoe's article, there was a steady increase in saucer sight-

---

3 J. Ronald Oakley, *God's Country: America in the Fifties* (New York: Dembner Books, 1986) 364.

4 The Editors of Time-Life Books, *Mysteries of the Unknown: The UFO Phenomenon* (Alexandria: Time-Life Books, 1987) 36-27.

5 Oakley 364.

ings; they were being reported at the rate of four a day during 1952. That same year witnessed perhaps the most famous sightings of the era: On the evening of 19-20 July, unusual flashes of light were reported over Washington, DC, accompanied by strange radar readings. Numerous airline crews reported unusual sightings. Air Force interceptors were dispatched to investigate but found nothing.[6] A second incident over the nation's capital occurred on July 26. Discussing the episodes with reporters afterward, Major-General John Samford, Air Force Intelligence Chief, asserted they resulted from temperature inversions and "radar images," supposedly ground lights reflected on the undersides of clouds.[7]

Shortly afterward, a new element was added to the pattern: "contactees," those people who claimed to have personally met aliens. The first such individual, George Adamski, who happened to operate the snack stand at Mount Palomar, said he had encountered a man with lustrous blonde hair shortly after he witnessed the landing of a spaceship. Both Adamski and his otherworldly friend conversed with each other telepathically. The alien, who said he was a Venusian and requested not to be photographed so as to remain hidden, had come to Earth because of atomic bombs. Following this initial encounter, Adamski began seeing others everywhere, especially in bars. Other contactees began telling their stories; eventually they began holding a yearly gathering at Yucca Valley, California, where they attracted paying visitors. Stressing intergalactic harmony as an issue, one contactee campaigned for the United States Senate, garnering 171,000 votes.[8]

Owing to the military ramifications of UFO sightings, it fell to the US Air Force to investigate them. The air force decided that the majority of the sightings were of weather balloons, planets, lightning, artificial satellites (after 1957, the year the Russian *Sputnik* was launched), regular aircraft, and other natural occurrences, in addition to the inescapable hoaxes and optical illusions. The air force conceded that it couldn't account for some of the sightings. Still, many people asserted that air force and civilian government officials were stonewalling or hiding the truth to prevent disclosing the government's incapacity to investigate or intercept UFOs.[9]

Both the atomic age and the flying saucer craze of the postwar era signified a popular unease about where science had brought humanity. Against this backdrop, Hollywood began the extraterrestrial invasion of Earth in the 1950s with *The Thing.*

The man behind the film was an old Hollywood hand, Howard Hawks, who specialized in films epitomizing rugged, undaunted masculinity. His work covered nearly every film genre that showed men in conflict: crime melodramas

---

6 Geoffrey Perret, *A Dream of Greatness: The American People, 1945-1963* (New York: Coward, McCann & Geoghegan, 1979) 155.

7 Mark A. Vieira, *Hollywood Horror: From Gothic to Cosmic* (New York: Harry A. Abrams, Inc., 2003) 165.

8 Perret 257.

9 Oakley 364-365.

(*Scarface*, 1932; *The Big Sleep*, 1946); war dramas (*The Road to Glory*, 1936; *Sergeant York*, 1941); air dramas (*Only Angels Have Wings*, 1939); rough battle-of-the-sexes comedies (*His Girl Friday*, 1940); and Westerns (*Red River*, 1948). "Hawks believed that the essence of drama," wrote Chris Steinbrunner and Burt Goldblatt, "was the pitting of strong, individualistic men against odds within a stark setting. He enjoyed working in the simplistic Western form where tough men faced (with few weapons except their own courage, loyalty, and camaraderie) a nearly overwhelmingly hostile nature." Hawks believed that the Western format could be transferred to science fiction.

Hawks was one of the first to recognize the possibilities the postwar science fiction publishing boom held for the movies, and he had purchased one such tale, *Who Goes There?*, originally penned in 1938 by John W. Campbell, Jr., editor of *Astounding Science Fiction* magazine. The latter was rechristened *Analog*, with Campbell its editor until he died in 1971.[10]

Written under Campbell's pen name, Don A. Stuart, *Who Goes There?* focuses on an American polar expedition that discovers a spaceship and its occupant that have been frozen in Antarctica for 20 million years. The spaceship is accidentally destroyed but the alien survives, carried back in a block of ice to the scientists' camp. The extraterrestrial's appearance is quite unsettling: blue-skinned, red-eyed, and clearly evil. Even encased in the ice, the alien is frightening to behold:

> "Three mad, hate-filled eyes blazed up with a living fire, bright as fresh-spilled blood, from a face ringed with a writhing, loathsome nest of worms, blue, mobile worms that crawled where hair should — "

The creature thaws out, but instead of decaying, comes back to life: a shape-shifting, telepathic monster possessing the ability to take control of the protoplasm of any living being — animal or man — transforming it into one of its own while still retaining the abilities and appearance of the original.

From here, the scientists seek a means to tell human and monster apart. Campbell's tale established a pattern for the scientific problem story, where reason, science, and resolve all merge to solve a problem. This kind of story would reappear in *Astounding/Analog*.[11]

Hawks' film differs from Campbell's story in that it (the film) is set in the Arctic, and the Thing, instead of being a shape-shifter, is an eight-foot, man-shaped vegetable, resembling the Frankenstein monster. The film opens when an extraterrestrial vehicle crashes in the Arctic. Upon being informed of the crash, Air Force Captain Pat Hendry (Kenneth Tobey) speculates that it might be the Russians, as they're "all over the Pole like flies." Locating an air force base in Alaska, the film reflected the widespread view that if the Russians attacked the United States, they would do so via the polar route. This, along with the flying saucer craze, reflected the Cold War anxieties then prevalent. The pilot of the alien ship

---

10 Chris Steinbrunner and Burt Goldblatt, *Cinema of the Fantastic* (New York: Galahad Books, 1972) 221, 223.

11 Alexei and Cory Panshin, *The World Beyond the Hill: Science Fiction and the Quest for Transcendence* (Los Angeles: Jeremy P. Tarcher, Inc., 1989), 272; Von Gunden and Stock 31.

is transported in a block of ice to a research station. After returning to camp with their guest, the scientists, led by Dr. Carrington (Robert Cornthwaite), and the soldiers, led by Captain Hendry, butt heads over what to do next. Carrington's party wants to thaw the alien out while Hendry wants to wait for orders from his commanding officer. Hendry sends out a message. Carrington tells the radio operator, "Richards, when you get your answer, I'll expect you to let *me* know." The Arctic lab, with its sense of isolation from the outside world, provides a perfect setting for the film.

Eventually, the Thing breaks free and flees into the icy polar wilderness, leaving death in its wake — and a hand that has been severed from its body by a husky. The scientists discover that the alien thrives on blood and, like any plant, can regenerate its severed part. They also find that when given plasma, the seeds found under the severed hand's fingernails spawn new aliens and grow at an astonishing rate. Carrington ponders this discovery:

> "A neat and unconfused reproductive technique of vegetation. No pain or pleasure. . . . No emotions, no heart . . . . Our superior in every way. . . . A being from another world as different from us as one pole from the other. If we can only communicate with it, we can learn secrets that have been hidden from mankind."

A clash now ensues between the scientists and the military over the Thing's fate: the former desire to preserve him to learn from it, while the latter, seeing it as a threat to humanity, want to destroy it. When Hendry begins searching for the alien, Carrington implores him not to harm it: "Captain, when you find what you're looking for, remember it's a stranger in a strange land. The only crimes involved were those committed against it. . . . All I want is a chance to communicate with it."

One of the most shocking scenes in the film, the one that unnerved the young John Carpenter so much, shows Hendry's men opening a door — and finding the Thing starring right in their faces! He roars, and takes a swipe at them with his clawed hand. Hendry's men immediately slam the door in the monster's face, riddle the door with machine gun fire, and secure it.

After Carrington grows some of the seed pods with blood plasma, his colleagues begin taking issue with him, arguing that the Thing could be the harbinger of an invasion of Earth — a notion Carrington dismisses: "There are no enemies in science. Only phenomena to study. We're studying one." His excitement over the discovery of the visitor has clouded his judgment.

To obtain nourishment, the Thing destroys the installation's heating system. Neither bullets nor the sub-zero weather affect it. The base secretary (Margaret Sheridan) must come up with a solution: What do you do with a vegetable? Cook it. Overruling the scientists, Hendry sets up an electric booby trap. Carrington makes one more attempt to communicate with the alien:

"Listen, I'm your friend. Look, I have no weapons. You're wiser than I. You must understand what I'm trying to tell you. Don't go any further, they'll kill you. They think you mean to harm us all. But I want to know you, to help you. Believe that. You're wiser than anything on Earth. Use that intelligence. Look at me, and know what I'm trying to tell you. I'm not your enemy. "

The Thing knocks Carrington aside, steps on the booby trap, and is destroyed. Scotty (Douglas Spencer), a newspaperman on the scene, informs the world:

> One of the world's greatest battles was fought and won today by the human race. Here at the top of the world, a handful of American soldiers and civilians met the first invasion from another planet. . . . And now, I bring you a warning. Everyone of you listening to my voice — tell the world. Tell this to everybody wherever they are: Watch the skies. Everywhere. Keep looking. Keep watching the skies.[12]

Hollywood legend aside, Orson Welles was in no way involved with *The Thing*. Official credit for directing the film goes to Christian Nyby, yet the evidence clearly indicates that Howard Hawks truly directed the film. Nyby, who was Hawks' film editor, desired to get into directing, so Hawks let him direct *The Thing*. But Nyby's subsequent directorial efforts, while ably done, failed to approach the potential of his directorial debut with *The Thing*. Nyby proved he was a superb director of TV action shows. Hawks, for his part, never admitted directing any portion of *The Thing*. Considering Campbell's story "an adult treatment of an often infantile subject," Hawks only used about four pages of it.

After cameras rolled on *The Thing*, Nyby, in Hawks' account, came to him with some problems, so Hawks consented to lend a helping hand. Hawks was on hand for every key scene, overseeing and making recommendations where he thought he should. "One imagines a 'suggestion' from Hawks at this point carried quite a bit of weight," wrote science fiction film historians Kenneth Von Gunden and Stuart H. Stock. They also wrote:

> *The Thing* really has all the marks of a Hawks film: tough, competent men, facing overwhelming odds; the humorous, overlapping dialogue; Nikki, the Hawksian woman, able to give as good as she gets from any man; the swift pacing; and the straightforward yet riveting camerawork.[13]

When asked years later about Nyby still saying he directed the film, Kenneth Tobey had this to say:

> "Chris has to sell himself. . . . I've told the truth in about fifteen newspapers, magazines, etc., and on the air, so I don't mind telling you what I told them: Howard Hawks directed it, all except one scene. Chris Nyby directed us coming through a door, and it's the worst scene in the picture. I've worked with Chris on television and he was very nice to me. (And *I* was very nice to *him*.) He was

---

12 Carlos Clarens, *An Illustrated History of the Horror Film* (New York: Capricorn Books, 1968) 122-123; *The Thing from Another World*, dir. Christian Nyby, Warner Home Video, 2003.

13 Von Gunden and Stock 31-32.

an editor prior to *The Thing*, and he was learning how to direct from Hawks. But Hawks didn't let him learn by *doing*."[14]

The Thing began shooting at the RKO studio on October 25, 1950, then moved to the California Consumers downtown icehouse in Los Angeles. Robert Corn-thwaite said:

> "That was where they'd shoot scenes where they had to have the breath showing. . . .Then we did go up, just before Christmas time as I recall [December 9, 1950], to Montana, where they had built the huge set for the flying saucer se-quence, and also the whole compound where the Arctic party was supposed to be — all the exteriors where the planes landed and so on. The locals made a big hoopla over us. Ken [Tobey] and Dewey [Martin] and I were adopted into the Blackfoot Tribe in a big ceremony with the chiefs, including the old chief who had signed the last treaty of peace between the Sioux nation and the United States."

The cast and crew waited for enough snow to fall to start filming, only to learn the snow didn't stay on the ground. "It was a high plateau up there at Cut Bank, Montana; that's why the US built a landing strip there for the takeoff to Alaska," Cornthwaite explained further:

> "...because the snow is blown off by the winds. . . . It never did [snow] — We never got a shot with actors. They did get a few brief shots with doubles. And then they had to rebuild the set (I think it was) Minot, North Dakota; and they were *thinking* about building a set up in the Yukon (I don't think they ever did). But they did shoot some stuff in North Dakota, apparently, which I was not with at all, it was all doubles. I had about six doubles in that picture before it was done."

Cornthwaite said the crew stayed at Cut Bank "a week or ten days, something like that." He added:

> "The whole cast was up there — that is, everybody that was concerned with the flying saucer scene. We shot that eventually in Encino, California, at the RKO Ranch. That was the last thing we shot, that was early March of 1951, and they had a date in April that they *had* to have the film ready by, for exhibition at Radio City Music Hall. Dimitri Tiomkin, who did the score, was composing the music as we went along, toward the end. I met him when we got together and rehearsed for him this flying saucer scene, so that he could compare the score for it. He had, of course, been watching the dallies and the rough cut, so that he could time his music by each frame of film. When we met and shook hands,

14 Tom Weaver, *Attack of the Monster Movie Makers: Interviews with 20 Genre Giants* (Jefferson: McFarland & Company, Inc., 1994) 346. A dissenting view comes from Robert Cornthwaite: "Here's the way I look at it: Howard Hawks was launching Chris, who had been his cutter on several pictures, as a director. But on a Hawks picture, there was only one boss; he was an absolute autocrat. There were a few — *very* few — occasions when Hawks was *not* on the set and Chris *was* the actual director. But Chris *always* deferred to Howard Hawks. . . Here was a great filmmaker, and Chris was not really in the same league. But as far as I was concerned, if it was between them that Chris was the director, then Chris was the direc-tor." Tom Weaver, *They Fought in the Creature Features: Interviews with 23 Classic Horror, Science Fiction and Serial Stars* (Jefferson: McFarland & Company, Inc., 1995) 117.

Dimi said, in his very thick Russian accent, 'you're just a boy!' He'd been used to seeing the old man on screen!"[15]

James Arness, who played the title role of *The Thing*, recalled a humorous incident one day when they'd finished filming at the ice house and were returning in a limo to the studio: "I hadn't cleaned off my makeup, and we got stalled in downtown traffic. As we waited at a light, the guy I was with thought it would be funny if I jumped out and bought a paper at a nearby newsstand. So, in all my makeup, I went up to the stand and said something like 'Hey, give me an *LA Times*, arg-gh-gh.' I growled, thinking the joke would be obvious. But the frightened newsman abandoned his stand, and pedestrians stopped dead in their tracks. People just couldn't figure out if I was real or what. Finally they decided I was in costume, just another Hollywood screwball, and went about their business."

There was another less than humorous episode after the film was released "I got a call one day from the studio," Arness wrote, "and it seemed a young boy had seen the movie in Georgia and gone catatonic. He was in a hospital and wouldn't talk to anyone. They asked me to go and see him, convince him the alien was not real and I was the actor. Of course I said yes, but before I could hop a plane, the boy recovered." As to why such a reaction happened, Arness theorized that "the picture was so realistic and people were genuinely scared when they watched it. Perhaps memories of the 1938 Orson Welles radio show *The War of the Worlds* still lingered in their minds."[16]

The air force declined Hawks' request for assistance with the film on the grounds that they had disproved the existence of flying saucers; why should they help make a film about one?[17]

While there is disagreement among film enthusiasts as to how Arness's makeup as the alien contributes to the film's impact, Hawks and makeup artist Lee Greenway knew that a bug-eyed monster wouldn't have been as effective. The best monsters are the most human looking, because the audience can relate more to them. Pre-production, Greenway conducted makeup experiments on Arness to come up with the creature's design. Arness had been chosen for the alien role in part because of his six-foot, five-inch frame. Greenway made approximately fifteen different test sculptures with mortician's wax. Each time he found one he liked, he and Arness presented it to Hawks for approval. According to one story, the final version caused a woman in a nearby car to faint at a red light while they were on their way to see Hawks. John "J. J." Johnson described how the makeup worked:

> "The makeover, which took about two hours to apply, entailed the use of a long piece of foam rubber that fit snugly over the actor's nose and cheeks, then wrapped around his ears and stretched on down to his neck. An air valve containing colored water was built into the appliance, which extended up over his

15 Weaver, *They Fought* 114-115.

16 James Arness with James E. Wise, Jr., *James Arness: An Autobiography* (Jefferson: McFarland & Company, Inc., 2001) 80.

17 Von Gunden and Stock 34.

forehead. The vein-like valve tubing was attached to a small football bladder partially filled with air. When Arness breathed, a belt that was tied around his chest would help expel air from the bladder causing small bubbles in the water. The colored water effect accomplished the two-fold purpose of adding to the intellectual carrot's eerie appearance and keeping Arness's head cool underneath the appliance. Once the apparatus was sealed down with spirit gum, Greenway then built up the forehead and stippled over the edges of the rubber prosthetic with a liquid adhesive. Greenway stuck around the set during filming to touch up any smudges to Arness's makeup."[18]

In addition to making up Arness, Greenway had to mold and bake a pair of dismembered alien right arms. One was used in the sled dog attack sequence in the snow, the second in Carrington's laboratory when it comes alive after feeding on canine blood. "Like the specially fitted claw gloves that Arness wore, these hands were made out of a plastic and rubber composition, but they weren't hollow inside."[19]

Kenneth Tobey emphatically asserted that Arness was so embarrassed about the makeup he wore as the Thing, "he never came and had lunch in the RKO commissary with us! (I have no idea where he did eat; maybe he brought his lunch.) But he was a *very*, very nice man."[20] "I think Jim has perhaps *always* been a little embarrassed about being an actor; I don't think he was ever what you would call a dedicated actor," says Robert Cornthwaite. Regarding *The Thing*, Cornthwaite adds:

> "Well, he's on-screen, what, two minutes or less out of the picture. It's kind of an embarrassment, to have the title role and not have a word to speak, and your on-screen time is minimal. Perhaps from that point of view, it was an embarrassment to him; I don't know, he never said so to me. I had very good relations with him. When we were doing that confrontation scene, in the tunnel, just before the Thing whomps Dr. Carrington, he said something complimentary about how I was doing, and he said, 'They'll have to come in for a big close-up of you here.' And I said, 'No, they won't.' He didn't understand Hawks' way to making a picture."[21]

The Thing was a landmark in that it was one of the first films ever to show a man completely set on fire. Because they couldn't use the typical rubber suit for the kerosene burning sequence, Lee Greenway employed Sinclair Paint to come up with a suitable fireproof replacement. For the filming of the scene, two stuntmen were used, each one wearing several layers of flame retardant clothing (specially treated boots, gloves, a mask). To brighten the flame effects, a flammable paste mixture was applied to the suit. The entire suit could endure fire for about two and a half minutes. Each stuntman had approximately a minute's worth of

---

18 John J. J. Johnson, *Cheap Tricks and Class Acts: Special Effects, Makeup and Stunts from the Films of the Fantastic Fifties* (Jefferson: McFarland & Company, Inc., 1996) 162-164.

19 Johnson 188.

20 Weaver, *Attack* 342.

21 Weaver, *They Fought* 121.

oxygen supplied through tubing from a cylinder of bottled air concealed just under the arm. Cornthwaite recalled:

> "I watched the entire filming of the fire scene, because it was fascinating and scary to be there on the set. They had two stuntmen playing the Thing, so that they could change off. They were equipped with about a minute's worth of oxygen, so once they were sealed in that suit, they had to shoot immediately. I remember one of the guys jumping up and down with impatience even though there was only so much oxygen."

One of the participants in the stunt, Tom Steele, said the effects chief nearly imperiled him:

> "Well, we worked three or four days with the special effects, with the suit and whatnot. The director said all he needed was two minutes of complete fire. So we did it and ran a test, and the director said, 'that's fine.' Then, when it came time to shoot it, the head of special effects [Linwood Dunn] told the fellow who was putting the liquid on me to put more on. But the other fellow knew me from Republic and wouldn't do it. We had a controlled fire and after two minutes it went out."[22]

For the final scene of the film, where the alien is electrocuted into nothingness, four actors were used: Arness, a shorter stuntman; Teddy Mangean, a midget actor; Billy Curtis; and, finally, a 12-inch miniature puppet.[23]

Despite appearing in only three '50s sci-fi films (*The Thing*, *The Beast from 20,000 Fathoms* — 1953 and *It Came from Beneath the Sea* — 1955) as well as one horror film (*The Vampire* — 1957), Kenneth Tobey seemed closely associated with the genre. He epitomized the dedicated military officer in '50s sci-fi.[24] Critic Manny Faber characterized his work in *The Thing* as a "fine, unpolished performance of a nice, clean, lecherous American Air Force Officer." "That," Von Gunden and Stock write, "comes off as a slightly left-handed compliment, but in *The Thing*, and most of his other films, Tobey conveyed a kind of clean-cut competence and masculinity that audiences always enjoyed — a kind of John Wayne-like strength without the physical height or swagger."[25]

Tobey had worked with Howard Hawks before on another picture, an experience that led to his casting in *The Thing*. He recalled, "I'd done a picture for Howard Hawks called *I Was a Male War Bride* (1949) that was supposed to be a daily job, but Gary Grant and Ann Sheridan laughed so hard at what I did (I have no idea *what* I did!) that Hawks kept writing in new scenes for me, And at the end of the picture he said to me, 'You know what, I'm gonna star you in a picture someday.' Nothing more was said. So I kept my eyes and ears open as far as his next picture, and when I read about *The Thing* in a paper, I called him and he said, 'I was just

---

22 Johnson 204-205.

23 Johnson 260.

24 Von Gunden and Stock 34; Bill Warren, *Keep Watching the Skies! American Science Fiction Movies of the Fifties*. Volume I: 1950-1957 (Jefferson: McFarland & Company, Inc., 1982), xii.

25 Von Gunden and Stock 34.

gonna call you. Come on in and see me.' So I don't know if there were any other people up for it. I know a lot of people *hated* me 'cause I got it."[26]

Tobey also had to pass muster with legendary billionaire Howard Hughes to appear in *The Thing*. He recalled:

> "I met him at about three-thirty in the morning! He had an aide call me at about two-thirty in the morning, and I'd come home a little... inebriated. I told the aide, 'I can't meet a man like Hughes at *this* hour' — I told the guy I'd been out playing and so forth. He said, 'He just wants to look at you.' I told him, 'Oh, I look *awful!*' — I'd just been awakened from sleep. The aide said, 'He just wants to *meet* you.' So I thought, well, I'd better go or he might say *no* [to casting Tobey in *The Thing*]. So I went over there and he took a look at me, and said, "Okay." That was it. [*laughs*]!...That was my Howard Hughes experience."[27]

Robert Cornthwaite also encountered Hughes — though not personally. He was slated for a photographic test to determine if he would look sufficiently old for the part of Dr. Carrington. Corthwaite noted:

> "After they got me into makeup, Mr. Hawks said to me, 'We'd like to do it in sound because I want Howard Hughes to hear your voice.' So we did a test in sound, in one take, and I raced back to Universal, back to work. And I didn't hear anything for a few days. Then my agent brought the [*Thing*] script one day to this ramshackle place where I was living; he threw it down and said, 'Well you've got the part.'" Cornthwaite also learned that his mother looked after Howard Hughes as a little boy when Cornthwaite's mother's father built oil rigs for the senior Hughes in Texas.[28]

The heroes of '50s science fiction films are military men or FBI agents who invariably distrust intellectualism and scientists; they shoot first and ask questions later when confronting aliens, even if the latter are friendly. "In those days," writes Nora Sayre, "almost no one was going to contradict the Pentagon or to accuse the FBI of malpractice."[29] Scientists were villains because they blocked the defenders of America by protecting the alien menace.[30] The latter clearly applies to Carrington in *The Thing*. Described by one film historian as "a borderline mad scientist," Carrington's scientific curiosity prompts him to act in the alien's interest, betraying the military and, ultimately, humanity's survival. He's a deluded appeaser, trying to negotiate with an implacable adversary. Carrington's deportment gives Hendry's men reason to distrust science and the Bomb. "Knowledge is more important than life. We split the atom," Carrington cries. "That sure made everybody happy," retorts one of Hendry's men. Not all scientists in *The Thing* are in Carrington's camp to be sure. But Carrington learns the hard way that it is Hendry, not him, who is in charge.[31]

---

26 Weaver, *Attack* 341.

27 Weaver, *Attack* 342-343.

28 Weaver, *They Fought* 113-114.

29 Sayre 196.

30 Sayre 198.

31 Biskind 127-129.

Above: Kenneth Toby, Robert Cornthwaite, John Dierkes, Edmund Breon, James Young in *The Thing from Another World*. Photo copyright by RKO Radio Pictures, 1951. Credit: RKO Radio Pictures/ Photofest.
Below: James Arness (as The Thing) in *The Thing from Another World*. Photo copyright by RKO Radio Pictures, 1951. Credit: RKO Radio Pictures/Photofest.

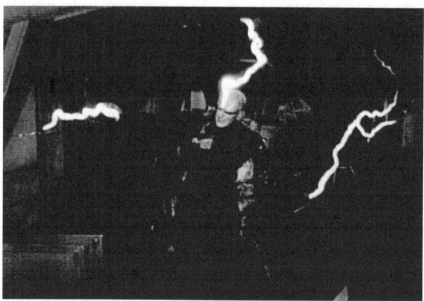

President Dwight D. Eisenhower arriving Apr. 22, 1954 at La Guardia Airport in New York, scheduled for a speech before the American Newspaper Publishers Association at the Waldolf-Astoria. No copyright provided. Credit: Photofest.

Indeed, the Hendry-Carrington struggle found a real-life counterpart in the 1952 Eisenhower-Stevenson presidential contest, which, in David J. Skal's words, "became a mass referendum on guts versus brains, men of action versus ivory tower intellectuals." Anti-intellectual sentiments weren't peculiar solely to the 1950s but trace back to what Skal calls "the puritanical distrust of prideful knowledge." Stevenson, in Richard Hofstadter's words, "became the victim of the accumulated grievances against intellectuals and brain-trusters which had festered in the American right wing since 1933." Moreover, the McCarthy era promoted an "at mosphere of fervent malice and humorless imbecility" in American affairs. The ordinary citizen "cannot cease to need or to be at the mercy of experts, but he can achieve a kind of revenge by ridiculing the wild-eyed professor, the irresponsible brain-truster, or the mad scientist. . . ."

Adlai Stevenson speaks in Hardford, CT (September 1952). No copyright provided. Credit: Photofest.

The Eisenhower-Stevenson contest — the military hero vs. the egghead — was reflected in '50s sci-fi films where the military resolved a crisis produced by "starry-eyed scientist intellectuals." Such a course was obvious given the recent American triumph in World War II. Yet Hofstadter felt the anti-intellectual sentiment of the '50s was merely part of a long tradition: "Filled with obscure and ill-directed grievances and frustrations, with elaborate hallucinations about secrets and conspiracies, groups of malcontents have found scapegoats at various times in Masons or abolitionists, Catholics, Mormons, or Jews, Negroes or immigrants, the liquor interests or the international bankers. In the succession of scapegoats chosen by the followers of Know-Nothingism, the intelligentsia have at last in our time found a place."[32]

In *The Thing*, Hawks preferred men of ideals who also took action ("practical men") over people who favored the abstract over reality. "In *The Thing*, it's the 'Scientist,' as symbolized by Carrington, who bears the brunt of Hawks' impatience with those who refuse to face what he at least considered the realities of life." Further: "*The Thing* is less anti-science that it is anti-Carrington, really anti-stupid. . . . *The Thing* ultimately stands against any attitude which places intellectual needs over human ones."[33] [34]*

The ultimate message of *The Thing* is there can be no appeasement of an implacable enemy. Only force will do. In the September 11 era, it's a message that is being promoted by a White House pushing an image of real-life Captain Hendrys doing battle with Islamic extremists, who, they say, like the Thing, are bent on world conquest.

Captain Hendry and his men managed to keep the threat of the Thing confined to a solitary Arctic base. Two years after the Thing's visitation, a greater, more catastrophic invasion descended on Earth.

The War of the Worlds

Except for *The Thing*, the majority of alien visitors in early '50s Hollywood films were friendly. That changed in 1953 with the success of Paramount's *The War of the Worlds*.[35] The inspiration for the film was H. G. Wells' 1898 science fiction novel of the same name. Set in Victorian times, Wells' story was a parable of the "alien" invasion of other cultures by industrially superior white societies, specifically the British. The latter, who were determined to broaden their empire, thought nothing of subduing weaker, less advanced peoples; it was their "white man's burden." In Wells' view, if man felt no guilt about murdering and oppressing his brother for almost any reason, then an advanced extraterrestrial race would do the same to humanity itself.[36]

A number of factors influenced Wells' novel. First, he was frequently in poor health and feared he would die young. Second, his early religious training exerted its continuing influence, suggesting to Wells that man might fall from his place of dominance. Third was the influence of scientific theorists who contended that

32 David J. Skal, *Screams of Reason: Mad Science and Modern Culture* (New York: W.W. Norton & Company, 1998) 181-182.

33 Von Gunden and Stock 36.

34 Hawks felt the anti-science angle made a better story. Steinbrunner and Goldblatt, 224.

35 *It Came from Outer Space*, dir. Jack Arnold, Universal Studios, 2002, "Feature Commentary with Film Historian Tom Weaver."

36 Von Gunden and Stock 41.

the law of entropy would result in the sun cooling and, consequently, the end of life on Earth and the other planets of the solar system.

The War of the Worlds easily fits into the "end of the world" tradition that contributed considerable religious imagery. The end of the world motif would reappear in Wells' writings: *In the Days of the Comet* (a collision between a heavenly body and Earth); *The World Set Free* (a colossal explosion); and *The Shape of Things to Come* (angels come to Earth to set up God's Kingdom).

The War of the Worlds was, moreover, one of several literary works showing the successful invasion of England: Sir George Chesney's *The Battle of Dorking* (1871); Sir William Butler's *The Invasion of England* (1882); William Le Quex's *The Great War in England in 1897* (1894); F. N. Maude's *The New Battle of Dorking* (1900).

All of the above expressed a predominant mood at the end of the nineteenth century known as *Fin de siecle* ("end of the century," which evoked a sense of the end of an age, or even the world), anticipation mixed with despair, nostalgic, decadent and fatalistic. Changes in art and in accepted conduct reflect the changing times; that which is old and commonplace vanishes or is replaced by things that are new, and seemingly strange or aberrant. Great change had characterized the nineteenth century, and there was a longing for a new beginning, a new century to rebuild the social and intellectual order.

The War of the Worlds was possibly the first book to depict humanity fleeing an implacable enemy, as well as the first book to depict humanity's first contact with a genuinely alien life form. In addition to being physically repulsive, *War*'s Martians consume human blood by injecting it into their veins — a practice Wells' narrator finds revolting. Still, he acknowledges: "I think that we should remember how repulsive our carnivorous habits would seem to an intelligent rabbit." This indicates an ability to take a different view of things, especially of how white men had enslaved "lower" races. As *War*'s narrator says, after hiding from the Martians: "Surely, if we have learned nothing else, this war has taught us pity — pity for those witless souls that suffer our domination."[37]

The effort to translate Wells' novel into a motion picture began when Paramount's Cecil B. DeMille bought it in 1925. After that, various plans were made to film it but all came to naught due to problems primarily in the areas of special effects and cost. The breakthrough came when George Pal joined Paramount in the early 1950s. With the completion of *When Worlds Collide*, Pal began searching through the studio's properties for another science fiction story, choosing *The War of the Worlds*. For the screenplay, Pal hired Barre Lyndon. For director, he tapped Bryon Haskin.

Owing to budget limitations, the story was updated to 1950s California, moving it from its original setting of England — a decision that didn't set well with many fans of the book. Years later director Bryon Haskin defended the switch: "A recent writer on science fiction films said it was bad to have removed the story from its identifiable background, but it was identifiable to Americans, and that's who we were making the picture *for*. In making our choice we did as Orson Welles had done. We transposed it to a modern setting, hoping to generate some of the

---

37 Von Gunden and Stock 94-96.

excitement that Welles had with his broadcast." "With all the talk about flying saucers," Pal explained, "*War of the Worlds* had become especially timely. And that was one of the reasons we updated the story."[38]

Linda Rosa, California, was chosen for the setting of the film. That out of the way, Barre Lyndon began penning the first draft of the script. Prompted by Pal, Lyndon dropped his original leading character, Major Bradley, for Pacific Tech nuclear physicist Dr. Clayton Forrester. Originally, Forrester was to be married, a father separated from his family, searching for them. The vice president in charge of production, Don Hartman, vetoed this idea, directing that Forrester have a "love interest." Pal reluctantly complied, directing Lyndon to write in the character of Sylvia Van Buren and toning down the violence in the first draft.

Hartman dismissed Lyndon's screenplay as a "piece of crap" and deposited it into a wastebasket. Associate producer Frank Freeman, Jr., came to the film's rescue, defending it to his father, Paramount president Y. Frank Freeman. DeMille spoke up in the film's behalf as well. The elder Freeman green-lighted the film.

After considering Lee Marvin for the role of Forrester, Pal opted instead for Gene Barry. Ann Robinson was signed to play Sylvia Van Buren.

A second-unit film crew began ten days of location shooting near Florence, Arizona in December 1951. Bryon Haskin and another crew were dispatched thirty-five miles northwest of Los Angeles to film the city's evacuation. In the hilly country encircling the Simi Valley, Haskin filmed the scenes of spectators viewing the atomic blast that failed to halt the Martian advance. The Arizona National Guard filled the role of Army troops.

Stage 18 served as the setting for the gully, which was the landing site of the first meteor. Segments of the LA evacuation were filmed on an unopened part of the Hollywood Freeway. Pal got the LA Police Department to seal off part of Hill Street on a Sunday morning to film scenes of Forrester searching for Sylvia. Principal photography was completed in mid-February 1952. During filming, Haskin was informed that Paramount had only the *silent* rights to the H. G. Wells book; filming would have to be terminated. Wells' son sold the "talkie" rights for another $7,000.

Stage 18 was cleared for four miniature sets with sky backings; of these sets the most complex was the LA street destroyed by the Martians. A back lot street was matched with 4-by 5-inch Ektachrome still pictures of LA's Bunker Hill, and then re-photographed on Technicolor film. A matte of the sky and background, done as an 8-by 10-inch blowup, was condensed to 35 mm film frame size, matched with the flame effects and Martian machines, and finally given live action.

The miniature street was constructed on a platform to permit the high-speed cameras to both film from street level and allow the cameras to get as close to the miniature buildings as needed. "Filming at approximately four times normal speed requires intense light levels, so the set was bathed in light."

To create an atomic bomb explosion, an assortment of colored explosive powders was placed on top of an airtight metal drum filled with explosive gas on

---

38 Brosnan 90.

Stage 7. Ignited by an electrical charge, the explosion climbed seventy-feet high, creating a perfect mushroom cloud on film.[39]

The War of the Worlds begins with a prologue explaining how the Martians' home world is dying, forcing them to search for a new world. They choose Earth. A meteor then falls near Linda Rosa, whose residents view the fallen extraterrestrial object as a potential boon to the local economy. Dr. Clayton Forrester, who was in the mountains with other Pacific Tech scientists, comes to have a look at the meteor and decides to stay when it proves radioactive.

That night, while everyone else is at a square dance and three deputies stand guard over the meteor, the latter begins unscrewing, revealing the cobra head and neck of the Martian machine. "It's a bomb. It's an enemy sneak attack," is the deputies' initial reaction to the sight. When they try to communicate with the Martians, the cobra head zaps them with its death-ray beam.

The military is called in to contain the invaders. When Sylvia's uncle, Pastor Matthew Collins, is incinerated by the Martians while trying to communicate with them, Sylvia screams and the troops open fire. Of that scene, Ann Robinson recalled:

> "My direction was, 'Now, Ann, when the red light hits your face, scream. Your uncle's being killed.' So I screamed once, and they said, 'Oh, my goodness.' So they did it one more time. By that time, I didn't have a third scream in me. I couldn't get it out."[40]

The Martians' heat rays and "skeleton beam" (so-named because they disintegrated whatever they hit) prove superior to the soldiers' tanks and other weapons, routing the Earthbound defenders. Forced to flee with the soldiers, Forrester and Sylvia take off in a small airplane, eventually finding sanctuary in an abandoned farmhouse. Their breakfast is interrupted by another Martian meteor crashing into the farmhouse. The scene in the kitchen of Forrester and Sylvia taking cover is reminiscent of civil defense footage of preparedness in the event of a nuclear attack. After Forrester regains consciousness from the meteor impact, both he and Sylvia have a close encounter with a Martian. Ann Robinson recalled:

> "Charles Gemora was the Filipino chap who played the monster. He must have made that costume to fit his own body, because he was a slight individual. He put that latex suit over his head and body — it came down to his hips. His fingers reached as far as his elbows, where there were three little rings attached to wires — that would make the suckered Martian fingers open and close. He knelt on a wooden dolly and very gently they rolled him into the scene. He couldn't see very well — in fact, maybe he couldn't see out of that tri-colored eye at *all*. Then that big arm of his was placed upon my shoulder — someone had to do it *for* him, place his arm on my shoulder, and then get out of the shot. I could hardly feel it, it was so gentle. We had to do that several times to get accustomed to it. Gene Barry pulled me away from him, Gemora got yanked out of the shot on the dolly and Gene threw a hatchet. Then in the next shot, you see the Martian's shadow run by and you see the hatchet sticking out of his chest. And

---

39 Von Gunden and Stock 98-100.

40 Von Gunden and Stock 91-93; *The Fantasy Film Worlds of George Pal*, dir. Arnold Leibovit, Arnold Leibovit Productions, Ltd., 1985.

> I always thought, 'This guy might have been nice!' Maybe we ruined a chance for peace because Gene Barry got overzealous and threw that hatchet! This Martian was just coming up behind me to tap me on the shoulder — he wasn't aggressive, he wasn't mean. Of course, the Martians *had* blown my uncle apart, along with a bunch of other people, but maybe *this* guy was the nice one who wanted to negotiate. And Gene 'thanked' him with a hatchet in the chest."[41]

Regarding the Martian's brief on-screen time in the film, author Robert Block explained that George Pal...

> "had enough foresight to realize that almost anything that was shown on the screen with the fairly crude special effects that were available would prove disappointing. So he heightened the audience's terror throughout. They saw what the monsters did but they didn't see the monsters — only for a few seconds on the screen. When it appeared, it had exactly the effect that he wanted, and showed, of course, George's genius for anticipating what was most effective with an audience."[42]

Forrester and Sylvia flee the farmhouse, making it back to Forrester's colleagues at Pacific Tech. Meanwhile, humanity fails to stop the Martians' worldwide advance. Nothing is mentioned of the Russians and the other communist bloc nations. "Are we to assume from this omission," wondered film historian John Brosnan, "that the Russians and the Martians were somehow in league with each other? If so, the term 'red planet Mars' takes on a whole new meaning."[43]

An attempt to destroy the Martians with the atomic bomb proves as fruitless as conventional weapons. The only remaining hope for mankind is "a biological approach": finding a weakness in the Martians' blood. Los Angeles is ordered evacuated, but as Forrester attempts to drive out of the city with instruments for biological research, a mob of looters overpowers him. They steal his truck and destroy his equipment. Forrester searches from church to church for Sylvia before finding her.[44] Man's weapons and science have failed to stop the Martians. Now, in the church, the minister prays, "O Lord, we pray thee — grant us the miracle of Thy divine intervention." As if on cue, the Martian ships begin crashing. "We were all praying for a miracle," says Forrester, as church bells sound. Over this, the film's narrator, Sir Cedric Hardwicke, intones:

> "The Martians had no resistance to the bacteria in our atmosphere to which we have long since become immune. Once they had breathed our air, germs which no longer affect us began to kill them. The end came swiftly. All over the world their machines began to stop and fall. After all that men could do

---

41 Weaver, *Attack* 298.

42 Arnold Leibovit, op. cit.

43 Brosnan 92. Filmmaker Nicholas Meyer elaborates on the Cold War theme of the film: "What's interesting about the movie. . .is what a product of the Eisenhower '50s that movie is. The Cold War and the McCarthy witch hunts played an enormous background role. It just permeated your thinking. . .Are the aliens in George Pal's Eastern European mind some version of the Communists?" "H. G. Wells: The Father of Science Fiction," *Special Collector's Edition: The War of the Worlds*, dir Byron Hansen, Paramount Pictures, 2005.

44 Von Gunden and Stock 91-93.

had failed, the Martians were destroyed and humanity was saved by the littlest things which God in His wisdom had put upon this Earth."[45]

Undoubtedly, *The War of the Worlds* is the most frightening alien invasion film of the 1950s. It was to its time what *Independence Day* was to the 1990s. Certainly *War*'s scenes of destruction, showing the Martians annihilating all before them, then proceeding to demolish Los Angeles with their heat ray weapon before being felled by the Earth bacteria, must have shocked and riveted audiences in 1953. The scenes of the Martians' attack on LA are like a premonition of the World Trade Center attacks on September 11.

The Martian attack in *The War of the Worlds* (1953). Photo copyright: Paramount Pictures, 1953. Credit: Paramount Pictures/Photofest.

Credit for bringing off the Martian attack so effectively in the film must go to the design of the Martian war machine with its manta-ray shape and snake-like death-ray emitter. Albert Nozaki, who designed the war machine, recalled:

"I would say the idea came almost full-bloom. . . . I was noodling one Sunday afternoon on a sketch pad, and the idea of this machine came like bolts in a comic section. One of the requirements. . . of this machine was that it had the menacing appearance. The manta ray concept did help some in that regard. Byron Haskin and Gordon Jennings — they both liked it immediately, and Pal particularly, I think, because it helped his concept of what this machine should

---

45 Biskind 117; *The War of the Worlds*, dir. Byron Haskin, Paramount Pictures, 1999. Forty-three years after *The War of the Worlds*, another virus, this time a computer virus, defeated the alien invaders of *Independence Day* (1996). "This, of course, explained IDIV's producer Dean Devlin, "is our allusion to the ending of *War of the Worlds*, when the alien invaders were killed by the common cold. And Roland (Emmerich) and I, as we were writing it,. . . .thought, "What would be the modern equivalent?" And we thought the modern equivalent would be a computer virus." *Independence Day: Five Star Collection*, dir. Roland Emmerich, 20th Century Fox Home Entertainment, 2000.

do in the picture. I think that was one of the things about Pal — that he made his concepts quite clear to us, I felt."[46]

Actress Ann Robinson believed the design of the Martin machine, in comparison to Klaatu's ship in *The Day the Earth Stood Still*, explained the personalities of the differing vehicles' occupants: "The machine we had in *The Day the Earth Stood Still*. . . was a flying saucer because the man [Klaatu] came to Earth to look after us, and take care of us and tell us to behave ourselves . . . where these people [the Martians] weren't coming to do anything but to harm us. . . Nothing looks more frightening in the ocean as this quiet, floating, beautiful sting ray. And then, of course, who likes the looks of a cobra with the full hooded head staring at you?"[47]

The original test designs for the Martian machine models featured three stilt-like legs of static beams of electricity. To blow sparks down the legs, the special effects crew employed a high velocity blower from a million volt electrical discharge. The tests on the special effects stage went well but the impact of utilizing a million volts of electricity on a litter-strewn sound stage with sparks flying would have endangered the crew, and the plan was dropped.

Made of copper, the Martian ships were painted a red to correspond to the Martian surface. Measuring 42 inches in diameter, they each had a wing-tip firing device, and a long snake-like neck with probing scanner. The models were both operated and supported by 15 very thin wires attached to a control trolley on an overhead track. This allowed the prop operators to control the models like they were puppets.

> These supporting wires also carried the electronic signals that controlled the cobra-like periscopes that shot laser-like heat beams. Jennings created the ray's light source by secreting a piece of red plastic shielding, a bulb, and a miniature fan in each machine. The slowly revolving fan blades alternately covered and uncovered the bulb's light, glowing through the plastic. This produced an eerie, pulsating effect, perfectly enhanced by a suitably haunting sound track.[48]

For the heat rays fired from the cobra head, burning welding wire was used. As it melted, a blowtorch behind it blew the wire out. The result was superimposed over the neck of the Martian ships.[49]

In addition to designing the Martian war machines, Albert Nozaki designed the Martian creature that briefly appeared on screen with Ann Robinson and Gene Barry. Once Nozaki completed the alien's design, Charles Gemora entered the picture to build it. According to legend, while Gemora was in George Pal's office adding finishing touches to the Martian costume, the latter knocked its creator to the ground. The incident prompted Pal to think the costume was too

46 Leibovit.

47 "Commentary by Ann Robinson and Gene Barry," *Special Collector's Edition: The War of the Worlds*, dir. Byron Haskin, Paramount Pictures, 2005.

48 Johnson 297.

49 Von Gunden and Stock 100.

risky for anyone else to wear so he suggested Gemora wear it. Gemora accepted the job.

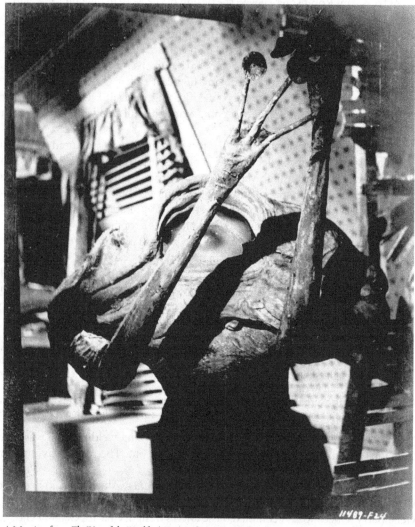

A Martian from *The War of the Worlds* (1953). Photo copyright: Paramount Pictures, 1953. Credit: Paramount/Photofest.

The Martian was fashioned out of papier-maché, wire, and sheet rubber stretched over a wooden frame. The arms vibrated with the help of rubbing tubing inside them. Gemora's hands reached as far as the elbows of the Martian's tentacles. Gemora built in glimmering eyes, throbbing veins, and operational gills on the front of the costume. Unable to stand upright while wearing the costume,

Gemora could move around on his knees. The alien always appeared to be gliding because Gemora was kneeling on a dolly pulled on the set.

To portray the Martian's death at the end of the film, the Martian's hand was covered with oil; when the arm's interior rubber tubing was deflated for the last time, death was simulated by changing the lighting from rust to green.

The Martian costume, according to Kenneth Von Gunden and Stuart H. Stock, was very delicate and barely made it through filming before coming apart. Director Byron Haskin "wanted to use the monster more than just the 20 seconds it appeared, but the six months it took for Gemora to build it apparently had cut too far into his shooting schedule."[50] The Martian was christened Louis Lump Lump.[51]

The great lesson promoted by *The Thing* and *The War of the Worlds* is that alien invaders can't be appeased, only destroyed. This wasn't the 1980s, when *E.T.* charmed everyone, but the '50s, when the Russians were said to be planning to attack the United States. Instead of directly confronting the Russian threat, Hollywood substituted extraterrestrial invaders. The great lesson then and now — with Islamic extremists cast in the role of the enemy — remains the same: appeasement is folly.

---

50 Johnson 134-135.

51 Brosnan 91. In her commentary on the film, Ann Robinson refers to the Martian as Willy Lump Lump. *Special Collector's Edition: The War of the Worlds*, dir. Byron Haskin, Paramount Pictures, 2005, "Commentary by Ann Robinson and Gene Barry."

Chapter 2. Hostile Aliens: The Mind Controllers

If *The Thing* and *The War of the Worlds* signified the threat of a Russian attack on the United States, the mind controllers signified a more insidious kind of invasion. In these films the aliens came to Earth to possess human minds. This signifies a total absence of emotion, individual feelings, freedom of will, and moral judgment.[1] In mythology, it evokes the concept of demonic possession. Besides Campbell's *Who Goes There*, other works dealing with the possession theme include Hal Clement's *Needle* (1949), Philip K. Dick's *The Father-Thing* (1954), and Robert A. Heinlein's *The Puppet Masters* (1951).[2]

When it came to the science fiction films of the '50s, the principal inspiration for the possession theme was the brainwashing of prisoners of war by the communists during the Korean War. Instead of resorting to physical torture of their captives, the communists subjected them to continuous repetition of communist slogans, phrases, and ideas as well as trying their loyalty by playing on grievances they may have had with Washington — particularly among black POWs. Even without being directly threatened, the captives knew that thousands of UN POWs had earlier been tortured and killed; hence, they gave in. Postwar surveys disclosed that only about 12% of American POWs "actively and consistently" resisted brainwashing. The great majority "cooperated in indoctrination and interrogation sessions in a passive sort of way, although there was a tendency to refuse to say anything obviously traitorous." Still numerous UN POWs signed "peace petitions" and other pro-communist documents that were circulated in the West. At war's end, twenty-one Americans and one Briton refused to be repatriated. By 1959 the Americans claimed to have identified seventy-five former POWs as communist agents. The former British vice counsel in Seoul, who was held captive

---

1 Clarens 134.

2 Von Gunden and Stock 139.

from June 1950 to 1953, was later exposed as an important Soviet agent inside the British Foreign Office. The fear that other traitors existed undetected within Western governments lasted for years.[3]

Invaders from Mars, released in 1953, presented the possession theme against the backdrop of a child's nightmare. Awakened from his sleep one night by a storm, a young boy David (Jimmy Hunt) sees a flying saucer land on a hill behind his home. The saucer burrows underground and anyone wandering near the landing site is sucked into the concealed vehicle. Once captured, the victims are taken over by the Martians with the aid of a crystal implanted into the brain. This allows the aliens to manipulate their newfound puppets into committing terrorist acts against a top-secret rocket project. ("A General of the Army turned into a Saboteur! Parents turned into . . . rabid killers! Trusted police become . . . Arsonists!")[4]

David begins to realize the presence of the alien menace. Seeking police assistance after his parents are subverted, he discovers that the former has been compromised as well. Ultimately, he finds allies in a woman doctor, Pat, and an astronomer, Kelston. The latter theorizes that the rocket being developed is seen as a threat by the Martians, who have come to Earth to execute a preemptive strike against it.[5] The Army is summoned, locating the Martians in a series of tunnels under the sand pit where their ship landed. In the ensuing battle, the aliens and their leader, a disembodied head in a glass sphere, are destroyed. At the film's conclusion, David wakes up to discover it was nothing but a dream; but then he sees the spaceship land behind his home again.[6] In the British version of the film, the Martian ship is destroyed just after lifting off, without any hint that the foregoing events were all a dream. The film ends with Kelston and Pat putting David to bed, with Pat commenting, "The little man has had a busy day."[7]

Told from David's point of view, *Invaders from Mars* is the story of a child's nightmare come true, where the adults, parents included, are the enemy.[8] The Martians take over authority figures (policemen, generals, parents). After being enslaved, the Martians' "puppets" act remote; they bear a red scar on the back of their necks, indicating where the Martians surgically implanted the control mechanism in their brains. The Martians' victims "act differently" than before. The Martians' control extends to their mutant servants, the latter "existing only to do his [the Martian leader's] will." The Martian leader issues commands, in Nora Sayre's words, "like a commissar. . . . All in all, the parallel between Martians and Communists is quite pronounced in this movie, where those who are

3 Clarens 134; Clay Blair, *The Forgotten War: America in Korea 1950-1953* (New York: Times Books, 1987) 966; Max Hastings, *The Korean War* (New York: Simon and Schuster, 1987) 288.

4 Brosnan 93; Malcolm Vance, *The Movie Ad Book* (Minneapolis: Control Data Publishing, 1981) 14.

5 Brosnan 93; Von Gunden and Stock 80.

6 Brosnan 93.

7 *Invaders from Mars.* Dir. William Cameron Menzies, Image Entertainment, 2002.

8 Brosnan 93.

programmed to be traitors to America are intent on perverting or suppressing the truth."[9] Moreover, the Martian-manipulated humans' acts of sabotage would, in light of September 11, be described as terrorism. The military's subsequent attack on the Martians' underground lair brings to mind America's military actions in Afghanistan and Iraq in the wake of 9/11.

Invaders from Mars (1953) Directed by William Cameron Menzies Shown from left: Hillary Brooke (as Mary MacLean), Charles Cane (as Police Officer Blaine), Douglas Kennedy (as Police Officer Jackson), Leif Erickson (seated, as George MacLean), Jimmy Hunt (as David MacLean. Photo copyright: Twentieth Century Fox, 1953.

The Martians' mutant slaves were played by 7-foot, 6-inch Lock Martin and 8-foot, 6-inch former circus performer Max Palmer.[10] Jimmy Hunt remembered what it was like working with them:

> "When we started working with the big mutants, it was a problem for them to physically pick us up and carry us around. It was such a long stretch for those guys. Anything that involved them was difficult since they weren't profession- als. It was hot, and because of the slits in their eyepieces they couldn't really see. These guys would always complain about them. They could only wear them for so long before they had to take them off. Poor guys would be crying."

Because he was both heavy and tall, Palmer would normally have to rest be- tween scenes. When it came to performing strenuous stunts, stunt actors like Pete Dunn and James Arness took Palmer and Martin's place, playing against midget soldier stand-ins to maintain the image of giant Martians.

---

9 Menzies; Sayre 199.

10 Von Gunden and Stock 87.

Female midget Luce Potter played the role of the disembodied Martian leader housed in a glass bubble transported by the mutants. Her makeup was limited solely to her head. A green-tinted, iridescent makeup was applied to her face while her head was fitted with a huge latex cranium headpiece — the latter the creation of makeup artist Anatole Robbins. Potter wore street clothes from the waist down. The three-fingered, moveable tentacles and glob-like trunk she stood behind was cast in rubber from a clay sculpture. Robbins merged her neck with the trunk base outfit. Then she was filmed straight on for close-ups, while in one shot she was matted into a medium shot of a globe. For distant shots of the Martian leader, a specially made sculpture (inside a globe the mutants carried) was used. The sculpture had a far thinner neck, and was completely immobile. Potter's acting in the film consisted primarily of moving her eyes to the right or left, or merely looking straight ahead. The alien leader did not verbally issue commands to its servants, but instead communicated telepathically to them.[11]

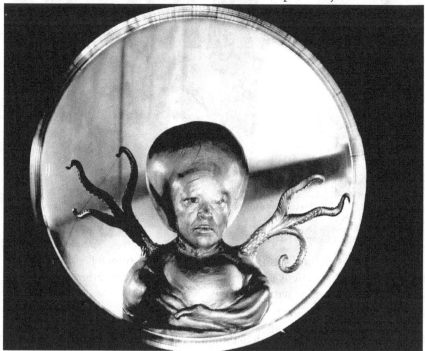

Invaders from Mars (1953) Directed by William Cameron Menzies Shown: Luce Potter (as the Martian 'Intelligence') Photo Copyright: Twentieth Century Fox, 1953.

To convey the film's mood of a child's nightmare, director William Cameron Menzies and art director Boris Levin subtly distorted the sets. The atmosphere of the police department hallway was made unfriendly by having a tall, narrow, threatening door at one end while, at the other, there was an especially high desk signifying "an almost Godlike authority." The only decorations to be found are

11 Johnson 257-259.

odd, out of place lamps and a clock. The walls are bare. This is the total opposite of Dr. Kelston's observatory. There the walls are covered with pictures, creating a friendly atmosphere. *Invaders from Mars* employed odd camera angles, well-planned shadows, and disproportioned sets to create a mood of claustrophobia and fear.

Though 20th Century Fox distributed *Invaders*, director Menzies didn't have access to any of that studio's resources; hence he utilized Republic Studio's enormous Normand sound stage. The latter served as the setting for a myriad of sets: the sand hill, the saucer interior, bedrooms, a living room, the police station with an adjoining office, a neighborhood backyard, and a gas station, Dr. Kelston's observatory, some front porch sets, and several backdrops. "The only interior sets not on that single stage were the tunnels through which the Martian soldiers lumbered back and forth."[12]

To create the sand whirlpool through which the Martians suck their victims down into their ship, a slit was cut under a piece of stretched canvas with sand on top. A hose running from a funnel placed inside the slit was affixed to an industrial strength vacuum, which drained the sand, creating the whirlpool effect. For scenes of the hole closing, the film was run in reverse.[13]

What makes *Invaders from Mars* so effective is the fact that it happens in a small town setting, making its tale of alien possession all the more frightening. Three years after *Invader's* release, another film about alien possession would take its terror to a greater level.

INVASION OF THE BODY SNATCHERS

Directed by Don Siegel, *Invasion of the Body Snatchers* may be the best of the alien possession films; it addresses two themes: the Cold War and social conformity. Set in a California community, the film shows what happens when alien seed pods from outer space descend on the town, transforming the inhabitants into emotionless duplicates. This theme clearly echoed the idea of communist "enslavement." Siegel had another message in the film: he was sounding the alarm against unthinking social conformity — what Erich Fromm termed "the escape from freedom" that characterizes industrial societies overall. "The enemy is them, *and* us."[14]

The film's opening credits are shown against a backdrop of moving clouds in the sky, suggesting the arrival of the pods from space. The movie then cuts to Dr. Hill of the State Mental Hospital being escorted by the police to the emergency room where he meets Dr. Miles Bennell (Kevin McCarthy), a seemingly psychotic man. After calming Bennell, Hill asks him to tell him what happened.[15] Bennell returned to Santa Mira, California, from a medical convention and found his of-

---

12 Johnson 70-271.

13 Johnson 277.

14 David J. Skal, *The Monster Show: A Cultural History of Horror* (New York: W. W. Norton & Company, 1993) 250.

15 *Invasion of the Body Snatchers*, dir. Don Siegel, Republic Entertainment, 1955; Von Gunden and Stock 137.

fice crowded with patients who are convinced that members of their family aren't acting as they normally would. Bennell is also reunited with his old girlfriend Becky Driscoll (Dana Wynter), who has just been divorced.[16] Dr. Dan Kaufman, the town psychiatrist, whose clients have been reporting experiences similar to Bennell's clientele, attributes the malady to "a strange neurosis. . . an epidemic of mass hysteria. . . .Worry about what's going on in the world, probably."[17]

Dana Wynter and Kevin McCarthy in *Invasion of the Body Snatchers*. Photo copyright: Allied Artists, 1956.

---

16 Douglas Brode, *The Films of the Fifties* (Secaucus, New Jersey: The Citadel Press, 1976) 171, 173.

17 Siegel.

Bennell's friends Jack and Theodora Belicec (King Donovan and Carolyn Jones) discover an unformed body in their home. The corpse ultimately assumes the appearance of Jack Belicec, right down to a cut on his hand.[18] Becky concedes her uncle has been acting differently since she returned. Eventually, Miles, Becky, Jack, and Theodora discover giant seed pods that are creating exact duplicates of them, which take over the original person while they sleep. Miles and Becky try to escape Santa Mira, only to find the entire town is determined to find them. They take refuge in Miles's office, where they see the townspeople obeying the orders of the police chief to spread the pod infection to neighboring communities.[19] Kaufman, himself now one of "them," returns, saying that it's futile to resist, and possession is painless. The pods, he explains, drifted through space, finally landing on Earth in a farmer's field. The seeds begat pods that can assume the form of any life form. The pod people will take over the world, making everyone the same unfeeling, unemotional beings they are. Kaufman explains: "There's no need for love. . . . You've been in love before. It didn't last. It never does. . . desire, ambition, faith — without them, life's so simple, believe me." The pods are incapable of love. Their sole objective is to survive.

Refusing to surrender, Miles and Becky flee to a cave above Santa Mira. When Becky falls asleep, she becomes a pod person, forcing Miles to flee to a highway. He hops aboard a truck, only to leap off when he sees it contains pods. He stands in the highway screaming, "*You're next!*"

Back at the emergency room, Bennell finishes relaying his tale to Dr. Hill.

"Will psychiatry help?" asks another doctor.

"If all this is a nightmare — yes," Hill says.

"Of course it's a nightmare," says the other doctor. "The man's as mad as a March Hare."

Just then an accident victim is brought in. He was involved in a collision of a truck and a bus. The truck driver was dug out from under a pile of "great big seed pods."

"Where was the truck coming from?" asks Hill.

"Santa Mira."

Hill immediately telephones the FBI. Bennell's story has finally been proven.[20]

Siegel's film was based on Jack Finney's novel *The Body Snatchers*. While the film's script closely adheres to the novel, the film and novel are different. The "frame" that begins and closes the film is absent from the novel, though the latter is told in the first person. Becky Driscoll is recently divorced in both film and novel, though in the novel she hasn't been living in England, a detail the film added to explain actress Dana Wynter's British accent. In the novel the Belicecs aren't captured by the pods, though the psychiatrist Kaufman is.

---

18 Siegel.

19 Siegel; Brode, *The Films of the Fifties*, 173.

20 Siegel; Brode *The Films of the Fifties*, 173; Von Gunden and Stock 139.

The novel features a character Budlong, a science professor, who explains more about the pods. When the latter assume human form, the original person becomes a kind of "gray fluff," with the pod disintegrating into the same mate-rial in the event the transformation is incomplete. The pods are far more hos-tile to human life in the original novel than they are in the film. Shown viciously ridiculing human ways, they are seemingly inhuman *and* anti-human. The bogus Kaufman tells Miles that pod people will disintegrate within five years. Since the pods intend to completely conquer Earth, they will eventually leave it *completely* lifeless and then conquer other worlds. Throughout the universe, only the pods will remain.

One scene in the film originated solely with Siegel, who remembered how, as a youth, he watched a helpless dog get run over by a car. This inspired the scene in the film where Becky screams when a dog is nearly run over by a truck, show-ing that she and Miles are still human.

The endings constitute the greatest differences between the novel and film. In Finney's book Becky isn't taken over by the pods, who are finally conquered by the sheer stubborn refusal of Miles, Becky, and others to give in to them. The defeated pods leave Earth for another world. The novel concludes with the pod people slowly dying off and Santa Mira returning to normal.[21]

Because *Invasion of the Body Snatchers* was released during the McCarthy era, nu-merous European and American media experts viewed the film as a commentary on the spread of communism. One critic maintained that the pods represented the notion of "communism, which gradually takes possession of a normal per-son, leaving him outwardly unchanged but transformed within."[22] As the "pods" take over, Miles exclaims, "They're taking us over, *cell* by cell," and "It's a malig-nant disease spreading through the whole country!" Communism was frequently equated with fatal maladies. Campaigning in 1952, Adlai Stevenson declared that communism was "a disease which may have killed more people in this world than cancer, tuberculosis, and heart disease combined." He further stated that America's adversaries sought "total conquest, not merely of the earth, but of the human mind."[23]

Don Siegel saw it differently:

> People are pods. Many of my associates are certainly pods. They have no feelings. They exist, breathe, sleep. To be a pod means that you have no passion, no anger, the spark has left you... Of course there's a very strong case for being a pod. These pods, who get rid of pain, ill-health, and mental disturbances are, in a sense, doing good. It happens to leave you in a very dull world but that, by the way, is the world most of us live in. It's the same as people who welcome going into the army or prison. There's regimentation, a lack of having to make up your mind, face decisions... People are becoming vegetables. I don't know what the

---

21 Von Gunden and Stock 139-140.

22 David Zinman, *50 from the 50's: Vintage Films from America's Mid-Century* (New Rochelle: Arlington House, 1979) 143.

23 Sayre 201.

answer is except an awareness of it. That's what makes a picture like *Invasion of the Body Snatchers* important.[24]

Fear of science and the atom is reflected in Bennell's initial explanation of the pods: "So much has been discovered these past few years, anything is possible. Maybe the results of atomic radiation on plant life or animal life. Some weird alien organism — a mutation of some kind."[25] Kevin McCarthy offered his own assessment of the film's meaning:

> I thought . . . this is about people who work on Madison Avenue. They have no hearts at all . . . these advertising people who just turn out material and sell things, and do it unemotionally. . . . I never felt that it had any political significance. It came afterward, after the fact. People began to find it politically suitable.[26]

"It was just supposed to be a plain, thrilling kind of picture," remembered Dana Wynter (Becky). Wynter stated further:

> That was what Allied Artists thought they were making. By the way, we realized — Walter [Wanger, the producer] and Kevin and people who *can* think about things — that we were making an anti-"ism" picture. Anti-"ism" — fascism, Communism, all that kind of thing. We took it for granted that's what we were making, *but* it wasn't spoken about openly on the set or anything like that. They were delicate times, and I think if Allied Artists had the slightest idea that there was anything deeper to this film, that would have quickly been stopped![27]

Invasion of the Body Snatchers grew out of several factors: the Red Scare, coming to terms with the new, postwar society, and the widespread fear of nuclear devastation — all of which shattered the well-established American notion that individualism counted. The Great Depression, World War II, America's retreat from isolationism to assume a leading role in the postwar world, and technological progress, had shaken that notion. The main themes of '50s science fiction films thus were depersonalization and dehumanization. There was also the possibility of nuclear destruction. "On the surface," noted Stuart Samuels, "there existed a complacency that disguised a deep fear of violence, but conformity silenced the cries of pain and feelings of fear."[28]

Out of these concerns arose three concepts: conformity, paranoia, and alienation. "For the most part," Samuels continues, "the decade celebrated a suburbanized, bureaucratized, complacent, secure, conformist, consensus society in opposition to an alienated, disturbed, chaotic, insecure, individualistic, rebel society.

---

24 Brosnan 127.

25 Von Gunden and Stock 147-148.

26 Siegel, *Invasion of the Body Snatchers: An Interview with Kevin McCarthy*.

27 Tom Weaver, *I Was a Monster Movie Maker: Conversations with 22 SF and Horror Filmmakers* (Jefferson: McFarland & Company, Inc., 2001) 301.

28 Stuart Samuels, "The Age of Conspiracy and Conformity: Invasion of the Body Snatchers," *American History/American Film: Interpreting the Hollywood Image*, eds. John E. O'Connor and Martin A. Johnson (New York: Frederick Ungar Co., 1979) 206-207.

Each of these three concepts dominating the 1950s finds obvious expression in *Invasion of the Body Snatchers*."[29]

Conformity became necessary if one was to be rewarded in an "increasingly affluent society," meaning individualism was a liability in this new world. Conformity became an anchor in an insecure, changing society. Miles Bennell is an "inner directed," self-reliant individualist who views the world by his own standards. The "pod people," on the other hand, are "other-directed," looking toward their own kind for signs as to how to behave.[30]

Conspiracy: In time of obvious crisis — war, or economic disturbances — perceptions may be simplified, as if there were a sharp line drawn between "good" and "evil." In time of confusion, however, that distinction isn't so clear. Subversion — real or illusory — is less apparent. Nothing is what it seems to be. Samuels writes: "Threats to the social order in the 1950s were not so much associated with personal violence as with an indefinable, insidious, fiendishly cold undermining of the normal. Conspiracy theories feed off the idea of the normal being deceptive." This is clearly the case with Miles Bennell's world. The "pod people" look just like everyone else. You can't tell the difference between human and alien.[31]

Alienation: From the start of American history, we extolled national harmony. This grew out of the concept popularized by Adam Smith and John Locke that there existed a natural and harmonious connection between individual wants and social demands, that those who act in their own interest move all of society toward natural perfection. Central to this idea was the conviction that no institutional barriers existed to frustrate people in achieving their aspirations and that America was free of such hindrances. Finally, natural harmony was grounded in the belief in abundance. If anyone failed to be successful, it was not due to the system but to that person's own deficiencies.

Confidence in natural harmony was shattered after World War II. Despite our victories, both in the war and over the Depression, and despite the discovery of atomic energy, a conflict developed between the trend toward individualism and collective group conformity, with the latter prevailing. Adherence to group conformity was rewarded, while films of the '50s depicted those who clung to individualism as people whose lives ended in tragedy and despair.[32] Indeed, Miles Bennell is depicted for most of the film as an individualist fighting for his freedom against the pods' collective conformity. He seems to be going insane, in his struggle, until the end when the authorities are finally convinced that his story is true, and he finds others who believe as he does.[33]

Invasion of the Body Snatchers is a film about an outsider's struggle to convince others that his vision is the truth. The film longs for what seems in retrospect like an uncomplicated past in place of the scientifically-oriented present, a past when

---

29 Samuels 207.

30 Samuels 207-208.

31 Samuels 209.

32 Samuels 210-211.

33 Samuels 214.

life was ordered and such notions as permissiveness, feminism, and political correctness were unheard of.[34]

The "frame" of Bennell and Dr. Hill together was not originally included in the film. The film was supposed to begin with Dr. Bennell returning home, and end with him shouting his alarm about the "pod people" on the highway. This would have left audiences shaken and disturbed as they walked out of the theater, underscoring the filmmakers' belief that the world was becoming more pod-like.

According to screenwriter Daniel Mainwaring, several "bad" preview audiences saw the film, apparently not comprehending it. This prompted the studio to request the addition of this frame so that audiences would make sense of the picture. Mainwaring convinced Siegel to film the frame and add Miles Bennell's voice-over narration so that another film crew would not do the job and completely change the film's original meaning.

Another version holds that there were three previews without the frame. Audiences laughed, initially, but became more interested in it as the story unfolded. Fearing the laughter meant the audience wasn't frightened enough, the studio demanded the frame and Wanger persuaded Siegel to do it. A final version of how that frame was put in maintains that Siegel himself decided to add it.

Whichever story is true, the main question is whether the frame helps or hurts the film. Siegel as well as numerous critics believe it revealed too much, thereby impairing the movie's effect. Consequently, the film has been shown without the frame, though Kevin McCarthy's narration must be incomprehensible to some audiences.[35]

Lift casts of Kevin McCarthy, Dana Wynter, King Donovan, and Carolyn Jones were made to represent their pod duplicates. As Don Siegel explained it:

> "Body molds were made in two halves, front and back. When the principals were cast for the body molds, the subject was laid on a slant board rather than being laid flat. In this position the breast and muscles fell into their natural position. Keys were put in the first half of the mold. When the second half was poured over the first half and then separated, they could be brought back together and would fit snugly in the correct position. The head was cast separately in the same manner. After the molds were dried in an oven, they were treated to accept foam rubber. Because of their size, the body and head molds were poured full of foam rubber and baked at a commercial rubber house. The heads were attached to their bodies, then hair, glass eyes, and fingernails were added. Skin tones were matched with rubber paint, and every detail was covered including eyelashes and teeth."[36]

When asked by Tom Weaver what it was like to have the plaster cast of her body made, Dana Wynter recalled:

> "Well, it was worse for Carolyn, because she had claustrophobia. For me, it wasn't bad, except they were 'funny,' the guys who made the thing. I was in this thing while it hardened, and of course it got rather warm! I was breathing

34 Biskind 139, 142-144.

35 Von Gunden and Stock 144-145.

36 Johnson 189-190.

through straws or something quite bizarre, and the rest of me was encased, it was like a sarcophagus. The guys who were making it tapped on the back on the thing and said, 'Dana, listen, we won't be long, we're just off for lunch!' In the end, we had to be covered except for just the nostrils and I think a little aperture for the mouth.[37]

As for a story that Siegel broke into her home and left a pod under her bed, Wynter says:

"That *is* a bit far out. Actually, he left it on my doorstep. He had a girlfriend who lived next door to me — I lived on Santa Monica Boulevard near the Mormon Temple in an enclave of five little cottages. Don Siegel was courting this girl, and he would pass my cottage all the time. And one night he just left it on the doorstep! . . . . I nearly broke my neck, because when you open your front door to go to your car, you don't expect to find something large on your doorstep."[38]

The sequence where the pods come to life in the greenhouse involved nearly 100 different camera setups. Siegel recalled,

"Good old fashioned soap bubbles saved the day. We would shoot our rubber pods coming to life, then, by cutting away to reactions from Kevin, Dana, King, and Carolyn, we would pick up our pods in a more advanced stage.

"We would obscure the faces with soap bubbles, then by cranking at high speed reversing our film, it would appear that the bubbles, as they burst, slowly took the form of the body they were taking over. Of course we had rubber impressions of the bodies and faces of our four principals. Actually, this was our main expense. Our crew found Dana and Carolyn particularly interesting, lying stark naked among our props.[39]

"For the climax where Miles Bennell shouts, "You're next!" on the highway, Kevin McCarthy did his own stunts. Of that scene, Siegel said:

"For one thing, he not only *seemed* tired, he was quite exhausted. When we shot the final of his screaming at the cars, it was just before dawn. Kevin was so tired, I was terrified that his timing would be off and he might fall down under the wheel of the cars and trucks. I put excellent stuntmen in as actual drivers of the various cars which were near Kevin. They were all warned of the dangers and handled themselves very well. I want very badly to make the sequence particularly believable and so again, with fingers crossed, I shot it all straight."[40]

IT CONQUERED THE WORLD

"Roger introduced me to the monster during a lunch break," recalls actress Beverly Garland. "He said that it came from Venus and that is why it was so short. I was shocked. It hardly came up to my knees. I pretended that I was going to kick it to teach it a lesson and to let Roger know how silly I thought it was.

---

37 Weaver, *I Was* 298.

38 Weaver, *I Was* 299.

39 Johnson 190-191.

40 Johnson 212.

Eventually, I grew to become rather fond of the monster. Her mechanical arms and legs really were rather neat, I must say."[41]

"Beulah" the alien and Beverly Garland in *It Conquered the World*. Photo copyright: American International Pictures, 1956.

Garland was reminiscing about her initial encounter with "Beulah," the otherworldly visitor who takes over human minds in *It Conquered the World*, released by American International Pictures, a studio whose forte was low-budget, high-

41 Melvin Matthews, Jr., E-mail to Beverly Garland, 4 Feb. 2004.

profit genre films, and produced and directed by the "King of B-Pictures," Roger Corman.[42] The film begins with Dr. Tom Anderson (Lee Van Cleef) warning the government that it mustn't continue with its satellite program. Otherwise "alien intelligence" will destroy the Earth

Anderson's warning is brushed aside and the satellite, under the direction of Anderson's colleague Dr. Paul Nelson (Peter Graves), is successfully launched. Three months pass, then the satellite breaks free of its orbit and heads into space. It then returns to Earth, bringing with it "Beulah" the Venusian. A "personal friend" of Dr. Anderson, the alien's arrival has been facilitated by Anderson, who sees the visitor as a savior of Mankind. Upon landing, the alien disables all power sources worldwide, then releases control devices that fly through the air, zapping key local officials in the back of the neck with electrodes, taking over their minds. The alien causes the town to be evacuated. All emotion is drained from its victims.

The alien enslaves Dr. Nelson's wife, who then releases a control device on her husband; the latter destroys it and shoots his wife, which frees her from Beulah's domination. Anderson ultimately turns against his extraterrestrial friend when it kills his own wife (Beverly Garland), destroying it with a blow torch to its eye; he dies along with the monster. At the end, Nelson muses:

> "He [Anderson] learned almost too late that Man is a feeling creature, and, because of it, the greatest in the universe. And he learned too late for himself that men have to find their own way and make their own mistakes. There can't be any gift of perfection from outside ourselves. And when men seek such perfection, they find only death, fire, loss, disillusionment, and the end of everything that's gone forward. Men have always sought an end to toil and misery. It can't be given. It has to be achieved. There is hope but it has to come from inside — from Man himself."[43]

Beverly Garland, who played Lee Van Cleef's wife in the film, came across in Corman's films as a tough, feisty type of woman. Garland explained further:

> "I think that was really what the scripts called for. In most all the movies I did for Roger my character was a kind of a tough person... I played the gutsy girl who wanted to manage it all, take things into her own hands. I never considered myself very much of a passive kind of actress — I never was very comfortable in love scenes, never comfortable playing a sweet, lovable lady. Maybe if the script wasn't written that way, then probably a lot of it I brought to the role myself. I felt I did that better than playing a passive part."[44]

---

42 Johnson 136; Skal, *The Monster Show* 256; *It Conquered the World*, dir. Roger Corman, RCA/Columbia Pictures Home Video, 1991.

43 Corman.

44 Tom Weaver, *Interviews with B Science Fiction and Horror Movie Makers* (Jefferson: McFarland & Company, Inc., 1988) 155-156.

As to whether her character in *It Conquered the World* was a feminist, owing to her toughness, Garland says now, "Probably so, but I didn't have the same awareness then, none of us did, that we do now."[45]

"Beulah," as the monster was dubbed, resembled a cucumber and was the creation of monster maker Paul Blaisdell. The creature's interior was designed like an airplane fuselage. The framework structure was fashioned from quarter inch plywood. With the frame completed, tiny wheels were installed. The wooden base was next covered with large panel slabs of foam rubber, which were then sealed together with contact bond cement, the latter a synthetic vinyl rubber glue. Once Beulah's facial features were completed, her exterior was covered with red lacquer. To enhance the alien's devilish features, black lacquer was added to the facial ridges. Finally, Blaisdell and his wife took a hammer to the monster to give the foam skin tone added flexibility and improved texture. According to Blaisdell, the monster had to be disassembled and reassembled outdoors because he couldn't get it through the door of his indoor workshop.

Blaisdell explained that the 6-and-a-half-foot long lobster-like arms were quite sophisticated and they operated with springs and wires. The claws could open and close. On the first day of filming, some of the grips damaged the arms, crushing the wiring and destroying nearly all the pincer mobility. There were other problems. Blaisdell could only see through small peepholes cut directly out from the center of Beulah's eyes. Moreover, because the monster was built low to the ground, Blaisdell could only duck-walk inside the alien. When Beulah and Garland were fighting in the cave, "Blaisdell was so low he couldn't really get an accurate fix on Beverly above him. On his first attempt at strangulation, Paul accidentally grabbed a breast" — much to the cast and crew's amusement!

Initially, Beulah wasn't supposed to be seen outside the cave, but Corman directed otherwise. Moreover, Corman wanted the monster to tip over at the end, a practical impossibility on account of its cone shape. Blaisdell believed such scenes would look ridiculous — and they did, according to sneak previews. Corman, according to *Variety*, "would have been wiser to suggest the creature, rather than constructing the awesome-looking and clumsy rubberized horror. It inspires more titters than terror." Beverly Garland found the monster hard to take seriously as well. As Roger Corman recalled:

> "Remembering my work from physics and engineering I realized that any living being from a large planet would have to work against the very heavy gravity of the planet, so I designed, or had designed, a very powerful, low to the ground monster. So Beverly Garland, my very good and very hip leading lady on the first morning of the picture, and making certain that I saw her, she walked over to the monster and looked down at it and said, "So you've come to conquer the world, enh? Take that," and she kicked it. Immediately I knew that from a standpoint of physics I was right, but from a standpoint of motion pictures I was completely wrong. And I said I'm going to shoot with Beverly alone for the morning and I want that monster eleven feet tall by afternoon."[46]

---

45 Matthews, e-mail.

46 Johnson 135-137.

Both *It Conquered the World* and *Invasion of the Body Snatchers* were originally filmed against the backdrop of the Cold War and anti-Communist hysteria. If they were filmed today, they might reflect concerns about terrorism. Both films present outside forces that would save humanity from its cares and worries by eliminating the very spark of life that creates these anxieties. In short, Beulah and the "pod people" offer a radical utopian society — a description Middle East expert Daniel Pipes applied to Islamism, characterizing the latter as "another radical utopian scheme," which, like Marxism-Leninism or fascism, "offers a way to control the state, run society, and remake the human being," "an Islamic-flavored version of totalitarianism."[47] In the same way, the mind controllers of '50s science fiction films sought to remake human society to their ends.

---

47 Daniel Pipes, "Distinguishing Between Islam and Islamism," www.danielpipes.org. 27 July 2003.

Chapter 3. Friendly Alien Visitors

Not every alien visitor to Earth during the 1950s was hostile to mankind and determined to annihilate us. Indeed, one such alien, Klaatu from *The Day the Earth Stood Still*, carried with him a peace message which, for its time, 1951, was quite daring, given the political climate in the United States. *The Day the Earth Stood Still*, of all '50s sci-fi films, was very much a political film.

As the film opens, Klaatu's saucer is picked up by tracking stations worldwide as it heads toward a landing in Washington, DC. Troops from Fort Meyer are rushed in to surround the ship after it lands. Indicative of the times, Klaatu's arrival ignites hysteria with a man running through Washington's streets screaming, "They're here! They've landed!"

Klaatu waits two hours after landing before emerging from his craft. When he offers a gift, a nervous soldier shoots him. This act of violence prompts Klaatu's robot companion, Gort, to destroy the soldiers' handguns, tanks, and cannons before Klaatu orders him to stop. When a soldier approaches Klaatu afterward, the latter says of the gift: "It was a gift for your President. With this, he could have studied life on the other planets."

Hospitalized, Klaatu is visited by a presidential aide to whom he reveals the purpose of his visit: to assemble representatives from all the Earth's nations to deliver a message concerning Earth's very survival. Such a conclave, the presidential emissary declares, is impossible, owing to the tense international climate of the moment. Such petty attitudes are repugnant to Klaatu, who decides to get out and study Earth people before reaching a final decision. Locked in his hospital room, he easily escapes, triggering a massive manhunt and scare headlines. Radio commentators describe him as "a monster at large."

After escaping, Klaatu adopts the name Carpenter from the name listed on the receipt attached to his suit from the cleaners at Walter Reed General Hospital, where he was taken after being shot. At the boarding house where Klaatu goes to live after escaping from Walter Reed, real-life newscaster Drew Pearson is shown on TV saying, "Though this man maybe our bitter enemy, it could be also a newfound friend."

On Sunday morning Klaatu joins his fellow boarders for breakfast, listening to radio commentator Gabriel Heatter hysterically describe Klaatu as "this creature," a "monster" who "must be tracked down like a wild animal . . . destroyed," a "menace from another world." One boarder, Mrs. Barley, turns to George, her husband, and tells him to turn the radio off as she's trying to concentrate on the magazine she's reading.

> GEORGE. Why doesn't the government do something? That's what I'd like to know.

> MR. KRULL. What can they do? They're only people just like us.

> GEORGE. People, my foot. They're *Democrats*.

> MR. KRULL. It's enough to give you the shakes. He's got that robot standing there, 8-feet tall, just waiting for orders to destroy us.

> HELEN BENSON (Patricia Neal). This spaceman, or whatever he is, we automatically assume he's a menace. Maybe he isn't at all.

> GEORGE. Then what's he hiding for? Why doesn't he come out in the open?

> MR. KRULL. Yeah, like that Heatter fella says. What's he up to?

> HELEN. Maybe he's afraid.

> MRS. BARLEY. He's afraid! (laughs)

> HELEN. Well, after all, he was shot the minute he landed here. I was just wondering what I would do.

> KLAATU. Well, perhaps before deciding on a course of action, you'd want to know more about the people here, to orient yourself in a strange environment.

> MRS. BARLEY. There's nothing strange about Washington, Mr. Carpenter.

> KLAATU. A person from another planet might disagree with you.

> MRS. BARLEY. Well, if you want my opinion, he comes from right here on Earth. (Pause.) And you know where I mean!

MR. KRULL. *They* wouldn't come in a spaceship, they'd come in airplanes.

Klaatu looks after Helen Benson's son Bobby while she and her boyfriend Tom Stevens (Hugh Marlowe) go for a date. Klaatu promises to take Bobby to the movies. Bobby has only two dollars. Klaatu exchanges two diamonds he's carrying for the two dollars. In Klaatu's world, diamonds are used for currency as they're easier to use and don't wear out. Bobby asks to see Klaatu's ship. While there, a newsman interviews Klaatu, asking him if he's scared by the spaceman. Klaatu replies, "In a different way perhaps. I am fearful when I see people substituting fear for reason." The newsman, obviously not expecting such an answer, cuts him off, moving on to another interviewee. Klaatu's words are a comment on the public's responsiveness to hysteria promoted by Washington, in the McCarthy era and more recent times.

While out with Bobby, Klaatu goes to visit Professor Barnhardt (Sam Jaffe). Seeing that he's not in, and noting that Barnhardt is working on a problem in celestial mechanics, Klaatu writes an equation on Barnhardt's blackboard and leaves a message for the professor to meet him. A government agent picks up Klaatu at his boarding house and takes him to Barnhardt's residence. Klaatu reveals his message: unless Earth curbs its experiments in atomic energy and rocketry (which threaten galactic peace), Earth will be eliminated. Barnhardt suggests a meeting of scientific minds, as well as leaders in other fields, where Klaatu can present his demands. Barnhardt also suggests Klaatu present some demonstration of his powers to dramatize his intention before the meeting. "Something dramatic but not destructive," says Klaatu. Two days from that date, around noon, the demonstration will be held.

Bobby later follows Klaatu back to his spaceship, where he makes preparations for his demonstration. Bobby tells his mother and Stevens when they come home, but they naturally don't believe him. Stevens goes to Klaatu's room and finds it empty, but discovers one of Klaatu's diamonds. Stevens has the diamond appraised by a jeweler, who discovers it's unlike any other in the world.

Klaatu's demonstration is to neutralize all electricity worldwide for thirty minutes — with the exception of hospitals and planes that are in flight. While he and Helen are immobilized in an elevator during the blackout, Klaatu reveals to Helen his identity and the purpose of his meeting. After the blackout, the military decides to capture Klaatu — dead or alive. Gort has been encased in a super plastic shell. Despite Helen's pleas, Tom turns Klaatu in to the Pentagon for his own self-interest, intending to make himself a celebrity. Tom's betrayal of Klaatu repels Helen, turning her away from him.

En route to Barnhardt's residence with Helen for the meeting of scientists, Klaatu is fatally shot by the military, but not before he gives Helen instructions to tell Gort not to destroy Earth in the event something happens to him. After delivering the message, Gort takes Helen aboard Klaatu's ship, retrieves Klaatu's body, returns it to the ship, and revives him. Klaatu then appears before Barnhardt and the assembled dignitaries and gives his final words:

I am leaving soon, and you will forgive me if I speak bluntly. The universe grows smaller everyday and the threat of aggression by any group, anywhere, can no longer be tolerated. There must be security for all, or no one is secure. Now, this does not mean giving up any freedom — except the freedom to act irresponsibly. Your ancestors knew this when they made laws to govern themselves and hired policemen to enforce them. We, of the other planets, have long accepted this principle. We have an organization for the mutual protection of all planets, and for the complete elimination of aggression. The test of any such higher authority is, of course, the police force that supports it. For our policemen, we created a race of robots. Their function is to patrol the planets, in spaceships like this one, and preserve the peace. In matters of aggression, we have given them absolute power over us. This power cannot be revoked. At the first sign of violence, they act automatically against the aggressor. The penalty for provoking their action is too terrible to risk. The result is we live in peace — without arms or armies — secure in the knowledge that we are free from aggression and war. Free to pursue more profitable enterprises. Now, we do not pretend to have achieved perfection. But we do have a system and it works. I came here to give you these facts. It is no concern of ours how you run your own planet. But if you threaten to extend your violence, this Earth of yours will be reduced to a burned-out cinder. Your choice is simple — join us and live in peace, or pursue your present course and face obliteration. We shall be waiting for your answer. The decision rests with you.[1]

Having delivered his message, Klaatu and Gort enter their ship and depart.[2]

Hysteria and fear of "aliens" (whether extraterrestrials or, by implication, anyone else who is "different") characterize the film, reflecting the country's mood during the early '50s with McCarthyism, the Korean War, and the Cold War. Parallels to today, where the distrust and fear are directed toward people of other races or religions, are readily drawn. People are "jittery" — to borrow a term from the film — over Klaatu's presence, a mood that accurately conveys real life under a perceived threat. Given that mood, the friendly, anti-war message of the film's "alien" made it exceptional among the era's predominantly hostile extraterrestrials and daring for its time.

Indeed, what made *The Day the Earth Stood Still* so daring for its time was its message that peace was possible only when no one had the ability to fight war.

After all, this was 1951: the Korean War was underway, and many believed that if any ideology was being placed in films it was pro-Communist ideology.

---

1 While one author, Jeff Rovin, characterizes Klaatu's oration as "the finest soliloquy [sic] in sf film history," John Brosnan emphatically disagrees:
But as the alien's civilization is supposed to be peace-loving it hardly seems logical or morally acceptable that it should threaten the natives on Earth with an even greater act of violence. Nor is their solution to our problems very attractive — namely that we should submit ourselves to the rule of a group of implacable, authoritarian robots like the one which has accompanied the alien to Earth . . . The idea of placing our basic human rights in the custody of a machine, or any "superior force," is not only an admission of defeat but also one which smacks of totalitarianism.
Brosnan 84.

2 *The Day the Earth Stood Still*, dir Robert Wise, Twentieth Century Fox Home Entertainment, Inc., Fox Video, 1998); Matthews, "Communists, Extraterrestrials" 16-17.

Before departing Earth with his robot companion Gort, Klaatu (Michael Rennie) delivers a solemn warning that Earth will be destroyed to insure galactic peace unless it abandons its warlike ways, at the conclusion of *The Day the Earth Stood Still* (1951). The film's peace message, quite daring given the prevailing political climate in America in the early '50s, resonates in the September 11 world.

On the other hand, popular attitudes toward science fiction made it the perfect vehicle for presenting controversial ideas, especially those seen as "pink" or "leftist," since no one paid attention to "that Buck Rogers stuff." One science fiction writer, William Tenn, who taught English and ethnic humor at Penn State, told his classes that he wanted to give up science fiction for other types of writing. What prevented him from doing this was that the McCarthy era had just begun, and he was allowed to write whatever he wanted to in science fiction because the establishment did not care one iota about this genre.[3]

Day was daring in other ways. It refused to take sides in the Cold War, but indicted *both* the United States and the Soviet Union. Klaatu wanted to see all the leaders of the world — not only the President of the United States; this was considered tantamount to treason. "And when it recommended empowering the Gorts of the world, those who are above the fray, the neutrals who would shortly give Dulles ulcers, it was merely rubbing salt in the wound." Moreover, the film came out in favor of peaceful uses of atomic energy. Asked by Bobby what powered his spaceship, Klaatu replies, "A highly developed form of nuclear power." "I thought that was only for bombs," says Bobby. "It's used for a lot of other things, too," says Klaatu. At this time Eisenhower's Atoms for Peace program still lay in the future; in 1951 the only talk people heard about the peaceful atom came from the Russians! The majority opinion believed that such proposals were Soviet pro-

---

3 Von Gunden and Stock 38-39.

paganda, and an unpatriotic slur on America's nuclear arsenal. "With all his talk about atoms for peace and collective security, Klaatu indeed sounded more like a Soviet agent than an emissary from outer space."[4]

In addition to its peace message, *The Day the Earth Still* is a modern retelling of the Jesus Christ story: Klaatu descends from the heavens to Earth, assumes the earthly name Carpenter, is betrayed by Tom Stevens, is killed, then revived, and returns to the heavens. "It was my private little joke," *Day's* screenwriter Edmund H. North explained. "I never discussed this angle with [producer Julian] Blaustein or [director Robert] Wise because I didn't want it expressed. I had originally hoped that the Christ comparison would be subliminal."

Just the same, the Breen Censorship Board took exception to Klaatu's resurrection on the grounds that "only God can do that!" In the film, Helen Benson tells Klaatu she thought he was dead. Klaatu agrees that he had been dead. "You mean he has the power of life and death?" Helen asks referring to Gort. "No," says Klaatu, "that is a power reserved for the Almighty Spirit." Klaatu is alive, but for how long, no one can say.[5]

Day's director, Robert Wise, was attracted to the film for several reasons:

> "Number one, it was (for once) an alien from outer space who was not an *evil* alien. Also, it was a science fiction film set on Earth here, and I thought that was marvelous. I liked the setting, the fact that it was in Washington, the heart of our country; I thought that made it very real, very believable, very mundane. I tried to heighten that with my casting, too. I wanted to make it just as credible and believable as it could possibly be, and I think that's one of its strengths."[6]

Initially studio head Darryl Zanuck wanted Spencer Tracy to play Klaatu — an idea that surprised Wise, who commented:

> I didn't think I ever heard of Spencer Tracy being mentioned for it — this is the first I've *ever* heard of *that*. When I came in on it, all three of us (Blaustein, Eddie North and I) had Claude Rains in mind. He was a fine English character actor and we thought he had the right quality. As it turned out, *fortunately* for us, he was in a play in New York [*Darkness at Noon*] and couldn't get out of it. We were starting to think of other people when we got this memo from Darryl Zanuck, who said, "I have just come back from England, and while I was there I saw a young man on the stage. He's a very good actor, I think, and he has a very interesting look. I think he's screen material and I've signed him to a contract with Fox and I think you should take a look at him for the lead in our film." That was Michael Rennie. Now, that was a big plus for us because here was a man who'd never been seen on the [American] screen before. That brought much more credibility to it than, for instance, if we'd had Claude Rains.[7]

As to whether those making such a liberal film in a conservative time were taking a risk, Wise observed:

---

4 Biskind 158-159.

5 Von Gunden and Stock 43-44.

6 Tom Weaver, *It Came from Weaver Five* (Jefferson: McFarland & Company, Inc., 1996) 343-344.

7 Weaver, *It Came* 345.

"No, there didn't appear to be any problem. I've been told many times, 'It seems kind of strange that Darryl Zanuck would go for something like this, him being a big Army man and very much a conservative,' but I think Darryl always looked at projects as entertainment and as possibilities for profit, and put aside any political considerations. The only time we ran into any sort of problem was when we thought we could probably get all the Jeeps and tanks and the equipment we needed in Washington from the Army. But when you want anything from the Army, you have to give them the script to read before they'll let you have the material, they have to approve the script. Well, they turned us down, they didn't like what the movie had to say. (Don't you think that's interesting?) But Fox had an office in Washington, a lobbyist, I guess, and *he* got a bright idea: He went over to see the National Guard in Washington, or just outside of Washington. And *they* had no problems with the script. So all the people, equipment, and soldiers and all that you see in those night scenes, chasing around in Washington, are actually the National Guard, not the Army."[8]

As to what the reaction would be if an alien *actually* landed on Earth, Wise was emphatic:

I think there would (obviously!) be . . . a lot more acceptance of the fact that there are other intelligences out there; there'd probably be much more research into it, and attempts to invite more aliens to our planet. The whole attitude that *we* are the only intelligent life in the universe would have been blown up! If all these things had really gone on, the world would not have any nuclear silos — all that would be gone, finished up. All that stuff would be behind us, and we wouldn't be having the problem we're having now with Korea and *their* threat of nuclear arms. I think it would be a much more peaceful world. I don't know that it would do much about Bosnia and *those* areas, but certainly I think the world would be free of the nuclear threat.[9]

Art directors Lyle Wheeler and Addison Hehr were responsible for designing Klaatu's robot companion Gort. After reading the story the film was based on and its description of Gnut (as it was dubbed in the story), Hehr chose to fashion Gort's metallic-looking yet flexible "skin" out of foam rubber. Once the foam rubber had been patterned into a suit, it was painted silver. The man inside the suit was an actor and former doorman at Grauman's Chinese Theater named Lock Martin. Once Martin had entered the suit, the full-length lacing that ran up and down each arm and down the back was pulled tight. For scenes where the robot was filmed from the back, walking away from the camera, a second suit that laced up the front was used. Martin wore gloves and boots as well as a helmet that brought the 7-foot, 6-inch actor's stature to well over 8 feet tall. Any concerns Blaustein and Wise had that the suit's bending and creasing as Gort walked would move the audience to laughter were quieted owing to careful editing.

The helmet Martin wore was nothing but a head covering. Thus, Hehr devised a mock-up head for special effects sequences. The mockup was equipped with a visor that could open and close and a pulsating electronic "eye." The mockup was used for close-ups of Gort's head.

---

8 Weaver, *It Came* 347.

9 Weaver, *It Came* 350.

When Gort used his ray beam to destroy a tank, the helmet mock-up, filmed against a special background, was utilized. Fred Sersen matted the ray in, while the destruction of the tank was shown using a sequence of matte paintings by Ray Kellogg and Emile Kosa. A matte is an element of a movie scene or shot that blocks out unwanted portions of the picture; a matte painting is the artistic replacement for the blocked-out portion; the plate is the live-action portion of the picture. The matte paintings hid the replacing of the tank by a melted one. Matte paintings by Kellogg and Kosa were also used to simulate the disintegration of the plastic block the Army had encased Gort in.

For scenes accentuating Gort's size, the studio's art department constructed a 9-foot fiberglass mock-up. This mockup, used in most long shots of Gort, served two purposes: to stress Gort's proportions and to lessen the time Lock Martin needed to be in the foam rubber suit he wore as Gort.[10]

Robert Wise recalled a stunt:

> "...one I'm proud we got away with." Lock Martin "could no more lift up Patricia Neal than he could lift up — the White House! And yet I had to have him pick her up in his arms and carry her into the spaceship. So we had to find *some* way to do this. This is what we did: When she fell, she fell down out of sight, behind a wall or a door or something. I had the camera pan Gort as he walked over to Pat, and the camera 'lost' him when *he* went behind the door. I held my camera on the door — *stopped* the camera, didn't move it, left it right there. Then we brought in a derrick and put the rig on Pat, the harness around her, and the wire on the derrick. We lifted Pat up; turned Gort around; and put her in his arms, with all her weight on the wire. Then I called *action* and started the camera again, panned as Gort came out, and there was the actual Pat Neal being 'carried' in his arms. We had to establish that that was Pat, and *then* we had a shot of Gort's back where he's walking away with her; he's carrying a lightweight dummy there, which we got away with."[11]

The Day the Earth Stood Still was released the same year as *The Thing*, and was its polar opposite. In an era that featured predominately hostile aliens, *Day* stood out for its benevolent alien and anti-war message. Unfortunately, it failed to become the model for future science fiction films.[12] Perhaps destructive aliens were bigger box office.

It Came from Outer Space

In contrast to Klaatu, who brought a message of peace to the people of Earth, the xenomorphs, who land on Earth in Universal-International's 1953 release *It Came from Outer Space* do so quite accidentally. They, in film historian Paul M. Jensen's words, "don't want to be here. They didn't come to meet us. They didn't come to tell us anything. . . . Their car broke down."[13]

---

10 Von Gunden and Stock 45, 47.

11 Weaver, *It Came* 349.

12 Douglas T. Miller and Marion Nowak, *The Fifties: The Way We Really Were* (Garden City: Doubleday & Company, Inc., 1977) 337.

13 Arnold, *It Came* "The Universe According to Universal."

The xenomorphs' ship crash lands next to an old mine near the fictional town of Sand Rock, Arizona. The xenomorphs' appearance is repellant by human standards: a floating, disembodied cranium, with a huge cyclopean eye in the center, and long, mangy hair on either side. The crash attracts the attention of John Putnam (Richard Carlson), an amateur astronomer, and his girlfriend Ellen Fields (Barbara Rush), a local schoolteacher. Putnam enters the crater at the crash site to investigate, and discovers the spaceship. When he investigates further, the spaceship door closes and a rock slide buries the ship from view.

No one believes Putnam when he tells them there's a ship buried under the rock, and the local press dubs him a "star gazer." "An intense young man," says a colleague of his. "Yeah, and an odd one too," says another. "More than odd," continues the former. "Individual and lonely, a man who thinks for himself." The town sheriff, Matt Warren (Charles Gray), is upset that Ellen didn't teach school that day because she was with Putnam. An old acquaintance of Ellen, Warren also knew her father when he (Warren) was working as a deputy under him. "I mean to keep an eye on her," Warren tells Putnam. "Trouble is, she keeps trailin' after you. See, this town doesn't understand you pokin' around out here in the desert, squintin' up at the stars, and now you come up with this story."

"This town!" says Putnam. "The reason I came out here to the desert was to try and get away from that kind of thinking."

"Putnam, you frighten 'em," says Warren, "and what frightens 'em, they're against, one way or another.... You want to destroy yourself, that's your lookout. But leave Ellen alone. She needs her job." Warren's sentiments echo America's distrust of intellectuals and nonconformists such as Putnam.

Two telephone linemen encounter the xenomorphs and are taken over by them. The aliens assume the physical appearances of humans to enable them to move freely among them, gathering the materials they need to repair their stricken ship. In town, Putnam discovers the xenomorph linemen. The latter tell him they don't want to harm anyone, especially him. No one will be harmed if he cooperates with them — otherwise "terrible things will happen." The xenomorphs also possess some miners, and are using Earth people, their duplicates, to help make their repairs. They also duplicate Ellen, using her as a lure to bring Putnam to the mine. They tell him that it isn't time for their two worlds to meet in friendship, as humans would be horrified by their appearance. "Had you fallen on our world, it might have been different. We understand more." Ellen and the others are being held hostage by the xenomorphs to ensure nothing will interfere with their repairs. Putnam finally persuades the xenomorph to appear to him as he truly is, and is horrified by the sight of it.

Despite Putnam's warnings, Warren organizes a posse, sets up a road block and kills one of the xenomorph duplicates. Shortly thereafter, Putnam encounters Ellen's double, who tells him, "They're on their way here. You brought them! ... You can no longer be trusted. I'm sorry. We did not want to use violence," whereupon she fires a ray at him, forcing Putnam to shoot her in self-defense. She plunges to her death in a crevice below. Putnam then discovers the aliens' ship and secures the release of the hostages and dynamites the mine entrance, allowing the xenomorphs time to complete final repairs and depart Earth. As they watch the ship streak across the skies, Warren observes, "Well, they're gone." "For good, John?" wonders Ellen. "No, just for now," says Putnam. "It wasn't the right time for us to meet. But there'll be other nights, other stars for us to watch. They'll be back."[14]

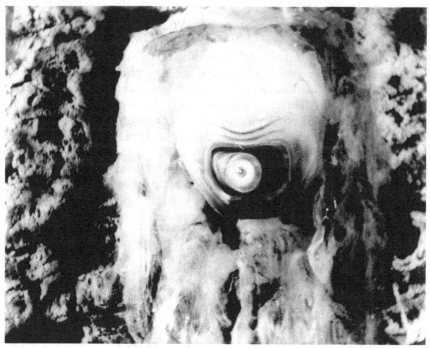

A xenomorph from *It Came from Outer Space*. Photo copyright: Universal International Pictures.

It Came from Outer Space was the creation of producer William Alland. Born in Delmar, Delaware, he began his entertainment career with a semi-professional Baltimore company, and went to Manhattan where he studied and performed at the Henry Street Settlement House. There he met Orson Welles and became a member of Welles' Mercury Theatre group. He later had a part in Welles' film classic *Citizen Kane*. After serving as a combat pilot in the Second World War, Alland was the Peabody Award-winning producer of radio's *Doorway to Life*. He began producing Westerns and science fiction films at Universal-International in the early '50s.[15]

According to Alland, the idea for *It Came from Outer Space* was very simple:

> "A spaceship accidentally crashes on Earth, and the beings in it take one look around at this place and say, 'let's get . . . out of here!' Because they sense that

---

14 Arnold, *It Came*.

15 Tom Weaver, *Monsters, Mutants and Heavenly Creatures: Confessions of 14 Classic Sci-Fi/ Horrormeisters!* (Baltimore: Midnight Marquee Press, Inc., 1996) 9.

we're an inferior breed — savage, brutal, stupid, beastly. They understand that we are a species that destroys anything that frightens us, that destroys anything we don't understand. I wrote this up in a couple of pages with the idea that they crash here, they want to get out, they realize that the Earth beings want only to destroy them, and they have the power to destroy *us* if they have to. (But they don't want to do that, they just want to get out.) And, ultimately, cooler heads prevail and they are allowed to leave. That's basically what I had."[16]

Once the studio green-lighted Alland's project, his next task was to hire a writer. Alland's choice, Ray Bradbury, was reluctant to undertake another movie assignment, having had such a terrible experience writing the screenplay for *Moby Dick*. But a lunch meeting with Alland changed all that. Bradbury turned in what Alland described as "an absolutely, *incredibly* beautiful treatment. Actually, you could have *shot* it, it was so photographic, so complete. It was almost like a silent movie — there was very little dialogue in it." Though the studio liked it, the latter vetoed Alland's idea to have Bradbury write the screenplay. Alland instead turned that chore over to Harry Essex on the condition that Essex adhere to Bradbury's treatment.[17]

It was Bradbury who created the archetypal '50s science fiction hero in John Putnam, played by Richard Carlson. In the way that Kenneth Tobey epitomized the dedicated military officer in '50s science fiction films, Carlson epitomized the scientist hero.[18] Tom Weaver observed:

> "Carlson did so many of the early '50s sci-fi films in such a short space of time that he set the pattern for many of these SF scientist-heroes who followed. In sci-fi movies of the '50s, scientists were depicted very differently than in the past. In the '30s and '40s, the scientists were usually the bad guy, or, at best, an off-the-wall character, like Colin Clive in the *Frankenstein* movies . . . .these Universal '50s movies made the scientist the hero, too, and Carlson was just right for that. He looked and acted just like an intellectual, which he probably actually was, but he also seemed to be reasonably athletic and outdoorsy. And he was good-looking enough that you could see why the leading lady would be interested. . . . At Universal, the scientist-heroes all looked like tennis pros — John Agar, Rex Reason, Grant Williams — all those guys."[19]

Asked if the film was more about paranoia and McCarthyism than space creatures, Alland replied:

> "Well, in all fairness to them [film historians], they are right. I *always* tried to have an underlying thematic idea in my films. Most of my films, if you'll examine them, have a plea for humanity, for decency. For being *human*, so to speak. I never tired to degrade my audience. Most of my films, as you will see, always had some [message]. . . . I consciously try to have a reason for telling a story, and the fact that people can 'read things' into some of my pictures is not necessarily wrong-headed. Many times we do things without knowing ourselves why we're doing them, and it takes somebody else to read into it something that perhaps is there, perhaps not. But *It Came from Outer Space* certainly *did* talk about hysteria, para-

---

16 Weaver, *Monster, Mutants* 18, 20.

17 Weaver, *Monster, Mutants* 20-21.

18 Warren xiv, xii.

19 Arnold, *It Came* "Feature Commentary with Film Historian Tom Weaver."

noia, all these things — that was the whole point. The point was that human beings destroy when they don't understand what. . .they're confronting. Human beings are *so* terrified of the unknown that, instead of facing it, they deny its existence, as we do about what's going on Earth right now. We're destroying the Earth so fast, it's pathetic, but we won't stand still long enough to face it. We *don't know* — and we don't *want* to know. In a sense, that's what *It Came from Outer Space* is about. The moral of *It Came from Outer Space* is: Don't destroy things just because you don't understand them. Don't try to read evil into what is not understandable. And don't be afraid of the unknown."[20]

Was it Alland, not director Jack Arnold, who came up with the notion of setting sci-fi films in the desert? *"Absolutely,"* said Alland, who added:

"The fact of the matter is that desert settings are marvelous for science fiction stories, that's all. Oh, it had nothing to do with *him!* Let me repeat! Any time Jack Arnold made a movie for me, when he arrived, the script was done, the sets were pretty much in progress already, the casting was done. All he did was take the script and start to shoot. He had v-e-r-y little input on *anything* else. He was a push-button director for me. Now I don't want to take anything away from him: He knew how to get a little shock out of the audience, by revealing a hand, or this, or that — although all that stuff was *in* the script. But he could accent that with the way he shot it, so I don't want to take anything away from his ability in *that* regard. But he was, himself, *not* a storyteller. He was a *director*."[21]

Apple Valley, located about 80 miles from Los Angeles, served as the setting for the desert scenes in the film. "Some of the sequences on the highway," Alland explained, "the scenes where the guys climb up the telephone poles and listen to the wires, were done on a sound stage with forced perspective. We had big telephone poles, and we used smaller and smaller ones in the background. It was remarkable, it worked like a charm and it was very cheap to do.[22]

Ultimately, *It Came from Outer Space* is about two cultures — one human, the other alien — in collision with each other.[23] That conflict, played out on the screen in 1953, now finds real-life expression in America's characterization of the clash between Islamism and the West — one painted as a radical utopian concept, the other as a "democratic" civilization.

This Island Earth

Two years after *It Came from Outer Space*, William Alland produced another space opera for Universal, *This Island Earth*. This film, along with *Forbidden Planet* (1956), seemed to signal a new chapter in Hollywood science fiction. Both films resembled the kind of stories SF readers had enjoyed since the 1930s: intergalactic adventures, dying or dead alien worlds, vast, extraordinary machines, and considerable super-science. Until now such stories had been confined to the printed page, and were only just being transferred to the movie screen. Yet, owing to the expense and intricate sets such films necessitated, these productions, while box-

20 Weaver, Monsters, Mutants 25.

21 Weaver, *Monsters, Mutants* 25-26.

22 Weaver, *Monsters, Mutants* 26-27.

23 Arnold, *It Came* "The Universe According to Universal."

office hits, weren't sufficiently profitable for other studios to lavish the kind of money needed for similar movies. Subsequently, American science fiction films declined in quality, ultimately falling into the hands of such exploitation produc-ers as Roger Corman, Bert I. Gordon, and Herman Cohen. The latter gave the genre a bad name that took years to change.[24]

Filmed in Technicolor, whereas most '50s sci-fi films were shot in black and white, *This Island Earth* was based on a novel by Raymond F. Jones. Jones's novel itself was born from three separate Cal Meacham novelettes first published in *Thrilling Wonder Stories* magazine. "The Alien Machine," the first in the series, in-troduced the reader to the central protagonist, Cal Meacham, and focuses on his efforts to learn who sent him the parts to build the machine at his lab at Ry-berg Electronics. At the end of the novelette, Meacham boards a pilot-less plane bound for a mysterious destination.

"The Shroud of Secrecy" follows the story to the point where Cal and heroine Ruth Adams learn that something is amiss among the research center's scientists, who are called the "Peace Engineers." "The Greater Conflict," the final chapter of the series, finds Cal and Ruth aboard a spaceship headed for the planet Metaluna and ends with Metaluna's destruction by the Zahgons. Jones's novel argues for the elimination of war, "exploring intellectual concepts no movie can encompass. The film does, however, retain the general tone of the novel's intelligence which elevates it above a mere space adventure film."[25]

By the mid-1950s, Universal-International had filmed successful low-budget, black-and-white sci-fi and horror films that required few special effects. Not wanting to be seen as a B-movie studio, U-I looked for a property that could be a prestige A-film. Sabre Productions, an independent film company, purchased the screen rights to the Jones novel, then hired a seasoned screenwriter, Edward G. O'Callaghan, to write the script. Upon seeing O'Callaghan's finished product, the primary focus of which was the interplanetary war, Sabre executives sought a bigger studio's backing, as it would be an expensive film to produce. U-I bought the film from Sabre in 1954, then tapped William Alland to produce it. Joseph (M.) Newman directed. Newman's earthbound scenes were fine, but Alland be-lieved the Metalunan scenes weren't. Alland thus asked Jack Arnold to re-shoot them on redesigned sets. Arnold received no screen credit.[26]

As the film opens, Dr. Cal Meacham (Rex Reason), an electronics specialist, is returning to his lab in Los Angeles. As his plane comes in for a landing, the engine "flames out," whereupon a mysterious green light envelopes the plane, taking con-trol of it and landing it safely. Back in the lab, Meacham finds that he has received a delivery, a conductor, that has unusual properties. A diamond drill won't pen-etrate it. He then receives a catalog from Electronics Service — Unit No. 16 — the same place the conductor came from. From it, he orders an "Interociter." Once as-

---

24 Brosnan 118.

25 Von Gunden and Stock 112, 114-115, 117.

26 Von Gunden and Stock 117, 119.

sembled, it acts as a television screen, transmitting the voice and image of Exeter (Jeff Morrow), leader of a team recruiting scientists for a special project.

Meacham boards a special one-seat pilot-less plane provided by Exeter that flies to Meacham's lab to fetch him. Upon landing at its destination, in Georgia, Meacham is greeted by an old colleague, Ruth Adams (Faith Domergue), who drives him to an estate where Exeter has assembled several distinguished scientists. Exeter has a high forehead and white hair, like his assistants. His goal, he says, is to end war. In reality, he's seeking new sources of atomic energy — and not for practical purposes.

Suspicious of Exeter's motives, Cal, Ruth, and Steve Carlson (Russell Johnson) attempt to flee Exeter's headquarters. A ray zaps Steve when he tries an evasive maneuver in his car. Cal and Ruth flee to a plane and take off just as Exeter's house is destroyed. The plane is drawn aboard Exeter's spaceship, after which Cal and Ruth are transported in it to Exeter's home planet, Metaluna, which is at war with a neighboring planet. Metaluna's ionization layer is being penetrated by the enemy's meteors. The layer depends on atomic energy, which depends on uranium, the supply of which had been exhausted on Metaluna, explaining why Exeter assembled all the Earth scientists. The Metalunans intend to relocate to Earth but not before brainwashing Ruth and Cal. A final attack on Metaluna prevents that, and Ruth, Cal, and Exeter board the latter's spaceship for the flight back to Earth. As they flee, Metaluna is finally destroyed. Ruth and Cal invite Exeter to return to Earth with them, but he declines. They board the plane and descend from the spaceship into the sky over the coastline. Exeter then crashes his ship into the sea.[27]

Unlike other science fiction films of the period, *This Island Earth* is pro-science in its attitude, crediting the achievements of the mind and viewing technology as the solution to some of humanity's problems. The special effects and color photography are superb. What shortcoming the film has perhaps is due to its absence of a theme. While the film is anti-war, that message is quickly weakened — especially as the final part of the film deals with an interplanetary conflict (though Exeter acknowledges the cost of the war to Metaluna).

Just the same, *This Island Earth* has a second message: the human mind is incapable of being creative under coercion. Exeter tells the Monitor, his Metalunan boss, that the thought transformer is morally abhorrent to the humans and impedes their creativity. Only a free and willing mind can seek out solutions to problems.[28]

Asked by one interviewer if *This Island Earth* was "just *Flash Gordon* in Technicolor," William Alland replied, "*Absolutely* — no question about it. Including that ridiculous Mutant! I didn't want that in the movie, but they said, 'You gotta have a monster!'" As to who insisted on the monster's presence in the film — Universal or director Joseph Newman — Alland said,

---

27 *This Island Earth*, dir. Joseph F. Newman, MCA Home Video, Inc., 1993.

28 Von Gunden and Stock 120.

"*Both!* It was outrageous, to clutter the movie up with that ridiculous thing. . . . The crab claws and all that crap! . . . But the special effects were tremendous, and that was thanks to the genius of Stan Horsley. Remember the spaceships zooming in and out, attacking the planet and all of that? None of that had been done before — and everything that came after *This Island Earth* were basically *copies* of it! You had never seen a fast spaceship, you had never seen a battle in space before you saw *This Island Earth.*"

Alland's appreciation of the film grew with that of the audience: "*You* guys are telling *me* how good it is, so, fine, I'll go along with you! And I will say that the war-of-the-worlds sequences are, for their time, incredible."[29]

Regarding his selection as Exeter, actor Jeff Morrow recalled, "My contract went into effect some time in February 1954, and just prior to that date Universal suddenly decided they wanted me to play the lead in a science fiction picture, *This Island Earth.* They sent me the script, I read it and went in to talk with the producer, Bill Alland, . . . and the writer, Franklin Coen." Attracted by the script, Morrow was disappointed to see that Exeter was written as a one-dimensional villain. He said:

"You had no idea why Exeter was doing any of this stuff, except that he was an ornery character. I didn't have to do the picture because it was going to start ten days before my contract went into effect, so this was one of the few instances in all the times I've signed for pictures that I had a little bit to say about it! I told them, 'I'm interested in doing it, but he's such a heavy. Can't we do something about it — show that he is, let's say, the epitome of a true scientist, and really concerned about the effect of what he does upon the world?' So we talked for about an hour, and there was a sort of general agreement that it wasn't a bad idea. And when we walked down the street to the parking lot, Frank Coen said, 'I'm so glad you were there, because I've been trying to sell them on that concept for a month!'"

When it came to makeup for his role, Morrow recalled, "They gave me a slightly enlarged forehead, which had to be put on very, very carefully, and then a white wig over that. It was the kind of look where, if you walked down the street, people wouldn't notice you, but then twenty feet later they would suddenly stop, turn around and say, 'He looked a little odd, didn't he?'" However, the white wigs Morrow and his fellow "aliens" wore proved to have unexpected problems. Morrow noted:

"The wigs we wore were so white that we were all very worried, especially the woman hairdresser, about how they would wind up looking on film. I did a test, and that was printed and delivered on a Monday — the same Monday that we started shooting the picture. And, as we predicted, when we saw the dallies, we saw that my hair came out pure white — it looked like cotton candy. It was terrible! Well, after the producers and executives all went into a bit of shock, they decided, 'We'll just print the film darker, and the hair won't look so white.' So they printed it darker, but then my skin looked as though I had been out in the sun all my life! The consequence was that every day, little by little, the hairdresser would twist and comb so that there was a wave in the white hair — not for any cosmetic appearance, but simply so there'd be a little light and shade,

---

29 Weaver, *Monsters, Mutants* 47-48, 49.

and it wouldn't look this ghastly pure white. They also softened the lights on the hair, and after a short time I looked fairly human."[30]

Looking back at the film, Morrow felt, "By and large, the film was quite good; as a matter of fact, I think it was slightly underrated by some of the New York critics. To the best of my knowledge, it cost about $750,000, the shooting schedule was about six weeks, and it had extremely good special effects, much in advance of most of the science fiction pictures of that time. It certainly had a lot more to say than practically any of the science fiction pictures that I've seen recently — ones that cost $25-$30 million — which are not only not-positive but extremely negative in their point of view. And, oddly enough, I know I did get more fan mail from that picture than any other I ever did."[31]

"Jeff Morrow was," to costar Rex Reason, "*the* professional — he was very stimulating to watch and to work with. He was 'in' his part, and he had a lot of respect for his fellow actors. And as a result of this, I was better — he was 'high,' and this called forth every bit of my attention and involvement as an actor. His few remarks to me during the shooting of *This Island Earth* helped me. He said, 'You know, you have looks, Rex, but if you think that you do have looks, it's going to take away from your acting. You're the kind of person who's going to have to work a little harder.' I did the best work I knew how on *This Island Earth*, and I think I held up my end of the picture to his satisfaction. He is to be categorized as an 'actor's actor.'" Faith Domergue "was quite a sport," says Reason. "There was a scene where I had to dunk her down into some dirty water and a chase where I had to yank her along, and she didn't ever complain. She never once played the 'Hollywood Queen' with me — she did a good job, she was a lovely lady and she was real nice. I'm sorry I didn't get to know her better."[32]

Universal's Stage 12, or "process stage," served as the site for the huge Metaluna surface set, while Universal Sound Stage 28 was transformed into a universe where the Metaluna model planet work was done. To create the effect for Metaluna's atmospheric shield ionized by atomic energy, red and green lights were projected onto a 22 by 115 foot sky backdrop painted with red and green streaks. By carefully varying the lighting, the streaks produced an unusual and luminous "ionized" effect. For the film's model effects, the production team utilized (and changed) a number of different kinds of backings. For the ship "fly by" shots over the huge Metaluna surface set, a black duvatine backdrop was suspended parallel to the model ship and the 200-foot dolly track used for passes over Metaluna. The duvatine fabric, made from wool, cotton, rayon, or silk, is a soft, short napped material with a diagonal parallel rib texture utilized mainly as it furnishes a less reflective, "sheen-less" backdrop. In contrast to the glimmering "ionized atmosphere" cyclorama, the majority of the backdrops required for the movie's special effects had to be opaque in origin: to film the sparkling meteors the set lights had

---

30 Weaver, *They Fought* 212-213.

31 Weaver, *They Fought* 214-215.

32 Weaver, *They Fought* 238.

to be switched off and the backdrop covered in black to subsequently double expose it (by optical printer) onto film of the saucer and Metaluna surface.[33]

Miniature engineering was the key to the film's flying saucer-like spaceships. Exeter's 18-pound model ship was fabricated from aluminum and photographed in front of a magnified color observatory picture of space. When it came to landing Exeter's spaceship on Metaluna, the miniature effects team built a gigantic 200-foot planet's surface set on Sound Stage 12. Moreover, the special effects team built a miniature version of the interior of the control room of Exeter's ship; no shots of this set appeared in the final film. A magazine article described the wiring system that was used to operate the Zahgon warships and Exeter's vessel:

Faith Domergue, Rex Reason, Jeff Morrow, and Regis Parton in *This Island Earth*. Photo copyright: Universal International Pictures.

First a 200-foot dolly track was laid out on the process stage, then a black duvatine backing was hung parallel to it. The straight line saucer and meteor fly-bys done on this setup required an overhead trolley (nicknamed a "stork"), below which a model could be hung; a system of three overhead guide cables; and the dolly cart. The stork, with model attached below, traveled along two of the cables and was pulled along by the third. The cables were led off to one side and down through a pulley system on the cart. As the cart traveled either way along the track, the stork did likewise, providing smooth forward or backward movements for whatever was hung from the stork.[34]

---

33 Johnson 276, 289-290.

34 Johnson 297, 299.

The Metaluna Mutant had a dual-brained head almost 30 inches in diameter. For extreme close-up shots, a separate head was built. The hands of the actor playing the mutant were located at the end of the second segment, which was equipped with a squeeze mechanism used to open and close the mutant's claws. Once the monster was completed, the studio's makeup department began painting its creation. The creature, which was initially to have been painted brown and yellow, was finally painted blue with red streaks highlighting its protruding veins.[35]

"Regis Parton," recalled Faith Domergue, "played the monster." Domergue said:

> "Reggie was an adorable guy. I would often bring my husband and children to the set. Reggie would pick up my children in his arms and walk around with them in his monster costume. My children were quite young at this time and when we all went to see the film in Rome, my children just could not connect the monster with the man who was playing with them on the set. They got hysterical when they saw their mother being attacked by the mutant. The sequence that stands out in my memory is when the mutant chases me around the platform of the spaceship.

> "Doing this scene with Reggie was much more violent than what appeared in the final version. I was thrown around that set and I was black and blue from head to toe. My body looked like someone had gone over me with a rubber hose. By this time, we were well into the film and I was excited about it all, the adrenaline was flowing with Reggie and me. He was a big guy to begin with and in the costume, he became even larger. I was given some nasty bruises when it was all over. It was even more exciting the way we originally shot it, but they wanted to get on with the rest of the spaceship sequences and not dwell so much on the struggle between the monster and me."[36]

When it came to the inclusion of the Mutant in *This Island Earth*, Domergue dissented from the majority opinion that it was a bad idea:

> "I thought the Mutants were wonderful — look how many were in *Star Wars*. Ours were the *first*. And, you know, Steven Spielberg must like our picture, because a few years ago I was watching *E.T.* [1982] with my daughter in Santa Barbara. To my surprise, when E.T. turned on that television, there were Rex and I [in *This Island Earth*], being pulled up into that flying saucer! It was very exciting!"[37]

Domergue also recalled that the space outfit she wore was skin tight:

> "We changed to them before we landed on Metaluna. I had problems getting into mine, and wearing panties under them would not work because they would show, as was the case with anything I attempted to wear with it. So I

35 Johnson 120.

36 Paul Parla and Charles P. Mitchell, *Screen Sirens Scream! Interviews with 20 Actresses from Science Fiction, Horror, Film Noir and Mystery Movies, 1930s to 1960s* (Jefferson: McFarland & Company, Inc., 2000) 69-70.

37 Tom Weaver, *I Was a Monster Movie Maker: Conversations with 22 SF and Horror Filmmakers* (Jefferson: McFarland & Company, Inc., 2001), 34-35.

told the girl who was dressing me that I had an idea, and simply removed all of my clothes and put the skin-tight silver costume back on over my bare skin. I jokingly told her that if she caught me in the zipper I was going to replace her. So she zipped me up and not a line showed. Then I went stark nude into my suit and it became difficult to sit down. At this point, I asked them to build special leaning slant boards to rest on for the scenes that had Rex, Jeff and me seated in our chairs aboard the spacecraft. Later I asked them to put armrests on my chair, so they added armrests onto all of them. It was quite painful to sit down while dressed in this costume because the zippers could jab into my flesh, so in order for me to sit down after our scenes were done, I'd have to strip down and wrap a blanket around me so my hairdresser could do my hair for another scene."[38]

One of the special effects used in *This Island Earth* was superimposure, used in two sequences. In the first, gasoline explosions filmed under controlled conditions were superimposed over the Metaluna landscape footage, and, in the second, to cover the crash of Exeter's ship into the ocean.[39]

"The thing that I felt was important about *This Island Earth*," recalled star Jeff Morrow, "was the fact that there was a sense of hope — that if we *do* ever come to meet people from another planet, in some way we'll be able to communicate on a human level of understanding. At least, let's hope to!"[40]

Half a century after *This Island Earth* and the other friendly alien films of the '50s, the need for "a human level of understanding" is more urgently needed now as never before as America sees itself beset by religious extremists. The fact that benign extraterrestrials were such a rarity in '50s science fiction cinema owes to a pair of considerations: the box office, and the political climate. Hostile aliens proved more lucrative with audiences, hence the film studios turned out more alien nasties. Moreover, in an age when Americans were being led to expect war with the Communists, aggressive aliens were more in tune with the message of the times. Seen in this context, Klaatu, a moderate alien voice in an unfriendly universe, stands out for his peace message. The xenomorphs merely came to Earth to repair their spaceship and leave as quickly as possible. Exeter epitomized the noble alien scientist concerned for the well-being of his human friends.

All this aside, the message the friendly aliens of the '50s have for us in the so-called Age of Terrorism is that all of us, irrespective of our nationality and spiritual beliefs, must recognize our common humanity and accept one another in a spirit of peace and brotherhood.

---

38 Parla and Mitchell 70.

39 Johnson 92.

40 Weaver, *They Fought* 219.

CHAPTER 4. VISIONS OF THE APOCALYPSE: THE END OF THE WORLD

"We sense we are very close to something apocalyptic, but that something positive will come out of it," said a Jerusalem-based Evangelical. "It's like a woman having labor pains. A woman can feel this pain reaching its height when the child is born — and then doesn't feel the pain anymore, only the joy of the happy event." Following the September 11 attacks, a Denver lay pastor at an inner-city ministry sent out an Internet letter recommending that people turn to *Revelation* to comprehend what was happening. He received what *Time* called "a huge — and frightened — response": "People were asking themselves whether they were ready to die. Very sane, well-educated people have gone back to the storm-cellar thing to make sure they have water and freeze-dried stuff in their basements."

A Texas pastor resigned his pulpit to devote himself full-time to recruiting Christians to become politically active. A Wyoming state senator retired from politics in part to spend more time helping people prepare for the Second Coming.

"I would go for years without anyone asking about the End Times," said the senior minister of the Fifth Avenue Presbyterian Church in midtown Manhattan. "But since Sept. 11, hardcore, crusty, cynical New York lawyers and stockbrokers who are not moved by anything are saying, 'Is the world going to end?', 'Are all the events of the Bible coming true?' They want to get right with God. I've never seen anything like it in my 30 years in ministry."[1]

These were some of the reactions to the September 11 attacks. That event, coupled with the anthrax scare that followed immediately thereafter, heightened the interest of those Christians familiar with End Times theology and expanded that interest to those previously unacquainted with it. Adding to the interest was the *Left Behind* series of books, based on the *Book of Revelation*. Written by Tim

1 Nancy Gibbs, "Apocalypse Now," *Time* 1 July 2002: 44-45.

F. LaHaye and Jerry B. Jenkins, the series specifies what is supposed to happen to those who are left behind on Earth to oppose the Antichrist after the Rapture of Christian believers into heaven.[2] Many people, noted *Time*, "are starting to read the *Left Behind* books not as novels but as tomorrow's newspapers. LaHaye believes that the Scriptures lay out a precise timetable for the end of the world, and the *Left Behind* books let us in on the chronology." The series follows the adventures of pilot Rayford Steele and journalist Cameron ("Buck") Williams as they help nonbelievers accept Christ during the rise of the Antichrist. The latter "does his best to kill as many of the new Christians as possible, and in some episodes it's all Rayford and Buck can do to stay alive and protect their wives."[3]

According to a *Time*/CNN poll, more than one-third of Americans said they were paying more attention to how the news might relate to the end of the world and had discussed what the Bible said about it. Fully 59% said they believed the events in *Revelation* would come true and almost one-quarter believed the Bible foretold September 11.

From its beginning, America cast itself as God's special nation and always had an interest in prophecy. Beginning with World War II, a series of events — the rise and fall of Adolf Hitler; the return of the Jews to Israel after 2,000 years; and war in 1967 when Israel took Jerusalem's Old City from the Jordanians — all pushed apocalyptic thinking to a wider audience and convinced many Christians and Jews of God's presence. Preoccupation with the end times was advanced even more with the publication of Hal Lindsey's *The Late Great Planet Earth*, which became the best-selling nonfiction book of the 1970s. "Lindsey's explanation of the Bible's warnings came just as a backlash was stirring against '60s liberalism, an echo of the eighteenth-century reaction to the Enlightenment. Lindsay caught the moment that launched a decade of evangelical resurgence, when for the first time in generations believers organized to put their stamp on this world, rather than the next."

This evangelical resurgence reached a greater peak with the election of Ronald Reagan. Yet the more Evangelicals became politically active and involved in worldly affairs, "the more interest in End Times theology drifted back into the realm of entertainment." September 11 changed that.[4]

Of course apocalyptic fears weren't peculiar to the September 11 era only. The 1950s were a time of both prosperity and unease. On the positive side, the economy was booming and Americans bought such consumer items as cars, freezers, refrigerators, and televisions, and flocked to the new suburbs. Ancient maladies such as polio were eradicated.[5] Nevertheless, a sense of unease blighted the national mood. Norman Vincent Peale noted an "epidemic of fear and worry" in America: "All doctors are having cases of illness which are brought on directly by fear, and aggravated by worry and a feeling of insecurity." The greatest source

2 Gibbs 42.

3 John Cloud, "Meet the Prophet," *Time* 1 July 2002: 50, 51.

4 Gibbs 42, 45-47.

5 Richard M. Fried, *Nightmare in Red: The McCarthy Era in Perspective* (New York: Oxford UP, 1990) 4-5.

of worry for some Americans was the Cold War, helped along by "civil defense" pamphlets that declared things such as, "Our nation is in a grim struggle for national survival and the preservation of freedom in the world." Moreover, the threat of nuclear destruction was constantly evoked, which left people, in one observer's words "in a state of suspension, waiting to see whether the Bomb is go-ing to fall or not."[6] Richard M. Fried, an historian of the McCarthy era, describes the way the fear was both promoted and then more or less allayed:

> "Newspapers published city maps with concentric circles showing levels of destruction expected from a nuclear blast. School-children learned in drills to crawl under their desks in the event of a bombing . . . In New York, Dr. Peale met a child terrified by the H-bomb. He calmed her with the simple positive thought that God would not let a bomb fall on New York. Popular magazines strove to put the new weapons in a less threatening everyday context." *Look* burbled that the H-bomb — about the size of a living room — was "one of the cheapest forms of destruction known to man."[7]

Given the prevalence of nuclear themes in '50s films, it is ironic that very few dealt with the end of the world.[8] *Five*, a film referred to as "a story about the day after tomorrow," and released by Columbia Pictures in 1951, deals with the five sole remaining survivors of the final conflict. Michael (William Phipps), the only survivor from New York, is an idealist. The pregnant Roseanne (Susan Douglas) is the only woman and signifies Earth's procreative potential. Charles (Charles Lampkin), the sole black among the group, is a bank teller. Mr. Barnstaple (Earl Lee), a banker who works with Charles, says that the two of them must move on. ("Vacations are delightful, but one has obligations to one's work.") Eric (James Anderson), a mountain-climber, retains his racial prejudices. The fight between Eric and Charles provides a civil rights' theme for the film.[9] Barnstaple succumbs to radiation poisoning. Charles is murdered by Eric, who, when he discovers that he has radiation sores on his chest, runs off.[10] [11]* The film concludes with Rose-anne (whose baby has died) and Michael as the only ones remaining. The impres-sion is that Roseanne and Michael will sire a new human race. The final shot that follows features a Biblical message: "And I saw a new heaven/and a new Earth./

---

6 Miller and Nowak 10.

7 Fried 6.

8 Kim Newman, *Apocalypse Movies: End of the World Cinema* (New York: St. Martin's Griffin, 2000) 99.

9 Matthews, "Communists, Extraterrestrials" 12; Douglas Brode, *Lost Films of the Fifties* (Secaucus: Citadel Press, 1988) 58.

10 Warren 29.

11 Racial tensions in a post-apocalyptic world were also present in *The World, the Flesh and the Devil* (1959), in which there were three survivors: Ralph, a black miner (Harry Belafonte); Sarah, a white woman (Inger Stevens); and Ben, a bigot (Mel Ferrer). Ralph and Ben begin fighting each other. Ultimately, everyone comes to their senses, "sort out their racial and sexual differences, and invent a new kind of family." Newman 133.

And there shall be no more death/No more sorrow. . . No more tears. . . /Behold! I make all things new!"[12]

Day the World Ended, produced and directed by Roger Corman, was similar to *Five*. The film opens with the words: "What you are about to see may never happen. But to this anxious age in which we live, it presents a fearsome warning. . . . Our story begins with THE END!" This is followed by footage of an atomic blast. A handful of survivors remain: Tony, a gangster (Mike "Touch" Connors); Tony's stripper girlfriend Ruby (Adele Jergens); Rick, a geologist (Richard Denning); Pete, an old miner and his burro; and Radick, a man whose skin seems to be mutating into "atomic skin." They all converge on a cabin occupied by a former Navy captain, Jim (Paul Burch), and his daughter Louise (Lori Nelson). Jim, foreseeing that nuclear devastation would come, has provisioned his home against such a catastrophe.

Louise begins hearing a mysterious voice. Radick begins staying out at night, mutating into an atomic-age creature, hunting in the woods. While Louise and Ruby bathe in a waterfall, Louise senses they're being watched in the bushes. As they leave for the house, they discover footprints made by some creature. Later Jim tells Rick of his experiences as captain of a ship towing animals during an H-bomb test. The animals that survived the test developed armor-plated skin against nuclear radiation — just as Radick is doing. Because of this, Jim asks Louise to marry Rick so they can have children and ensure the continuance of the human race.

Another human mutant, his skin changing like the animals — a stage two mutant — appears, saying there are others who wouldn't give him food. He dies immediately thereafter. Radick is stage one. The mutant calling Louise begins coming closer to the house. When Radick takes Pete's burro to eat, the mutant kills him. Meanwhile, Louise keeps hearing the "voice" calling to her, coming closer to the house.

When Pete tries to leave the house to look for gold, Jim chases after him. Pete knocks him out, causing Jim to be exposed to the radioactive vapor. Pete succumbs to it himself. Jim takes to his couch. Tony tries to take Louise for himself. When Ruby intervenes, Tony stabs her to death.

The mutant finally summons Louise into the night, kidnapping her. The mutant, multi-eyed, with horns coming out of his head, is stage three. Taking her to the pond, the monster avoids the water out of fear.[13] Louise enters the pond,

---

12 Matthews, "Communists, Extraterrestrials" 12-13.

13 Lori Nelson recalled working with the "monster":
The actor inside the monster suit was very small, and not very strong. He was kind of wimpy-armed, not muscular at all, and not much taller than me. We were doing the scene by the lake, and he was carrying me down the bank. He was kind of staggering around — his knees were buckling. I think he stepped in a hole or tripped on a stick — he fell and I fell on top of him. I landed on his chest, and because the costume was made of rubber I started to bounce up and down. I started laughing, and I could hear the "mutant" laughing, too — muffled — within the suit! Luckily we fell down on the bank, right on the edge of the water; that was a good thing, because I don't know how well that monster suit would have stood up if got wet. Also, he might have drowned, the suit was so heavy. Weaver, *They Fought* 229.

where the monster won't go. Rick does the same when his rifle proves useless against it. A rainstorm begins, forcing the monster to flee. The rainwater, now free of radiation, destroys the monster by dissolving it. When Tony prepares to shoot Rick, to get Louise, Jim shoots him to death. Jim's radio has picked up a transmission, indicating there are other survivors. After telling Rick and Louise about the broadcast, Jim dies. Rick and Louise leave the house for the new world. Louise takes a last look at the photograph of her and her first boyfriend. The next shot shows the dead mutant — implying that it was Louise's boyfriend. Rick and Louise then depart into the wilderness as THE BEGINNING flashes on the screen before the final fade out.[14]

When Worlds Collide

The world came to an end, literally, not by a nuclear holocaust but a cosmic catastrophe, in George Pal's 1951 film *When Worlds Collide*. The film is a doomsday parable for the nuclear age of the '50s — the precursor of what became known in the '70s as "disaster films." Collisions with cosmic rocks had been featured as early as *The Comet* (1910) and *The Comet's Comeback* (1916), which capitalized on Halley's Comet's initial appearance in the twentieth century. Pal's film, based on a 1930s novel by Philip Wylie and Edwin Balmer, upgraded the concept for the atomic age and showed both the end of the world and a feverish race against time to save a handful of survivors before calamity strikes.[15]

Times Square flooded in *When Worlds Collide*. Photo copyright: None given but most probably Paramount Pictures.

14 *Day the World Ended*, dir. Roger Corman, Columbia TriStar Home Video, 1993.

15 Newman 133.

The opening shot features a Biblical quotation: "And God looked upon the earth, and behold, it was corrupt; for all flesh had corrupted his way upon the earth. And God said unto Noah, The end of all flesh is come before me; for the earth is filled with violence through them; and, behold, I will destroy them with the earth. . ."

Mount Kenna Observatory in South Africa makes an astonishing discovery, requiring a courier to deliver photographs to the United States in utmost secrecy. Bellus, a star larger than Earth, and Zyra, a new-found planet orbiting Bellus, are on a collision course with Earth. Zyra will pass near Earth, followed by Bellus, which will collide with Earth. The findings are confirmed in New York. The scientists go before the United Nations and the US Congress for their "Noah's Ark proposal" to migrate to another planet, but are rebuffed. In the end private enterprise — industrialists — provide the funding and resources to build the vessels. A wheelchair-bound businessman, Stanton (John Hoyt), interested only in saving his own skin, agrees to provide the remaining funding to finish the ship — only if he's allowed to choose who goes to the new world. The chief scientist, Dr. Hendron, forces him to relent and still gets the money.

The scientists and other technicians gather in a remote area where the galactic ark is under construction. Stanton brings rifles with him to the camp, predicting that when doomsday arrives, those not fortunate enough to make it to Zyra will rise up, storming to get aboard the ship — a notion Hendron dismisses because he believes that people are more civilized than that. As Zyra approaches, a religious revival sweeps the world. When Zyra passes near Earth, volcanoes erupt, oil wells ignite, glaciers collapse, tidal waves crash into the shore, flooding is rampant and New York is engulfed in flooding and a tidal wave.*[16]

A raffle is held to determine who will be taken to the new world. The raffle results in hard feelings and fights among those left behind. Arming themselves with Stanton's rifles, those not chosen rush the ship before takeoff. Hendron refuses to take Stanton aboard, sacrificing both of them so the 40 select people can takeoff. As the ship moves down the ramp, Stanton rises from his wheelchair in a vain effort to board it. The ship roars into space just as Bellus collides with Earth.*[17]

Having used all its fuel, the ark glides to a crash landing on Zyra. Once there, they find the new world habitable. The passengers and their animal companions disembark into a lush, Garden of Eden environment as their first sunrise on the new world dawns. The final shot flashes onto the screen the words, "The first day on the new world had begun. . ." as a heavenly choir accompanies it.[18]

---

16 Owing to the film's meager budget, stock footage — evidently from forest fire stories — was utilized to depict global destruction; scenes of New York being inundated by tidal waves were actually effects shot. Warren 64.

17 The supposedly 400-foot long Noah's Ark spaceship was, in reality, a remote-controlled model, nearly 4 feet in length. Johnson 297.

18 *When Worlds Collide*, dir. Rudolph Mate, Paramount Pictures, 2001.

THE NEXT VOICE YOU HEAR. . .

In addition to churning out science fiction films during the '50s, Hollywood also produced religious epics such as *The Robe, The Ten Commandments, A Man Called Peter*, and *Ben-Hur*. Religious films depicted valiant Christians locked in battle against despotic and godless Roman villains — a clear metaphor for Communists.[19] Like the science fiction films, the religious pictures were a reflection of '50s America and the Cold War. The '50s witnessed a religious revival in America. For numbers of Americans the Church was both a house of worship and a class-room to learn about the nature of communism. By 1950, the ratio of American families boasting church membership stood at 57%; a decade later, it had risen six points. Between 1949 and 1953 the number of Bibles sold also rose. Evidence of Congressional piety could be found in the new prayer room in the Capitol, the addition of "under God" to the Pledge of Allegiance, and the engraving of "In God We Trust" on all coins.

Far more than the presence of the Red threat lay behind the official promul-gation of what theologian Will Herberg dubbed "civic religion." World War II, the Holocaust, the postwar tensions of family life, and the assault on small-town conventions kindled a yearning for religion's two great benefactions — solace and meaning. Theologians Norman Vincent Peale, Rabbi Joshua Loth Liebman, Monsignor Fulton J. Sheen, Billy Graham, and Francis Cardinal Spellman became national figures.

In middle America, patriotism and the church were synonymous; church at-tendance, which had spiraled downward immediately after World War II, rose owing to two factors: confidence (in God-sent American prosperity) and unease (over nuclear war and communist spying). People downed religion like a tran-quilizer and lavished money into the coffers of religious organizations.

In addition to releasing stupendous religious epics, Hollywood released what has been called "one of the most curious oddities ever released by a major studio": *The Next Voice You Hear...*[20]

The film focuses on a California aircraft factory worker, Joe Smith (James Whitmore), his pregnant wife (Nancy Davis), and their 10-year-old son (Gary Gray). At the beginning of the film, the Smiths hurriedly down their breakfast without taking time for devotions. Joe's car invariably conks out when he starts it up for work. Once he arrives at his job, Joe hears the "advice" of his hated foreman, Mr. Brannon (Art Smith): "An honest day's work for an honest dollar."

That evening, at 8:30, the regularly scheduled radio broadcast is interrupted by a strange announcement: "This is God. I will be with you for the next few days." Radio listeners the world over hear the same message, each in his or her own language. Joe's wife feels it's "one of those mystery voice shows" or "maybe

---

19 Matthews "Communists, Extraterrestrials" 24.; James T. Patterson, *Grand Expectations: The United States, 1945-1974* (New York: Oxford UP, 1996) 329.

20 Richard J. Barnet, *The Rockets Red Glare: When America Goes to War. The Presidents and the People* (New York: Simon and Schuster, 1990) 299-301; Douglas Brode, *Lost Films of the Fifties* (Secaucus: Citadel Press, 1988).

one of those Orson Welles things." Her son thinks it's a neighborhood kid trying to be a radio announcer.

James Whitmore, Nancy Davis, and Gary Gray in *The Next Voice You Hear*.   Photo copyright: MGM.

The Voice speaks again at the same time on subsequent nights. To those doubting He is who He says He is, He furnishes a token miracle: a cloudburst. He tells skeptics and dawdlers, "Create for yourselves the miracles of kindness and goodness and peace. You are like children going to school. You have forgotten some of your lessons. I ask you to do your homework for tomorrow."

An announcer discloses that the Federal Communications Commission has begun a nationwide investigation. The Voice has also been heard in other parts of the world: Europe, China, and Japan. Is this some ploy on the Russians' part? An attempt to record the Voice is unsuccessful.

Joe progresses from skepticism and annoyance to alarm. He shocks his son by getting drunk, which causes the boy to run away from home. Ultimately, Joe finds his son at Brannon's home, where father and son reconcile their differences, and where Joe and Brannon also make peace between themselves. On the seventh day, God is silent, prompting Joe's minister to conclude that God is resting. (This may be due to the fact that the people of Earth have repented.) Mrs. Smith gives birth to her second child, and the film concludes with words from John 1:1, "In the beginning was the Word: and the Word was with God: and the word was God."[21]

---

21 Matthews, "Communists, Extraterrestrials," 24-25; Sayre 206; Miller and Nowak 87.

Chapter 5. Atomic Mutants: Animal and Human

In addition to suggesting the imminent end of the world, atomic energy represented another threat to humanity's existence: atomic-age mutations. If irradiated marigold seeds could produce gigantic blossoms, then, Hollywood reasoned, atomic testing could cause similar malformations in anything.[1] In the early years of the atomic age, Americans had been secure in the knowledge that they alone possessed the Bomb. That changed after Russia exploded its own bomb in 1949, which triggered an arms race to build super bombs. Americans believed that God, the government, and good luck would safeguard them from nuclear devastation. Added to this was the fact that for over 100 years, war's horrors had only happened in other countries, not America.

Americans became accustomed to living in an atomic world and all that went with it: bomb tests, civil defense messages and drills, maps of the United States showing those places the Russians would be likely to attack, and maps of New York and other big cities showing the levels of destruction from the center of an atomic blast. Jokes about atomic energy and atomic war became the norm, and people living near atomic test sites in the desert became inured to the sounds of the tests.

As the race progressed to build bigger and improved H-bombs, questions arose as to the health and genetic dangers of radioactive fallout. In the opinion voiced by the United States government and its scientists, although little was known about fallout, it didn't appear very dangerous; and even if it were, America had to take the risks owing to the Russian weapons programs. It was in the "national interest" for American testing to continue.

Newspapers and magazines frequently featured stories on the results of nuclear tests, yet mostly minimized the dangerous effects and maintained that security reasons necessitated continued nuclear testing. A few conservative peri-

1   Skal, *The Monster Show*, 248.

odicals sought to persuade their readers that the hazards were insignificant and that opponents of testing were poorly informed alarmists, communist dupes, or communists and fellow travelers. Moreover, the government and media emphasized the peaceful uses of atomic energy that resulted from weapons research. Americans were constantly informed that atomic energy would light entire cities, transform medicine, and allow the creation of wonderful gadgets and conveniences that would improve life in the new atomic age.[2]

The Eisenhower administration sought to emphasize the peaceful atom. Announcing what became known as Atoms for Peace, in an address before the United Nations in 1953, President Eisenhower declared that the United States would share its nuclear knowledge with other countries "to apply atomic energy to the needs of agriculture, medicine, and other peaceful activities. A special purpose would be to provide abundant electrical energy in the power-starved areas of the world." Under Ike's proposal, the UN would create an International Atomic Energy Authority to hold stocks of fissionable material, donated by America, the Soviet Union and Great Britain, and to "devise methods whereby this fissionable material would be allocated to serve the peaceful pursuits of mankind," so that "the miraculous inventiveness of man shall not be dedicated to his death, but consecrated to his life."

Atoms for Peace was primarily directed toward production of electricity. "The United States," Catherine Caufield has written, "was determined to take the lead in the race for nuclear power, so that its designs and equipment would dominate the infant world market for nuclear power plants." In the wake of Eisenhower's proposal to the UN, Congress amended the 1946 Atomic Energy Act to further commercial nuclear power development. Within a week of the new legislation's enactment, Eisenhower initiated construction of the first American commercial nuclear power plant, in Shippingport, Pennsylvania.[3]

The atom also made its presence felt on everyday items. The earliest and most widespread symbol of atomic imagery was that of thin metal rods with tiny colored or gleaming spheres attached at the ends, and occasionally at connections as well. This design appeared in wrought-iron bookcases and lamps, and originated in the laboratory and the chemistry class. The sphere-and-rod look appeared on other items. "In a lattice, such a pattern could form a very transparent screen which nonetheless demarcated areas with some dignity. Such screens were often used in churches and public buildings." This pattern was also found in such household items as fabrics, chinaware, and glasses. This was only the beginning, people were told, for there would be such inventions as atom-powered wristwatches and cars. Emblazoning atomic imagery on commonplace objects was an attempt to domesticate the reputation of a destructive force.

One household item was particularly associated with nuclear destruction: the push button. It was widely believed that the President of the United States had

---

2 Oakley 358-361.

3 Catherine Caufield, *Multiple Exposures: Chronicles of the Radiation Age* (New York: Harper & Row, 1989) 148, 150.

such a button available to him to initiate an atomic war the same way a house-wife could start her vacuum cleaner. A similar button existed in the Kremlin.[4]

On a more esoteric level, the United States was exploding atomic bombs. The US detonated five in the South Pacific in the immediate postwar period; the Russians detonated one in Siberia in 1949. The Korean War upset American plans for a new series of Pacific tests in early 1951. Logistical and security considerations prompted the American government to seek a domestic test site. The place ultimately chosen was a 1,350-square-mile government-owned tract of the Nevada desert, located 65 miles northwest of Las Vegas. The first atomic test at the new site occurred at dawn, 27 January 1951, followed by a second one the next day and three more during the following eight days.

As the tests progressed, nearby residents' worries quieted. While concerned about the tests, Governor Charles Russell of Nevada remained proud of his state's contribution to national security: "No matter who's right, it's exciting to think that the submarginal land of the proving ground is furthering science and helping national defense. We had long ago written off that terrain as wasteland and today it's blooming with atoms."

The Atomic Energy Commission encouraged bomb-watching as something entertaining and educational. In the words of *The New York Times*: "In the wake of a detonation, the atomic cloud can be seen attenuating across the sky. It may come over an observer's head. There is virtually no danger from radioactive fall-out." In Caufield's book, the author adds that: "For local families, school groups, and tourists, a pre-dawn expedition to Mount Charleston, 50 miles from the test site, became a popular outing."

In late 1951 the Army established Camp Desert Rock, next to the test site, so that soldiers from all branches of the military, could participate in the tests. Despite insufficient record-keeping the Defense Department subsequently reckoned that, from 1945 to 1963, between 250,000 and 500,000 troops participated in atomic tests. Subsequently, many of the atomic veterans developed health problems, which they asserted resulted from exposure to radiation during their military duty. Six thousand of them filed claims with the Veterans Administration; all but 44 were denied on the grounds that no evidence existed establishing a connection between radiation exposure and health problems. Congress belatedly enacted legislation in 1988 requiring the government provide health benefits to any atomic veteran who developed a form of cancer known to be radiation induced.[5]

Against this backdrop, Hollywood churned out atomic mutation films that came to symbolize the nuclear-age anxieties of the 1950s.

THE BEAST FROM 20,000 FATHOMS

The atomic mutants of the 1950s owed their ancestry to the Depression-era monster King Kong. Reissued in 1952, the '30s smash about a giant ape brought from his primitive island home to New York, where he runs amok before being

---

4 Thomas Hine, *Populuxe* (New York: Alfred A. Knopf, 1986) 132-133.

5 Caufield 103-108.

shot down from atop the Empire State Building, was an even greater hit, earn-ing $3 million in ticket sales, prompting *Time* to dub the simian "Monster of the Year."[6]

The Beast from 20,000 Fathoms. Photo copyright: None provided but was released by Warner Bros.

Two men were watching the returns of *King Kong*: Jack Dietz and Hal E. Chester, the heads of a low-budget outfit, Mutual Films of California. Among the properties they were considering was a *King Kong*-inspired one: *The Monster from Beneath the Sea.* For art direction, they contacted veteran film designer Eugene Lourie. The latter, having wanted to direct a film for some time, saw this as his opportunity to fulfill his desire. Working with some writers, Lourie developed a script that expanded the Dietz and Chester concept. According to Paul Mandell, the script was prepared by Lourie and another writer who had been blacklisted. Lourie refused to reveal the man's name to Mandell. Final credit for the script goes to Fred Freiberger and Louis Morheim, though the shooting script bears the signatures of Morheim and Robert Smith, the latter perhaps a pseudonym.

The film opens with a nuclear test at the Arctic Circle.[7] "What the cumulative effects of all these atomic explosions and tests will be, only time can tell," says the top scientist on the experiment, Professor Tom Nesbitt (Paul Christian). The blast releases a prehistoric creature, a rhedosaurus, which makes its way to its

---

6 David Kalat, *A Critical History and Filmography of Toho's Godzilla Series* (Jefferson: McFarland & Company, Inc., 1997) 12.

7 Warren 99-100.

ancestral home, New York City. Once ashore, the rhedosaurus wreaks devastation, bringing with it germs that prove dangerous to the troops fighting it. The
beast is finally overcome with a radioactive isotope fired into it, destroying both
it and the germs it harbors.[8]

The crowd scenes showing people running from the monster "were shot partly on location in New York City and partly on the back lot of Paramount Studios,"
Director Eugene Lourie explained:

> "I went to New York . . . [to shoot process plates and some of the mob scenes].
> We shot on a weekend when there would be not much traffic. We had hired
> extras to play stevedores and dockworkers, and when we saw them we saw that
> they were puny men, they did not look like a stevedore should look. So we hired
> some real stevedores. When we were done, they asked for me to pose with them
> in a photo to their wives; this would prove that they were working [in the film],
> not getting drunk in a bar."

Lourie added:

> "The next day we shot on Wall Street with a crowd of twenty-five people.
> There were supposed to be many more, but the production manager said that
> it was a Sunday and extras would have to be paid double, so twenty-five was
> all we could afford. But I knew that we would be shooting [additional crowd
> scenes] at Paramount, so it was unimportant. The largest amount of extras I re-
> member at Paramount was four hundred for one day. [Producer] Bernie Burton
> was the editor on it, and as he was cutting the film he said, 'Gene, you don't give
> me any prerogative. You shot the scenes [in such a way] that I can only put them
> together the way you shot them.' I said, 'That was the idea!'"

Lourie added that the monster's demise at the end of the film greatly affected
his young daughter. "She was about six years old when I took her to see the picture. And coming home, she started to cry and said, 'You are bad, Daddy! You
killed the big nice Beast!'" Consequently, in Lourie's later film, *Gorgo*, "I tried not
to kill the beast. Gorgo escapes alive back to the sea. My daughter should have a
writer's credit."[9]

The finished film both pleased and somewhat surprised its producers. "They
were all *extremely* happy with the picture," Lourie recalled. "But when Dietz saw
that it was better than they expected, he didn't want to release it through a small
organization. He went to Jack Warner and offered *him* the picture. But Warner
didn't want to release the picture; he wanted to buy it outright. And he *did* buy
it outright, for $450,000, and Warners changed the title to *The Beast from 20,000
Fathoms*. Then, when the returns started coming in, Jack Dietz was very *unhappy*
that he had lost the rights, because it was number one at the box office. Each time
he read about it in *Variety*, he said, 'Oh, I am stupid!'"[10]

An unresolved question is how much the film drew its basis from Ray Bradbury's short story in *The Saturday Evening Post* (reprinted as "The Foghorn" in

---

8 *The Beast from 20,000 Fathoms*, dir Eugene Lourie, Warner Home Video, 1991.

9 Weaver, *They Fought* 204, 205, 207.

10 Weaver, *They Fought* 205.

Bradbury's *The Golden Apples of the Sun*). Lourie told an interviewer that Bradbury's story was acquired during production and that almost none of Bradbury's tale of a dinosaur attracted to the foghorn of a lighthouse was utilized in the final film. "However," according to film historian Bill Warren,

> "Bradbury told me another story. He and (film animator Ray) Harryhausen had been close friends for 15 years, and had often talked of collaborating on something. When Harryhausen finished his first feature, Bradbury said he was eager to show it to his old friend. After the screening, Bradbury mentioned that he was wondering when he'd be paid for the use of his story. Harryhausen was aghast; he had no idea of what had occurred. (It isn't clear if he didn't know of the similarities to Bradbury's story, which seems unlikely, or if he assumed that Bradbury had been paid for it.) In any event, Bradbury says that he was not paid for the rights until the film was completed. The fact that the title was changed from "The Monster from Beneath the Sea" to the same title the short story had in its magazine appearance strongly indicates that a settlement was made. Bradbury's name was featured prominently in the advertising for the film.

> "I don't think anyone is covering up or trying to gather glory for himself. Bradbury and Harryhausen are both decent, honorable men and have remained close friends all along. Memories simply become uncertain after so many years. The screen does credit Bradbury, the film has the same title as his short story, and he was called America's greatest science fiction author in the advertising. In any event, no one was hurt; the film certainly helped Harryhausen's career, and probably also helped Bradbury's.[11]

Recalling her co-stars in the film, leading lady Paula Raymond said, "It was a very happy set and we all got along well. Paul Christian was sort of distant but everyone from Cecil Kellaway and Kenneth Tobey to the director, Eugene Lourie, was simply wonderful. I played Kellaway's assistant in the picture, and Cecil was so very charming." Raymond continued, "I guess I was one of the first of a long line of lady scientists in these types of films."[12] Regarding the film's success, Raymond said, "That same year, Warner Brothers also released *House of Wax*, which was made in color and 3-D. Studio head Jack Warner thought for sure that *House of Wax* would fare better at the box office, but it turned out that *The Beast from 20,000 Fathoms* out-grossed *House of Wax*, which surprised even Jack. And back in those days, there were no residuals given to actors. When the film was in preparation, it was not deemed to be an important production. The public's attraction to it made it important as a film and as an impressive artistic piece for its time. It's definitely a nine on my one-to-ten scale because it's so credible in its execution."[13]

Ray Harryhausen, the man who brought the rhedosaurus to life, is a legend in motion picture special effects. The roots of his career trace back to his youth, when he began animating, utilizing whatever was available. His special interest was animals and dinosaurs. After viewing *King Kong* when he was 13, Harryhau-

---

11 Warren 103-104.

12 Parla and Mitchell 207.

13 Parla and Mitchell 205.

sen borrowed a camera and started fabricating animals without wire on wooden armatures. He met *Kong*'s creator, Willis O'Brien, who became his mentor, despite the fact that Harryhausen didn't require much encouraging on the subject. Harryhausen also met two of O'Brien's model makers, Marcel Delgado and George Lofgren. Both of them subsequently worked with Harryhausen on *Mighty Joe Young* (1949). From O'Brien, Harryhausen learned the importance of studying anatomy in constructing stop motion monsters. Anatomy was a subject Harryhausen was already familiar with, having studied art and anatomy at Los Angeles City College. Harryhausen, moreover, worked on George Pal's puppetoons, where he gained experience with movement and gesture knowledge. When his career took off in the '50s, he gave up wooden-jointed armatures with fur-coat coverings for metal ball-joint sockets cast with foam and sponge rubber.[14]

Harryhausen's rhedosaurus for *Beast* had a grey liquid latex skin coating with textured scales, and glued-on spikes. The dinosaur design was not the first one suggested for the film, a giant octopus being considered before the dinosaur was agreed on. "The producers," Harryhausen explained in a magazine article, "had a rough script to begin with but wanted to give it more substance. When I was called in I brought some fresh ideas to it. Then Ray Bradbury's *Saturday Evening Post* story came out which was bought, and parts of it were injected, as well as the maintenance of the title."

The price tag for the film was $200,000. Harryhausen explained, "I didn't get much out of it and it was sold for $450,000 to Warner Brothers who made over five million on it. In those days you were lucky to work." Harryhausen's fee for his work on the film was $10,000 (some sources say $5,000), along with the necessary supplies to finish the job. Harryhausen reported that Jack Dietz considered filming the movie in 3-D, but a lack of money necessitated abandoning this approach.

Prior to filming, Harryhausen was in his garage studio testing his effects on 16 mm film. For the scene where the rhedosaurus attacks and destroys a lighthouse, Harryhausen employed rear and front projection. The "front" process screen adaptation doesn't need much light, and since the beast would only be seen in silhouette, it seemed to be the right approach.

One of the innovations Harryhausen created for the film was shadow effects. "Anything that stands in sun light," John "J. J." Johnson explains, "casts a shadow, and although he could have easily gotten by without them, they add one more element of realism to the action. When using rear projection behind a stop motion model (like the Rhedosaurus) on a miniature set, the light that comes through the screen illuminates the monster. In turn, the monster's mass blocks off part of this light heaving a shadow on the foreground set which is recorded during filming even though the sequence is photographed one frame at a time."

Many elements came into play in the roller coaster sequence that concludes the film. The actors and the background plates were shot at Long Beach's Pacific Ocean Park. In the foreground, a tiny roller coaster set was erected for the monster to demolish. Once the stop motion work was completed, the fire that

14 Johnson 56-57.

destroys the rhedosaurus was superimposed onto the animation. "When viewed all at once, however, these separate elements are difficult to distinguish. Those who can tell the difference are too busy enjoying the thrills and action anyway."[15]

Harryhausen's special effects technique, called by many names, is frequently known as "Dynamation":

> Location footage of people reacting in terror (or whatever) to a to-be-animated figure is shot, usually under Harryhausen's direction. Back in his studio, he projects this footage on a screen from behind, masking off the elements that the animated figure will be moving behind — foreground action, buildings, mountains, etc. This rear-projected footage is re-photographed by Harryhausen a frame at a time as he animates the creature (also a frame at a time) in front of this process screen. The film is wound back and now the masked-off areas are exposed, the previously-shot area is itself masked off, and the scene is filmed once again. The result is that the animated creature is placed *between* the foreground and background of one shot — sandwiched between layers of reality. (Getting a person to move in front of the animated creature is more complicated, but basically a variation on this procedure.) This process is not only inexpensive, it is relatively simple and very appropriate for a picture like *The Beast from 20,000 Fathoms*, which emphasizes the documentary aspects of the story.[16]

Though it helped usher in the atomic-age mutant films, *The Beast from 20,000 Fathoms* was not an atomic mutant, rather a dinosaur awakened by an atomic blast. The first true atomic mutant film lay waiting in the wings to be released by the same studio that released *Beast*.

THEM!

That film had to surmount several obstacles to make it to the screen: Warner Brothers tried to sell the screenplay to another studio. Then, after changing its mind about selling it, Warners cut the film's budget just prior to shooting. All this notwithstanding, the film earned more money for Warners in 1954 than any other release that year.

Remembered as "that picture with the big ants," and of one of the first "atomic mutation films," *Them!* stood out among films of its genre for combing "mystery, horror, convincing background, documentary-like approach, and excellent performances."[17]

Two New Mexico state policemen find a little girl wandering aimlessly in the desert. Subsequently, they discover her parents' car destroyed. In the ambulance, she reacts to a mysterious sound coming from the desert. Checking a cabin owned by Gramps Johnson, the state troopers find it has been pulverized and its owner murdered. Like the wrecked car, money wasn't stolen from the cabin; only sugar is missing. One of the state troopers who remains at the cabin hears the same sound the girl heard in the ambulance. Going to investigate its source, he fires shots into it, then screams in agony.

---

15 Johnson 59-62.

16 Warren 101, 103.

17 Von Gunden and Stock 104.

The giant ants of *Them!* emerge from their desert hideaway in New Mexico. Photo copyright: Warner Bros.

The little girl's father was an FBI agent on vacation. FBI agent Robert Graham (James Arness), called in to the case, sends a plaster cast of a mysterious print found at the car wreckage to FBI headquarters for identification. Gramps Johnson's death was attributed to formic acid in his body. The Department of Agriculture sends Dr. Medford (Edmund Gwenn) and his daughter Pat (Joan Weldon) to help with the case. The Medfords were summoned after the FBI, unable to identify the cast, sent it to the Agriculture Department. The elder Medford asks when the first atomic bomb was exploded in the area. To Graham and State Trooper Ben Peterson's (James Whitmore) annoyance, he declines to tell them why he asked that question. At the hospital, using a glass of formic acid, Medford jolts the little girl out of her shock. She screams "Them!" over and over again.[18]

18 Sandy Descher, who played the hapless little girl, offered these recollections about working on *Them!*: "Well, it was a very difficult shoot, particularly for a child so young. I had a double and stand-in. . . she was a midget. As a matter of fact, she doubled for me for years until I outgrew her. Anyway, the shoot was difficult because of the weather. It was very hot in the desert, and we had a lot of sand that was supposed to be blowing. In particular it was difficult for me to maintain that catatonic state. I had to keep my eyes open, and sand was always blowing in them. I remember Mr. Douglas (the director) was directing me from under the camera. Suddenly he fell into a cactus bush, but he kept going. I didn't ruin the scene, and he didn't cry out until the shot was over. It was quite amusing. He wound up with a number of stickers in his rump, and he had to have them pulled out with tweezers by the make-up man. . . James Arness and James Whitmore were quite delightful to me on the set. So was Christian Drake, the other patrolman. I used to ride on their shoulders on location. I have some home movies showing that." Of her screaming scene, "I remember the scene we had in *Them* where I was in the hospital, and I remember they presented me with a serum with a scent, and I started screaming. They used some-

Afterward, the Medfords, Graham, and Peterson travel to the desert, where they discover the source of their problems: a giant ant, created by lingering radiation from the first atomic bomb blast. There are more of them in the desert. "We may be witnesses to a Biblical prophecy come true," says the elder Medford. "And there shall be destruction and darkness come upon creation. And the beasts shall reign over the Earth."

A helicopter search of the desert reveals the ants' mound and the remains of their victims. Graham and Peterson use bazookas to fire phosphorus shells on the surface of the mound to keep them there, then use cyanide bombs to flood the nest, killing them. Accompanied by Pat Medford, Graham and Peterson then descend into the nest. (Initially, Graham didn't want Pat to go with them but Pat has the scientific background to study the nest — a strong woman for the '50s!). Once inside the nest, they discover that not all the ants were destroyed and kill them. In the queen ant's chamber, they find that some of the eggs had already hatched and departed on their wedding flight, with the potential to create other colonies elsewhere. At a briefing in Washington, Pat's father warns that, unless the queen ants are destroyed before they establish other colonies, "Man, as the dominant species of life on Earth, will probably be extinct within a year. . ."

A pilot who reported seeing "flying saucers shaped like ants" in Texas is confined in a mental hospital until the government says he's well. A ship at sea, infested with the ants, is sunk by the US Navy. The queen ants and their colony are eventually tracked to the Los Angeles sewer system.[19] Peterson and Graham lead an Army team into the sewers to destroy the ants and find two missing children who were playing with their father when the ants attacked them, killing the father. Peterson rescues the boys, but he is killed by one of the ants. Graham and the soldiers find the queen's nest and destroy them. As they die, Graham asks Pat "if these monsters got started as a result of the first atomic bomb in 1945, what about all the others that have been exploded since then?"

"I don't know," is all Pat can say.

Pat's father has the last word: "Nobody knows, Robert. When Man entered the atomic age, he opened a door into a new world. What we'll eventually find in that new world, nobody can predict."[20]

---

thing that did smell quite strange. It wasn't ammonia. It was something else that smelled really strange. They tried to create something different, and it helped me a lot with that particular scene." Parla 49-50, 51.

19 When an emergency press conference is held, placing Los Angeles under martial law, a reporter asks, "Has the Cold War gotten hot?" The people of Los Angeles are directed to stay in their homes. When I watched this film in February 2003, the United States was at "Orange Alert" in light of possible terrorist attacks in connection with an Islamic holy day. People were stocking up on food and being told to tape their windows as a precaution against a terrorist attack.

20 *Them!*, dir. Gordon Douglas, Warner Home Video, 2002. Originally the script was to have Medford say: "Our dilemma is that we must apparently continue these atomic experiments if we are to preserve peace on Earth. We have no alternative. For the final results — we have no choice except to wait and see — and pray that decisions we make today (looks at Mike and Jerry — the two boys rescued from the ants) will not destroy them

Confronting the giant ants in the underground tunnels in *Them!*. Photo copyright: it says MGM but most likely is Warner Bros.

Them!'s producer, Ted Sherderman, had been a staff officer to General MacArthur during World War II, and was greatly disturbed about the use of the atomic bomb at Hiroshima: "I just went over to the curb and started to throw up," he explained. Upon seeing the story treatment for *Them!*, he saw two advantages: "Everyone had seen ants and no one trusted the atom bomb, so I had Warner buy the story." It was Sherderman who took George Worthing Yates's screenplay and revamped it, transplanting the ants from New York subway tunnels to Los Angeles storm sewers, and cut out a final confrontation between soldiers and the mutant monsters on a Santa Monica amusement pier. According to director Gordon Douglas, the production team regarded their assignment with utmost seriousness. They "weren't trying to make a comic strip or be cute about it. . . . We talked a great deal about the bombs these scientists were playing around with." Due to budget cuts, the film was shot, not in 3-D and color, the original intention, but black-and-white — a move that displeased Douglas: "I put green and red soap bubbles in their eyes," he said of the twelve-foot-long mechanical bugs. "The ants were purple, slimy things. Their bodies were wet down with Vaseline. They scared the bejeezus out of you."[21]

tomorrow." Dennis Fischer, *Science Fiction Film Directors, 1895-1998* (Jefferson: McFarland & Company, Inc., 2000) 166.

21 Skal, *Screams of Reason* 184-185.

Unlike *The Thing*, where the scientist was at odds with the military over how to deal with the monster, *Them!* presented the scientists working in concert with the military and law enforcement to destroy the menace. The scientist, feeling remorse for unleashing the Bomb upon the world, devises the method for destroying the monster. This reflected the real-life guilt many scientists felt about their involvement in developing the atomic bomb and its use in World War II.[22]

Indeed, the scientist is the hero of *Them!*. The police are inadequate to deal with the ants, requiring experts (scientists). When the ants murder the little girl's FBI father, they have attacked federal authority, bringing a federal response in the form of the Medfords, a general, and FBI agent Graham. The federal representatives form an alliance with a local authority — state trooper Peterson. Science supersedes military authority as the elder Medford gives orders to the general and traditional sex roles as Pat Medford forces Graham and Peterson to take her inside the ants' New Mexican nest, and then orders them to destroy the queen ant's chamber.[23]

The mutant ants owed their design to Larry Meggs of Warners's Art Department. His initial ant, a 3-footer, was screen-tested with some tiny railroad cars. This "big ant" failed to impress studio chiefs. Just the same, considering that rival studio Universal-International was planning to release *Creature from the Black Lagoon* in the spring of 1954 as a follow-up to *It Came from Outer Space*, the Warner executives wanted to remain competitive with a monster movie of their own and green-lighted *Them!*.

Two fully operational mechanical ants were built. Warners's principal ant builder was Dick Smith. His creations were equipped with built-in pulleys, gears, and levers that operated the head, antennas, pinchers, and legs. These were connected to cables operated off-screen by technicians. The latter greatly amused Gordon Douglas as they worked so closely together they frequently bumped into each other while running the ant. The second mechanical prop, a three-quarters ant displaying head and thorax mounted on a camera crane, was seen mainly in close-up shots such as Peterson's death in the ant's mandibles. The full body ant was used mostly in long shots and some overhead glimpses such as the ant holding a human rib cage in its pinchers. While the ant occasionally seemed to be walking, it had a motor inside that moved the legs back and forth; still, it was necessary to tow it on a camera dolly as it was incapable of walking on its power. Asked by director Douglas, "Does it look honest?," his editor merely said, "As honest as twelve foot ants can look." Several other ants, minus motors, were used for clustered ant attacks. They were far lighter, and constructed so that blowing wind machines could make their heads move.[24]

The ants' sound, according to Douglas, was an amalgamation of numerous different sounds: bird whistles "and things pitched up which were mixed and

---

22 Brode, *The Films of the Fifties*, 27.

23 Biskind 123-126.

24 Johnson 17-18.

combined on the soundtrack. The insistent sound of the initially unseen ants," Dennis Fischer notes, "definitely aids in creating an atmosphere of eeriness."[25]

Them! was only the beginning. In its wake came a whole menagerie of over-sized bugs in such films as *Tarantula* (1955), *The Deadly Mantis* (1957), *The Beginning of the End* (1957), and *Earth vs. the Spider* (1958), as well as a giant octopus in *It Came from Beneath the Sea* (1955).[26] Of these films, *The Deadly Mantis* comes the closest to September 11. The overgrown mantis is released from an icy prison, wreaks havoc in the Arctic, makes its way to Washington, DC, and is shot down over New York where it is finally destroyed in the "Manhattan Tunnel." The film accentuates America's Arctic security systems, with the mantis acting as metaphor for a Russian attack on the United States. When the mantis flies over the Capitol, it buzzes the Capitol building, then attacks the Washington Monument. For that scene, a real mantis was used, with the insect climbing a model of the landmark. A puppet mantis was used for the remainder of the film.[27]

While *Them!* gave rise to the atomic mutation film, its giant ants would be dwarfed by another atomic mutant.

GODZILLA

The ultimate nuclear age monster came not from Hollywood, but from the only nation in history to actually experience atomic war — Japan. There was a significant difference between how American science fiction films approached the Bomb and how the Japanese viewed it. While '50s American science fiction films' treatment of radiation reflected the era's nuclear anxieties, it was, according to film historian Bill Warren, mainly a gimmick the way other technical innovations of earlier times were used by Hollywood. By contrast, the Japanese were the only people to experience nuclear war firsthand — thus their feelings about nuclear weapons were far deeper. "In the Japanese context, the monster is less a reaction *to* the bomb than a symbol *of* the bomb."[28]

During Japan's "Golden Age" of movie making after World War II, such films as *Rashoman* (1950), *Ugetsu* (1953), *Gate of Hell* (1953), and *Seven Samurai* (1954) received international acclaim and such filmmakers as Akira Kurosawa, Kenji Mizoguchi, and Yasujiro Ozu were hard at work. It was also during this same period that the Japanese fantasy film, particularly the Japanese giant monster movie (*kaiju eiga*), emerged, where, in the United States at least, it was viewed "as the lowest of the lowbrow."

While Japanese monster films were usually classed together with American sci-fi films of the same era, in reality they were far different, though the Japanese films, at first, copied the American product. Japanese monster films, despite being regarded as films "so bad they're good," virtually ruled the science fiction film world from the late '50s through the late '60s. During that era, Japanese monster

---

25 Fischer, 166.

26 Skal, *The Monster Show* 248.

27 Warren, 337-338; Fischer 331.

28 Kalat 13-14.

films were characterized by what were then state-of-the-art special effects that greatly surpassed the most extravagant American sci-fi features: *Fantastic Voyage* (1966), *2001: A Space Odyssey* (1968).

During the late '50s and early '60s, while American science fiction films declined in quality, Japanese sci-fi films proliferated, and, to the Japanese at least, they were not second-rate. Between 1958 and 1967, most American science fiction films were photographed in black and white, whereas almost all Japanese science fiction films produced after 1955 were shot in color for the anamorphic wide screen (variations of Fox's CinemaScope, but, in Japan, called Nikkatsu Scope and Shochiku GrandScope). Moreover Toho, the main player in Japanese science fiction films, released many of them between 1957-1965 in Perspecta stereophonic sound.

The players in American science fiction films of the '50s and early '60s could be classified as B-movie actors, has-been leading men, rising stars waiting to be discovered, and actresses who were usually concluding their contracts or being led into "bigger" parts. Japanese fantasy films featured big-name stars. Because of poor American dubbing, such stars were condemned by American reviewers.

Aesthetically speaking, Japanese science fiction films bloomed between the mid-'50s and late-'60s. One film historian observed that Japanese monster makers were sophisticated men toiling in a highly unsophisticated genre. At the same time, American science fiction films were helmed by those who usually were hacks who had worked on serials, B-Westerns, two-reel comedies, and other similar genres who moved into sci-fi when the demand for their earlier film genres faded in the early '50s. "In terms of camera placement, staging, directing actors — the kinds of things directors do — American sci-fi directors often displayed a remarkable lack of imagination. In Japan, however, even the schlockiest of schlock looked good. Even the most undistinguished of directors knew where to put the camera, position the actors, and splice it all together, no matter how mindless the resulting film."

The Japanese film industry had programs to find and cultivate behind-screen and on-screen talents. In the assistant director program, a neophyte began as a grip, performing all sorts of menial tasks. As one rose from fourth assistant director to third assistant director, assistant directors worked more closely with their teachers, learning all aspects of filmmaking. Ultimately, assistant directors become directors; during the "Golden Age," they were normally assigned a short feature, 43-65 minutes in length. The "New Face Program" was basically comprised of annual talent contests open to anyone. The winners received studio contracts. After receiving acting, singing, and dancing lessons at the studio, the recruits were gradually placed in the studio's film in what were walk-on roles. Those roles became bigger and better if the fledgling performers possessed talent and/or popularity.[29]

---

29 Stuart Galbraith IV, *Monsters Are Attacking Tokyo! The Incredible World of Japanese Fantasy Films* (Venice: Feral House, 1998) 17-21.

It was from Japan that the greatest nuclear age monster of all would emerge. In his native country, he was known as *Gojira*. American audiences knew him as Godzilla.

The Godzilla saga began one night in 1954 when Japanese producer Tomoyuki Tanaka was returning home after a film, *Eiko no Kanatani* (*Behind the Glory*), a Japanese-Indonesian co-production, had been canceled because the Indonesian government declined to issue work visas to the Japanese actors.

"Now I had to come up with something big enough to replace it," Tanaka subsequently explained. As he stared out the window of the airplane flying him home at the Pacific Ocean below, he wondered what lay beneath its waves. He had an inspiration: Why not make a monster movie?

Several considerations influenced Tanaka's decision. *King Kong*, which had done so well upon its re-release in America in 1952, was re-released in Japan the same year to similar box office success. *Kong*'s success in Japan persuaded Warner Brothers to release *The Beast from 20,000 Fathoms* in Japan in 1953, and it became a box office success there as well.

A final motivation for Tanaka's monster epic was drawn from real-life headlines: the *Lucky Dragon* affair.[30] On 1 March 1954, the United States exploded Bravo, the first full-scale hydrogen bomb, on an islet near Bikini Atoll in the Pacific. Bravo had the force of 15 million tons of TNT, one thousand times greater than the bomb that fell on Hiroshima. "It spewed radioactive debris many miles up into the stratosphere and thousands of square miles across the Pacific." Within a short time of Bravo's detonation, fallout from the blast fell on the nearby island of Rongelap. Within 24 hours of Bravo, the inhabitants of Rongelap were exhibiting signs of acute radiation sickness, including nausea, vomiting, diarrhea, and itching of the eyes. Nearly everyone had burns on their skins. Subsequently, many of them lost all their hair. Two days after Bravo, the Americans relocated the Rongelapese to Kwajalein atoll, the command center for the tests. (In 1957 the United States returned the Rongelapese to their home island. In 1985, after appealing to the environmental group Greenpeace for assistance, the Rongelapese were relocated to another atoll in the Marshall Island group.)

A far grimmer fate awaited the crew of a Japanese tuna trawler, *Fukuryu Maru* (the *Lucky Dragon*). The morning the H-bomb was exploded, the *Dragon* was anchored 90 miles east of Bikini, 40 miles outside the official danger zone. Three hours after Bravo, the vessel was showered by a fine white ash that continued falling for roughly five hours; the ash was so thick there were footprints on the deck where the *Dragon*'s crew walked. Unsettled by the episode, the crew decided to return home. Before doing so, they washed down the ship, which likely saved many lives.

It took two weeks for the *Lucky Dragon* to return home to Japan. By then, every member of its crew was ill from radiation sickness. Some of the crew members, not realizing they were afflicted, went home. Others went to the hospital,

---

30 J. D. Lees and Marc Cerasini, *The Official Godzilla Compendium* (New York: Random House, 1998) 11-12.

where doctors quickly diagnosed their condition, ordering every crew member be brought in for observation.

The incident was a major news story in Japan and ignited a nationwide tuna panic. To calm public anxieties, the government had to examine all fish catches for radiation contamination. Inspectors destroyed one million pounds of tainted fish. The incident heightened anti-American sentiment, as evidenced by letters to newspapers and violent street rallies. Seven months after Bravo, all of the *Lucky Dragon's* crew remained hospitalized, receiving blood transfusions. One of the crew died at the end of September.*[31] His widow received a check for $2,800 from the US ambassador to Japan "as a token of the deep sympathy" of the American people. Subsequently, the United States paid $2 million reparation for the loss to the Japanese fishing industry.[32]

The entire affair enraged the US Atomic Energy Commission chairman Lewis Strauss; he came to believe that it was *he*, not the *Dragon's* crew, who was the real victim in the affair. The fishermen, Strauss told President Eisenhower, were part of a Communist scheme to spy on and embarrass the United States. "If I were the Reds," he told presidential press secretary Jim Hagerty, "I would fill the oceans all over the world with radioactive fish. It would be so easy to do!"[33]

"In *Gojira*," noted film historian Stuart Galbraith IV, "several vessels encounter the monster (kept off screen for the first half of the picture), and a group of stricken sailors reach an island community before succumbing to Gojira's radioactive residue. However, (director Ishiro) Honda and the screenwriters treated the nuclear references with kid gloves." "We skirted the issue, frankly speaking," Honda explained:

> "...because we felt that putting a real-life accident into a fictional story with a monster appearing in the midst of it wouldn't sit well in the world of a film entitled *Gojira*. That being the case, it was a matter of squeezing out the feeling I, as the director, was trying to cultivate, namely an intense fear that, having departed from the foundation of the atomic bomb and with scientific advances, having passed through various developments, has now become an environmental problem. Since those days I felt the atomic terror would hang around our necks for eternity."[34]

Honda's original intention was to tie the *Lucky Dragon* incident to the film by having the opening sequence show the doomed ship floating, completely lifeless, back to its home port just like the death ship in the classic silent horror film *Nosferatu*. "Fearing that the issue of the *Lucky Dragon* was simply too acute to address so directly," wrote film historian David Kalat, "Honda abandoned the sequence,

---

31 The deceased, Aikichi Kuboyama, the *Dragon's* chief radio operator, was quoted in newspaper accounts as saying, "Please make sure that I am the last victim of the nuclear bomb." The cause of his death was leukemia. Cancers and other illnesses thought to be attributable to the Bomb claimed five additional crew members. Steve Ryfle, *Japan's Favorite Mon-star: The Unauthorized Biography of "The Big G"* (Toronto: ECW Press, 1998) 21.

32 Caufield 112-114.

33 David Halberstam, *The Fifties* (New York: Villard Books, 1993) 348.

34 Galbraith, *Monsters* 23.

opting instead to let his monster movie merely suggest such recent horrors." Kalat also said, "Ironically, this piece of recent history is best known among *Godzilla* fans. In a way, *Godzilla*-fandom has helped with the process of 'oral history,' keeping memories alive that have otherwise fallen through the cracks of American education."[35]

Japanese science fiction writer Shigeru Kayama was tapped to prepare the film's screenplay, while Tanaka searched for an appropriate title for what was known at this point as the "G" (giant) project. Special effects were entrusted to Toho's special effects chief Eiji Tsuburaya, who had been greatly influenced by *King Kong*. The film's original designation, *Kaitei Niman Mairu Kara Kita Dai Kaiju* (*The Big Monster from 20,000 Miles Underneath the Sea*) was condensed to the much shorter and simpler *Gojira* after Tanaka learned about a corpulent, lumbering press agent in the studio publicity department who was dubbed by some of the staff "Gojira" — a fusion of the Japanese words for gorilla (*gorira*) and whale (*kujira*). After pondering the name, Tanaka chose to christen the monster "Gojira."[36]

The screenplay that ultimately emerged differed greatly from Kayama's initial concept. The final script — which featured the nuclear mutation component and the character of Dr. Serizawa — was concocted by Takeo Murata, Tsuburaya, and director Ishiro Honda. Honda, who had been with Toho since the 1930s, save for the intrusion of World War II, had visited Hiroshima after the war; greatly affected by what he saw there, Honda desired to make a movie about it. Honda went on to work on a number of Akira Kurosawa's films. *Gojira* gave Honda his first chance to bring his impressions of Hiroshima to the wide screen.

Instead of using costly stop-motion animation, the technique used in *King Kong*, Tanaka opted for Tsuburaya's miniature models and a man in a latex suit to play *Gojira*. When it came to designing the suit, "I asked Eiji Tsuburaya... to make ten or so models... in clay," Tanaka explained. "We picked one design from that." The final choice resembled a *Tyrannosaurus rex*, with the dorsal spines of a *Stegosaurus*. The beast's appearance was based on the scientific knowledge of the day, subsequently regarded as erroneous.

The first step in constructing the monster suit was pouring latex into plaster molds to fabricate arms, legs, torso, and tail. To give the suit bulk, it had an inner lining of cloth stuffed with bamboo for rigidity and urethane foam for mass. An opening along the dorsal fins, sealed by a zipper, enabled the actor to enter the suit. It was painted charcoal gray. The initial costume was far too stiff. A second one was somewhat better. The actor's head was situated in the suit's neck, while Gojira's head was mounted on a brace above the actor's head. While the suit actor could scarcely control its facial expressions, he could open and close

---

35 Kalat 33-34.

36 The identity of this man, his job at the studio, and where he worked were never disclosed. It may be because such a man never existed in the first place. "I expect the [monster's] name was thought up after very careful discussions between Mr. Tanka, Mr. Tsuburaya and my husband," director Ishiro Honda's widow explained in the 1990s. "I am sure they would have given the matter considerable thought." Regarding the man called *Gojira*, she said, "the backstage boys as Toho loved to joke around with tall stories, but I don't believe that one." Ryfle 23.

the mouth from inside. The tail, attached to wires, was operated off-camera by technicians. For scenes showing *Gojira* trampling buildings, the actor wore only the feet and legs on suspenders. A large robotic model, with working eyes, was built. For close-up shots of the beast, a smaller puppet was used.

Models of Tokyo's streets and buildings were built at 1/25 scale, with careful attention to detail. Reproductions of Tokyo's landmarks were constructed with full-scale interiors to make the damage to them from Gojira's onslaught look realistic.[37]

Haruo Nakajima and Katsumi Tezuka both wore the monster suit in the film. Nakajima, who would play the role through the early 1970s, prepared for it by observing bears at Ueno Zoo. For both actors, playing the monster required great perseverance. To make the action look believable, Tsuburaya shot the majority of the film at a higher frame rate than the usual twenty-four frames per second. Played at normal speed, the monster moved realistically. To correctly film the scenes at such a high frame rate, it was necessary for the special effects lighting director to light the stage more brightly than normal. "Under the hot lights, and without ventilation inside the costume, the actor inside could scarcely withstand three minutes of filming." Nakajima fainted more than once during filming, and when studio technicians took off the costume, they frequently drained a cup of his perspiration as well. Adding to his discomfort, Nakajima suffered blisters from rubbing against the rubber suit, agonizing muscle cramps, and shed twenty pounds.[38]

Akira Ifukube, a greatly renowned classical composer and professor of musical composition at Tokyo Music University, composed the film's musical score. Ifukube's score matched the emotional impact of the film's visual elements. Ifukube also made another contribution to *Gojira:* the monster's roar. After several unsuccessful tests to produce the roar were made, Ifukube rubbed a contrabass with a resin-coated leather glove, then reverberated the resulting sound to produce the singular sound that became Godzilla's roar. Another contribution Ifukube made was the monster's thunderous footsteps, created by beating a kettle drum with a thick rope knotted at the end.[39]

Some of Toho's most budding talents appeared in *Gojira*. The romantic triangle of Dr. Serizawa, Emiko, and Ogata were played, respectively, by Akihiko Hirata, Momako Kochi, and Akira Takarada. Emiko's father, Dr. Yamane, the paleontologist, was essayed by Takashi Shimura.[40]

---

37 Lees 12-14.

38 Kalat 16.

39 There are additional versions of how Godzilla's footsteps were created. Ifukube contented that they were devised with the aid of a primitive amplifier that produced a piercing clap when struck, designed by a Toho sound engineer. A number of Japanese texts, however, reported that, in reality, the monster's footsteps were the "BOOM!" of a recorded explosion with the "OOM!" deleted at the end and processed through an electronic reverb machine. The resulting sound was similar to a large bass drum — "or a monster's foot crashing down on the Tokyo pavement." Ryfle 32.

40 Lees 14-15.

In advance of the film's opening, Toho adapted a radio play from the film script, which aired as a serial over Japan Broadcasting from July 17 through September 25, 1954. The film itself premiered to the movie going audience on November 3, 1954, and was a major success.[41]

Several Japanese ships are sunk by a mysterious blinding light. The vessels belonged to the Southern Sea Steamship Company. A ship rescuing survivors and taking them to Ohto Island is sunk. One of the survivors who drifts ashore on a raft says "a monster" sank his ship. An ancient islander says Godzilla is responsible for the lack of fish in the area to catch. Another islander says "there must be some kind of animal in the sea, that's why we can't catch anything." In the old days, the islanders used to sacrifice girls to Godzilla to keep him from eating the island inhabitants. An ancient exorcism ritual is the sole remaining practice from that time. But the ritual isn't enough. A mysterious disturbance that evening does the following: it wreaks havoc on the island as it destroys houses; a helicopter that brought a survey team to investigate the ship's disappearance is pulverized; and a tidal wave occurs.

Several islanders, brought to Tokyo to tell what happened, say an animal was responsible for the destruction. Professor Yamane, a paleontologist, proposes a full-scale expedition be mounted to discover the answer. Once on the island, the survey party finds the water on only one side of the island contaminated by radiation as well as a footprint of a huge animal. The footprint also contains a supposedly extinct trilobite. A villager then rings a warning bell. The creature is emerging from the island's Mount Hachiba: "A creature from the Jurassic Period!" says Professor Yamane who saw the strange being. Godzilla then emerges from behind the mountain, forcing everyone to flee.

Back in Tokyo after the expedition, Yamane speculates that Godzilla was an intermediate between marine reptiles and evolving terrestrial animals. Ohto Island folklore calls the creature Godzilla. "It probably survived by eating deep sea organisms occupying a specific niche," says Yamane. Possibly nuclear testing removed Godzilla from his natural habitat, citing the trilobite, the sample of sand in the trilobite's shell, a sample matching deposits from the Jurassic period. The sand contained Strontium-90 resulting from an atomic bomb. Godzilla absorbed massive amounts of radiation. One of the audience members urges suppression of Godzilla's existence, because he believes a delicate international situation would unfold and worsen the situation if such news were publicized; this touches off an angry debate at the meeting.

The news of Godzilla's existence is revealed. "Atomic sea life and radioactive fallout, and now this Godzilla to top it all off!" notes one Tokyo commuter. "I guess I'll have to find a shelter soon," says a fellow passenger. "Find one for me, too," says the first passenger. A third remarks, "The shelters again? That stinks" — a reference to the bombing of Japanese cities during World War II.

A naval expedition is sent to depth charge Godzilla, and apparently succeeds in ridding the world of him. However, he emerges in Tokyo Bay, and ultimately comes ashore to ravage Tokyo, and then returns to the sea. While the residents of

---

41 Kalat 17.

Tokyo are evacuated, an electrical barb-wire fence is erected along the shoreline to destroy Godzilla as soon as he emerges from the sea. Yamane wants Godzilla to live so he can be studied. When Godzilla returns from the sea, he easily breaks through the wire, and then proceeds to turn Tokyo — in a television announcer's description — "into a sea of flames," before returning to the sea. The destruction resembles Hiroshima after the atomic bomb fell there in 1945.

Godzilla confronts the power lines around Tokyo. Photo copyright: Rialto Pictures.

After Godzilla's second attack, Yamane's daughter Emiko tells her true love Ogata that Dr. Serizawa showed her an invention of his, an Oxygen Destroyer, that, placed underwater, removes all the oxygen and destroys all the life in the water. He won't tell anyone about his discovery until he finds a beneficial use for it. Emiko pledges to keep his creation a secret. Emiko and Ogata go to Serizawa to get him to use the destroyer against Godzilla. He initially refuses, and a scuffle breaks out between him and Ogata. However, Serizawa relents when he sees the devastation of Tokyo on television, but he destroys his notes on the Oxygen Destroyer so they will not fall into the wrong hands.

Ogata and Serizawa descend to the ocean bottom where Godzilla rests. Serizawa activates the Oxygen Destroyer, obliterating Godzilla, and also severs the air hose to his diving suit, killing himself so the secret of his invention will die with him.[42] Yamane believes that Godzilla isn't the sole surviving member of his

42 Viewing the initial screening of *Godzilla* on the Toho lot was, for actor Akira Takarada, an emotional experience: "I shed tears. Godzilla was killed by the oxygen destroyer, but Godzilla himself wasn't evil and he didn't have to be destroyed. Why did they have to pun-

species and that further nuclear testing will unleash another Godzilla upon the world. Quite right. Godzilla was the only '50s monster to outlast the decade.[43]

Most people, especially in the West, view Godzilla within the context of nuclear weapons but later Japanese commentators felt differently. Film historian Tomoyasu Kobayashi noted that Japan never received American assistance against the monster invasions it endured on film — despite the fact that in real life the United States pledged military aid to Japan under the 1954 Mutual Security Act. From this Kobayashi feels that the Japanese are the only ones who can protect their homeland. In a subsequent film, *Godzilla vs. the Thing*, the US Navy does battle with Godzilla in defense of Japan but this was solely because the distributor, American International Pictures, asked the scene be included in the English language version of the film.

Writer Norio Akasaka viewed Godzilla as a "representation of the spirits of soldiers who died in the South Pacific during the Second World War. . . After coming from the South Pacific to destroy most of the Ginza and the Diet building, [Godzilla] stops suddenly in front of the Imperial Palace, then turns right and heads back out to sea with this look of painful sadness on his face." Akasaka equates this with Yukio Mishima's story, "The Voice of the Hero Spirits," in which ghosts of dead kamikaze pilots ascribe responsibility for Japan's spiritual decline to the Emperor. Akasaka sees Mishima's story and *Gojira* as critiques on Japan's moral decline since World War II.

Current-affairs commentator Yasuo Nagayama views Godzilla as symbolic of Takamori Saigo, leader of a nationalist revolutionary movement in the late nineteenth century. "Like Godzilla, Saigo was famed for his imposing physique," wrote journalist Jim Bailey, "conquered in a path than ran from south to north, was ultimately defeated and underwent a transformation in his reputation from villain to hero." Nagayama observed: "Saigo and Godzilla were not enemies of the people, but enemies of mistaken government policies."[44]

In 1955, *Gojira* was screened without translation in a Los Angeles theater. Among those to see it were American International producer Samuel Z. Arkoff and B-movie maker Alex Gordon. Both were interested in releasing the film in America, but it was Joseph E. Levine who acquired American distribution rights. Before US audiences saw the film, Levine Americanized it. Rather than release a subtitled version, which would have played mainly in art-houses, Levine filmed new scenes with British director Terry Morse and filled the starring role with Raymond Burr, destined to become famous to television audiences as Perry Mason.[45] *Godzilla, King of the Monsters*, as the American version of *Gojira* was titled,

---

ish Godzilla? Why? He was a warning to mankind. I was mad at mankind and felt sympathy for Godzilla, even if he did destroy Tokyo." Takarada further declared, "Mankind woke Godzilla, and today we have similar issues: air pollution, the ozone layer. That is also Godzilla. They're the same in that they were all brought on by mankind." Galbraith, *Monsters* 50, 52.

43 *Godzilla* [*Gojira*], dir. Ishiro Honda, Toho Video, 1954.

44 Kalat 22-23.

45 Lees 16.

debuted in the United States on April 26, 1956, earning what was then an aston-ishing sum of $2 million dollars in its initial American release.[46]

The Incredible Shrinking Man and the spider. Photo copyright: Universal International Pictures.

In America, Bosley Crowther's *New York Times* review dismissed the feature as "an incredibly awful film. . . . The whole thing is in the category of cheap cinematic horror-stuff, and it is too bad that a respectable theatre has to lure children and gullible grown-ups with such fare." *Godzilla*, in *Newsweek*'s opinion, was "a 400-foot-high plucked chicken" who "cannot act his way out of a paper bag." While deploring the acting, *Variety* liked the "excellently lensed" special effects. When, in 1982, the original, uncut Japanese version of the film debuted in the United States, the critics were far more kind. Finding it "still scary after all these years," Carrie Rickey observed in the *Village Voice*: "At once mythical, topical, melodra-matic, and fantastic, *Godzilla*. . . is only a rubberized miniature, yes, but the is-sues at stake are all too global." Howard Reich of *The Chicago Tribune* termed the original "an eerie metaphor for nuclear war. . . . The movie is a parable on life and death issues, and therefore its sledgehammer means of communication power-fully underscore the message."[47]

Unlike the American atomic mutants, which never inspired sequels, Godzilla was the only '50s monster to outlast the decade. Why? "There's a reason for that,"

---

46 Kalat 28; Lees 16.

47 Stuart Galbraith IV, *Japanese Science Fiction, Fantasy and Horror Films: A Critical Analysis of 103 Features Released in the United States, 1950-1992* (Jefferson: McFarland & Company, Inc., 1994) 13.

notes science fiction critic and historian John J. Pierce. Where the American mutants were merely "special effects extras, . . .Godzilla was an *individual*. More than that, he had *soul*. . . . Godzilla lives on and on because he can always be reborn in whatever guise works best for the time, and be invested with whatever greater significance suits our psychological needs." Pierce concludes: "Godzilla is, and always shall be, a monster for all seasons."[48]

INCREDIBLE SHRINKING AND COLOSSAL MEN

Radiation could mutate man as well as nature. Such was the case with a pair of late '50s films — *The Incredible Shrinking Man*, directed by sci-fi veteran Jack Arnold, and *The Amazing Colossal Man*, directed by exploitation specialist Bert I. Gordon.

The Amazing Colossal Man. Photo copyright: AIP.

A Universal film, *The Incredible Shrinking Man* opens with its protagonist, Robert Scott Carey (Grant Williams), vacationing on a boat with his wife when a mysterious white mist envelops the boat. Six months pass, and Carey notices that his clothes don't fit right. His doctor notices both his height and weight have declined. Carey's wife doesn't have to stretch like she used to, to kiss him. A follow-up visit to his doctor reveals that Carey is shrinking in size. There's no medical precedent for his condition. His doctor refers Carey to the California Medical Research Institute, which discovers the cause of his predicament: Carey

---

48 John J. Pierce, "Godzilla Beyond the Atomic Age: A Monster for All Seasons," Lees and Cerasini 17.

was exposed to an insecticide which, combined with radioactivity in the white mist, has caused his body to start shrinking.

Out of work, facing unpaid bills, Carey sells his story to the press, which soon descend on his home, making him a prisoner. Carey's condition puts a strain on his marriage. The institute finds an antitoxin that halts his shrinking but doesn't restore his size. He meets a circus midget who temporarily renews his interest in life but then his shrinking resumes. Carey ultimately begins living in a dollhouse. Attacked by his own pet housecat, he is forced to flee but when he tries to block the door to his cellar, against the cat, Carey is knocked down into the basement. His wife, finding his torn shirt, thinks the cat killed him. She eventually moves out of the house. Alone in the cellar, unable to reach the outside world, Carey's only recourse is to survive as best he can. He nearly drowns when a leak in the water heater floods the cellar. When his wife and brother come downstairs to get a trunk, he's too small to attract their attention. To get food, he's forced to kill a spider sharing the cellar. His shrinking continues. Ultimately, he accepts his fate. At the film's conclusion, he says:

> "What was I? Still a human being? Or was I the man of the future? If there were other bursts of radiation, other clouds drifting across seas and continents, would other beings follow me into this vast new world. [I was] so close to the infinitesimal and the infinite.

> "But, suddenly, I knew they were really the two ends of the same concept. The unbelievably small and the vast eventually meet — like the closing of a gigantic circle. I looked up as if somehow I would grasp the heavens, the universe, worlds beyond number. God's silver tapestry spread across the night. And in that moment, I knew the answer to the riddle of the infinite. I had thought in terms of man's own limited dimension. I had presumed upon nature. That existence begins and ends is man's conception, not nature's.

> "And I felt my body dwindling, melting, becoming nothing. My fears melted away. And in their place came acceptance. All this vast majesty of creation, it had to mean something. And then I meant something, too. Yes, smaller than the smallest, I meant something too. To God, there is no zero. I still exist."[49]

The ending disappointed some critics, who wanted to see a miraculous cure for Carey's affliction. One felt: "A curious pseudo-poetical, semi-religious ending is a shock, a frustrating evasion of the solution that the strange little film demands." Another believed the film had a "very contrived ending."

"You had to do something with the hero," explained Richard Matheson, whose screenplay for *Shrinking Man* was adapted from his own novel. "You couldn't let him just disappear. That would be nothing. I wanted to say, 'There are universes within universes.' And I don't think that was inconsistent with the story."

"But, in fact," wrote film historian David Zinman, "it was director Arnold who wrote that soliloquy." Arnold explained that studio executives wanted the film to end with the shrinking man returning to normal size.

---

49 *The Incredible Shrinking Man*, dir. Jack Arnold, MCA Home Video, Inc., 1988; Zinman 140.

Arnold told them "if you do that, you may as well throw the picture away." "Well," they replied, "you can't let him die."

A compromise was reached with Carey's closing speech, which Arnold claimed authorship of. "I felt it was an upbeat ending. . . . He [the shrinking man] had taken on an almost Christlike appearance. And it seemed an almost religious atmosphere. . . . [He was saying that] all life is in the eyes of the beholder. There is no difference between the finite and the infinite. Life is a circle. It completes itself in a whole."

According to Matheson, the film out-grossed Universal's earlier box-office hits of the 1950s, *To Hell and Back* (1955) and *Away All Boats* (1956). "They had a lot of expensive sets left over and they asked me to write a sequel. I did and they called it *The Fantastic Little Girl*. It told about his wife getting small and going down to join her husband. But for some reason, it was never made."[50]

To achieve the illusion of normal-sized objects made gigantic in comparison to the shrinking man, Arnold doubled some objects in size, while others were constructed twenty-five times as big. Some were built on a scale of one hundred to one. A paint can was 25 feet high, a slice of stale sponge cake 18 feet tall. A pencil the shrinking man employed as a spar to hold himself above water in his flooded cellar was 21 feet long.*[51]

The majority of *Shrinking Man's* special effects took place on a set duplicating the basement of Carey's residence. For a long sequence, nine sound stages were required. As one unit, the set would have measured over a mile long and almost three-quarters of a mile wide. One special effect proved challenging — creating giant water drops. The shrinking man was to be flooded out of his matchbox home. "We tried everything," Arnold recalled. "We got up on the top of the sound stage and rigged a device that released water a small amount at a time. But the water would spread out on the way down and look useless." The solution originated with a childhood prank Arnold used to play. "I discovered that they [rubber condom contraceptives] made dandy bombs when you fill them with water," Arnold explained. "I used to drop them on top of people from windows. And I remember that they used to hold a tear-shaped form on their way down."

When Arnold tested one on the set and the trial proved successful, he ordered one hundred gross of them and rigged a treadmill to release them at a faster rate. The scene concluded with actor Grant Williams being deluged with a flood of water from a tank. When the production office asked Arnold if he indeed had ordered the contraceptives, he said, "Fellows, it was such a hard picture, and we all worked so hard that we decided to have a big party at the end of it."

The film's lead role required Grant Williams to enact his part in pantomime alone before a black velvet sheet. His image was then reduced and edited into scenes of a cat or spider to make it seem the animals were gigantic.[52]

---

50 Zinman 140.

51 Other enormous props used in the film were a full size reproduction of a giant wall, a street-sized ledge, a giant spider's web, a giant pair of scissors, and a huge ball of cord. Johnson 277.

52 Zinman 137.

Jack Arnold was an old hand at working with spiders, having directed one in the 1955 giant monster epic *Tarantula*. When it came time to direct the "giant" spider in *The Incredible Shrinking Man*, Arnold said:

> "We flew in 60 Panamanian tarantulas because the domestic ones were too small and we couldn't keep a sharp focus on them. They were tremendous beasts, six inches in diameter! In the scene where he [Grant Williams] impales the spider after enticing him down from his web, I shot the spider first. It's very hard to direct a spider. I used jets of air as I had done previously with *Tarantula* (1955). I would probe him in the direction I wanted him to move with spurts of air."

According to film special effects historian John "J. J." Johnson: "Some critics contend that the use of a tarantula, instead of the normal spider you might find in a basement, hurt *Shrinking Man*'s credibility." Another author, Dana Reemes, disagrees: "The story required Carey to confront a black widow spider, but a real black widow was too small to photograph." Johnson continues: "Arnold agrees that he took 'dramatic license' by filming a tarantula instead, and it's a good thing too, because the chilling spider attack is one of the horror highlights of the decade." Several of the tarantulas gave their lives for the sake of art when they were "cooked" to death by the bright lighting required for filming them.[53]

What made *The Incredible Shrinking Man* a success was the fact that it dwelt on the horrors of the nuclear age as they affected one ordinary man who just happened to be touched by the hand of fate.[54] The success of *Shrinking Man* inevitably sired an imitation. Produced and directed by Bert I. Gordon, *The Amazing Colossal Man* (1957) took the mutation process in the opposite direction. Gordon specialized in sci-fi tales predicated on some aspect of gigantism, frequently resulting from exposure to radiation. Monsters fashioned from clay, in his view, weren't believable. Instead, Gordon opted for makeup to disfigure faces and employed perspective photography to change size. Moreover, he believed actors, not stuntmen, could give a monster character through voices and body movement.[55]

Aside from *The Incredible Shrinking Man*, *The Amazing Colossal Man* was also inspired by the novel *The Nth Man*, the central character of which is a man two miles tall. Charles B. Griffith was hired to write the script. The end product of his labor was a comedy that would have been too expensive for the studio, American International Pictures, to produce. In Griffith's version, an unhappily married man drinks an experimental serum. He grows to gigantic size until a cure for his condition is found. Gordon, who had directed an earlier giant man film, *The Cyclops*, came aboard for this project. Because he and Griffith didn't get along, a new scenarist, Mark Hanna, entered the picture.[56]

Like *The Incredible Shrinking Man*, *The Amazing Colossal Man* deals with how the nuclear threat affects one man. The film begins at Desert Rock, Nevada, where troop maneuvers with a plutonium bomb are being conducted. When the coun-

---

53 Johnson 252-253.

54 Brode 206.

55 Warren 317; Johnson 91.

56 Fischer 243.

ter reaches zero, the bomb fails to detonate. When a plane crashes at the test site during the stalled countdown, Colonel Glen Manning (Glen Langan) rushes out of his bunker to rescue the pilot. At this moment, the bomb finally detonates, exposing Manning to a full dose of radiation.

Miraculously, Manning survives the night of the blast and surgery, growing new skin to replace the skin destroyed in the explosion. The scientist who developed the bomb ascribes Manning's survival to chance that "afforded him a certain amount of protection." Later, Manning's fiancée, Carol, is told she can't see him due to security reasons. She checks with the hospital, only to find he's not there anymore. Discovering that the doctors who treated Manning have been reassigned to an Army rehabilitation and research center, Carol drives there, where she finds Manning is growing 8 to 10 feet daily. His cell growth is out of balance: new cells are growing while the old ones that normally would die aren't, causing his abnormal growth. When Manning regains consciousness and realizes what has happened to him, he wonders, "What sin could a man commit in a single lifetime to bring this upon himself?" His heart isn't growing fast enough to keep up with his growth. The scientists researching his condition discover a serum that can be injected into the bone marrow.

Manning's mind snaps. He escapes, wrecking havoc in Las Vegas, then is injected with an oversized needle. The injection fails, and Manning kidnaps Carol, à la *King Kong*, then proceeds to Boulder Dam, where he's persuaded to free Carol, and then is shot by the Army, plunging to his death in the waters below.*[57] But this wasn't the end of Glen Manning: he was resurrected for a sequel, *War of the Colossal Beast*.[58]

Special effects in the film were somewhat disappointing. In those scenes where actor Langan worked with prop miniatures fashioned by Paul Blaisdell, he looked natural. Yet when director Gordon used a positive matte of Lagan behind Vegas scenery slides, his image seems washed out. "Because Gordon was fudging with his split screen matte processes, any dark tones on Langan's body would become transparent."

Because of this, Gordon decided to have his colossal man become bald and why he appears in an expandable *white* sarong in the film. To "bleach" out any shadows that might appear on his body, Gordon bathed Langan in high key lighting, diminishing shadow detail. "Most high key work starts with the white clad subject's being filmed in a low contrast ratio white room." In film historian Bill Warren's words:

> "Throughout, the special effects by producer-director Gordon are awkward and unconvincing. In every sequence in which Langan appears with normal sized people, he's a superimposed matte or on one side of a very rigid dividing line, separating him from the other half of the split screen. In the matte scenes he's always dim and pale, sometimes even transparent, so that instead of creat-

---

57 For the final scene where the colossal man falls from Boulder Dam, Gordon photographed Langan bending over a chair. "The chair was then matted out, and the stooped-over image of Langan was superimposed over Boulder Dam footage." Johnson 92.

58 *The Amazing Colossal Man*, dir. Bert I. Gordon, Columbia Tristar Home Video, 1992.

ing the illusion of a giant man, the poor effects actually work contrary to this intent, calling attention to themselves and destroying the illusion."[59]

Like a dark shadow, the nuclear threat hovered over the '50s. No one could escape its presence — be it real life (the "downwinders" and atomic veterans who attributed their proximity to atomic test sites as the cause of serious illnesses; the crew of the *Lucky Dragon* who chanced to be in the path of radioactive fallout from Bravo); or movie fiction (the people who trembled before the onslaught of giant mutant monsters overrunning their communities or those individuals who shrank or grew in size from radiation exposure). Much the same way, half a century later, Americans' minds are filled with a new threat — terrorism. And, once again, it seems, no one is safe.

59 Johnson 91-92.

Chapter 6. The Road to September 11

From the perspective of half a century, the science fiction films of the 1950s were made in an era that looks far more ordered and leisurely than the high-tech, fast-paced world of the early twenty-first century — if one overlooks 'the Cold War–Red Scare concerns. What changed the perception of the '50s from an age of anxiety to "happy days" was the contrast with the chaotic and disillusioning '60s and '70s that followed. The maelstrom only intensified over the remainder of the twentieth century, culminating in the culture war, political correctness, and September 11, when foreign terrorists struck at the seemingly untouchable United States.

Not only has America changed politically, socially, and internationally since the '50s, its movies have changed as well. Fifties films depicted a world of black-and-white morality, one where heroes were heroes, men and women knew their respective roles, moral deviants were out of sight, the traditional nuclear family was the norm, and America was certain of its moral rightness. All of that changed, in the years that followed: morals became confused, heroes became anti-heroes, families broke up, people "tuned in, turned on, and dropped out," or "came out of the closet," movies bore "R" and "X" ratings, and special effects were transformed in ways previously undreamed.

In other ways, movies haven't changed. Above all, they remain a storytelling medium. When it comes to the enduring popularity of monster movies, "It's always about good box office," says actress Beverly Garland. "Fright films have always done well and continue to do so."[1] Fifties science fiction still exerts an influence on modern films. Some of them were remade in updated versions. Others presented old themes in new versions. A look at some science fiction films from the late '70s to the early 2000s will show that many of them correspond to the themes already explored in this book.

1 Matthews, e-mail.

HOSTILE ALIEN INVADERS

The threat of alien invasions did not disappear with the end of the 1950s. Indeed one of that decade's most notable invasion films was given a new, updated treatment in the early 1980s: *John Carpenter's The Thing.*

One may recall that the original 1951 version of *The Thing* was inspired by John W. Campbell, Jr.'s "Who Goes There?", but the final product in no way resembles Campbell's story. The monster in Howard Hawks' film was a living, humanoid "vegetable" resembling Frankenstein's monster that derived sustenance from blood, whereas Campbell's monster was a shape-shifting alien that could assume the identity of any human being, creating distrust and paranoia among the members of the Antarctic scientific team that encounters the alien.[2]

A quarter of a century after the original film, television producer Stuart Cohen purchased the rights to the original Campbell story, taking it to producers Lawrence Turman and David Foster. The pair obtained a development deal for the story with Universal Pictures. For a director, Cohen suggested John Carpenter who, like Cohen, admired the original film. Universal, however, vetoed Cohen's suggestion. After the success of *Alien* and Carpenter's own film *Halloween*, Carpenter was brought aboard as director of the new version of *The Thing.*[3]

After seeing the Howard Hawks film as a child, Carpenter read the short story in high school and, as he explained, "realized it was a lot different than the movie." Campbell's tale "was basically an Agatha Christie kind of Ten Little Indians. This creature is in your midst, and he's imitating either one or all of us. Who's human and who isn't? And that kind of an idea really fascinated me."[4]

Carpenter was drawn to *The Thing* because it afforded him the opportunity to make a horror movie dealing with issues of trust, and also to "dramatize a formless, insidious evil."[5] Carpenter's *Thing* would be the initial installment of his "apocalypse trilogy," followed by *Prince of Darkness* and *The Mouth of Madness.* Moreover, *The Thing* would mark Carpenter's third collaboration with actor Kurt Russell, the pair having previously worked on the TV movie *Elvis* and the feature film *Escape from New York.*[6]

Bill Lancaster, who had penned *The Bad News Bears*, was assigned the task of scripting *The Thing.* In executing this assignment, he paid great attention to Campbell's story, both in shaping scenes like "the blood test" and the characters' names and Campbell's aim of fashioning an atmosphere of paranoia. While it is true that Lancaster did add considerable action and gore to the story, this was

---

2 John Kenneth Muir, *The Films of John Carpenter* (Jefferson: McFarland & Company, Inc., 2000) 25.

3 *John Carpenter's The Thing*, dir. John Carpenter, Universal Home Video, Inc., 1988, "Production Background Archive."

4 Carpenter, *John Carpenter's The Thing*, "John Carpenter's The Thing: Terror Takes Shape."

5 Muir 25.

6 Carpenter, *John Carpenter's The Thing*, "Feature Commentary with Director John Carpenter and Kurt Russell."

required as those who would view the film had already seen *Star Wars*, *Halloween*, and *Alien*.

The Carpenter-Lancaster partnership on the script was, in John Kenneth Muir's words, "a very positive one. Lancaster wrote the first 40 pages of the script, which John Carpenter loved, and then he went back to finish it up on his own."[7]

Set in 1982, *John Carpenter's The Thing* focuses on an American scientific team in the Antarctic. As the film opens, a helicopter from a nearby Norwegian camp is flying above the frozen landscape in pursuit of a fleeing husky dog. The latter makes its way to the American installation, where it is taken in and quartered with the other dogs there. Once inside the American camp, the husky turns out to be the alien shape-shifter, able to replicate any living being — human or animal.

The American scientists now begin a desperate search to determine which of them is The Thing. The film concludes with only two survivors left: MacReady (Kurt Russell) and Childs (Keith David), MacReady having destroyed the otherworldly menace with dynamite.[8]

Todd Ramsay, film editor on the project, noted:

> "The reviews were mixed, I think, with the audience. There was an alternate ending to the film that was shot. I had spoken to John about this. I had said that I felt, 'Well, gee — this is a terribly nihilistic ending. It's very much of a downbeat. Perhaps we should protect ourselves, while we have the principal — Kurt — and just shoot an ending where we see that he survives. John was open to this, so essentially what he did was he staged a scene in which Kurt has been rescued, and is sitting in a kind of a small office structure, and he's just had a blood test, so we know that he's not infected. He has survived this ordeal, rather than the kind of mutual death that concludes the film now. He just shot this for protection. We never previewed this. The issue did come up at the conclusion of the two previews as to whether we should perhaps try this ending, see how it flew with the audiences, and/or make other adjustments on the film. And I think John essentially at that time, felt that he had achieved in the movie what he wanted to do. He had made the story of "Who Goes There?". . . I think he felt he had accomplished that . . . so that's the way the film went out."[9]

Despite the great expectations everyone had for the film's success, *John Carpenter's The Thing* was a box office flop when it was released in the summer of 1982. Several factors explain its troubled reception. The film faced strong competition from several other summer releases that year: Steven Spielberg's *E.T.: The Extraterrestrial*, Nicholas Meyer's *Star Trek II: The Wrath of Khan*, Tobe Hooper's *Poltergeist*, Clint Eastwood's *Firefox*, and Ridley Scott's *Blade Runner*. Consequently, Carpenter's film suffered a swift demise: after three full weeks, it had earned a mere $13.8 million. Such a sum, considering that the film's budget was $10 million, minus advertising costs, was devastating.

---

7 Muir 25.

8 Carpenter, *John Carpenter's The Thing*; Muir 99, 103.

9 Carpenter, *John Carpenter's The Thing*, "John Carpenter's The Thing: Terror Takes Shape."

What this meant was that, for the first time in his film career, Carpenter had a dud. Even worse, he was subjected to severe critical condemnation on the grounds that the film was, in Muir's words, "a pointless gore-fest."[10] *Newsweek* opined: "There's a big difference between shock effects and suspense, and in sacrificing everything at the altar of gore, Carpenter sabotages the drama. *The Thing* is so single-mindedly determined to keep you awake that it almost puts you to sleep." The script "is so low on characterization that even a first-rate cast of character actors. . . is unable to work up any team spirit. . . Even the star, Kurt Russell, has to play second fiddle to the special effects. . . It's the new Esthetic — atrocity for atrocity's sake — and it ill becomes a neoclassical action director like Carpenter."[11]

Writing in *The Los Angeles Times*, Linda Cross said: "Bereft, despairing, and nihilistic. . .the most disturbing aspect of *The Thing* is its terrible absence of love. The film is so frigid and devoid of feeling that death no longer has any meaning. . . ." While praising the film's technical aspects, Cross concluded that "what we are finally left with is the film's abiding paranoia and its gruesome empty effects."

Alan Spencer felt that the movie "smells, and smells pretty bad. It bears plenty of Carpenter's trademarks as a director. . . has no pace, sloppy continuity, zero humor, bland characters. . . ." Carpenter, Spencer declared, "was never meant to direct science fiction horror movies. Here's some things he'd be better suited to direct: Traffic accidents, train wrecks and public floggings."

Here and there, minority voices of support for the film were heard. "A slick thriller with expertly handled monster scenes that are as scary as they are sickening. . . ," observed David Stared, "a complete throwback to the most paranoid attitudes of the past, as if the popularity and influence of *Close Encounters of the Third Kind* never existed." And Pat H. Brioschi commented:

> "Abounding in primal fears, *The Thing* constantly surprises. *The Thing* does benefit from the strong presence of Russell. . . . Dean Cundey's cinematography is hauntingly atmospheric, making the bases' dimly lit maze of rooms. . . claustrophobically real. . . . A tour de force for twenty-four-year-old Rob Bottin, creator and designer of special make-up effects . . . when viewed at a distance from the E.T. syndrome, *The Thing* should enjoy critical respectability as a riveting exercise in horror."[12]

Until *The Thing*, Carpenter had enjoyed critical and box office acclaim. That *The Thing* was at least fifteen years ahead of its time gave the hostile critics the chance to cut Carpenter down a bit. Finally, the fact that both *The Thing* and *E.T.* came out simultaneously hurt the former film.[13] *The Thing*'s cinematographer, Dean Cundey, felt that, at the time of its release, *The Thing*:

> "...was an innovative, very kind of unusual journey for an audience. And I think that it came across an interesting phenomenon. . . [We] also had a very

---

10 Muir 27.

11 David Ansen, "Frozen Slime," *Newsweek* 28 June 1982: 73.

12 Muir 98-99.

13 Muir 27.

friendly alien that came to visit the earth, in the form of *E.T.* And it was a case of an audience, at the time, feeling probably more comfortable with a friendly alien. And the fact that the sort of dark edge of *The Thing* was something that wasn't sort of appreciated at the time. I think the audience's sensibilities always sort of change, and they're now sort of prepared to accept an alien that isn't so friendly, in the shape of *The Thing*."[14]

With the passage of time, *John Carpenter's The Thing* began to find its supporters. The editor of *The Encyclopedia of Science Fiction*, Peter Nicholls, ranked it among the top ten sci-fi films of all time. Alan Dean Foster believed that John W. Campbell, Jr., would have loved the film as Carpenter faithfully adapted his original story for the big screen.

The 1990s brought further rehabilitation to Carpenter's production. *Terminator 2: Judgment Day* (1991) presented audiences with a shape-shifting robot from the future. The T-100's transformations closely resembled (though not as viscerally) those of *The Thing*. Moreover, the shape-shifter's death scene was nearly the same as that of Carpenter's monster. A comic book version of Carpenter's story, picking up where the film left off, was issued the next year. Television's *The X-Files* presented an episode that utilized stock footage of the installation built for *The Thing* as well as echoed the latter's storyline: drilling in the Arctic, a team recovers a prehistoric extraterrestrial life-form that invades the human bloodstream, changing the identities of its victims. *Star Trek: Deep Space Nine* introduced viewers to alien shape-shifters, whose presence can only be revealed by blood tests. All of this was evidence that Carpenter's film was finally receiving recognition.[15]

At the core of *John Carpenter's The Thing* are two themes: the frailty of human flesh, and man's dehumanization in the modern era. The former is established early on when viewers see a dead Norwegian whose eye has been shot out and a member of the American team being treated for a gun-shot wound. When MacReady and another team member find another dead Norwegian, they find his skin permanently "separated" at the neck and his blood frozen like an icicle, hanging from slit wrists — demonstrating that man is vulnerable, this time to the environment (the cold). This vulnerability is once again demonstrated by the autopsies in the film, showing how people can be separated a piece at a time. The human anatomy is significant, as it will determine who is human and who is "the Thing."

These scenes of wounds, frozen dead bodies, and autopsies are the prelude to The Thing's appearance, which takes Carpenter's "frailty of the flesh" theme even further. The human body can hide an alien life form capable of distorting its host. The warning here is that disease can transform us. The alien as disease concept is further stressed in a scene adapted from Campbell's original story, where a blood test is utilized to detect the creature's presence. This scene resonates with modern America, where blood tests locate infections: hepatitis and AIDS. In Carpenter's film, MacReady uses a blood test to determine who among his com-

---

14 Carpenter, *John Carpenter's The Thing*, "John Carpenter's The Thing: Terror Take Shape,".

15 Muir 28.

panions has been taken over by the monster. Edward Guerrero felt this scene in the film, as well as the whole movie, directly referred to the then dawning AIDS epidemic in America:

> "Once the Thing absorbs the person, it dissembles flawlessly while spreading and taking over the bodies of other victims. In this sense, the monster's mode of operation clearly parallels the AIDS virus' geometric spread. . . . The great fear that drives much of the film's action is that of not being able to detect those who have been penetrated and replicated by the thing."

Moreover, Guerrero felt that, in reality, the film symbolized the homosexual lifestyle: the all-male cast of characters inhabit a self-indulgent (pot smoking, alcohol consuming) same-sex liberal life-style, making themselves vulnerable to "infection."[16] The AIDS parallel wasn't lost on Carpenter and *The Thing*'s star Kurt Russell, both of whom refer to it on the DVD commentary of the film.[17]

Carpenter's second theme in the film was coming to the surface as the '80s was dawning: an individual can *appear* normal at first glance, but under the surface be very different. Numerous middle-class Americans felt they really didn't know their neighbors, a feeling arising from the commuter lifestyle, air travel and the American habit of relocating from one's birthplace; consequently, those in a suburban district might differ, morally and ethically, from each other.

Both versions of *The Thing* reflected the times they were made in. Hawks' film, made shortly after World War II, depicted a unified team of men, committed to basic American values and ingenuity, vanquishing the monster. Carpenter's version came along just as the '70s (the "me" decade) had ended and the '80s (the yuppie era) was dawning. In place of unity and comradeship was a Social Darwinian ethic of me-first, get ahead, make all the money you could, distrust your fellows, and watch out, for they might have AIDS. Carpenter's film, Thomas Doherty believed, portrays a societal trend, an:

> interpersonal implosion. Radically destructive of the ethos of the original, the second film features a collection of autonomous, angry, unpleasant and self-interested individuals, as chilly as the stark Antarctican landscape they inhabit. That men could live in close quarters, in total isolation, depending on each other for survival and succor — and not develop a fraternal bond defies . . . dramatic logic.

As well as depicting the transformation of American core values over thirty years, *The Thing* shows that man may not be able to vanquish disease. At the film's end, MacReady faces the prospect that the alien may still exist, and that he will have to share the world with it — a new social order. Man and alien's only bond is that they must now confront the oncoming winter together. There is also a sense of isolation in the film on two levels: the isolation the men feel due to their fear of alien infection; and the isolation of *geography*, which is underscored by the barrenness and chill of the Antarctic wasteland. It is this isolation that enables

---

16 Muir 103-105.

17 Carpenter, *John Carpenter's The Thing*, "Feature Commentary with Director John Carpenter and Kurt Russell."

the scientists to fight The Thing to a standstill.[18] Actor Charles Hallahan, Dr. Norris in the film, felt that the film had a psychological level of isolation, where "each one of those men had his own little trap, little prison that he lived in, cut off from anything else except the guys around him. And then the introduction of this alien, which couldn't be seen but could be sensed, intensified that experience for each and every guy in it."[19]

Being a fan of Howard Hawks, John Carpenter infuses his *Thing* with homage to the original *Thing*.[20] Early in the film, MacReady discovers a block of ice ("James Arness's bed," Russell called it in the DVD commentary track) at the Norwegian station after the Thing escapes to the American camp. Similarly, the original Thing was returned to Carrington's base in a block of ice.[21] Norris, MacReady, and the other members of the American team view film of the Norwegians planting thermite charges around the spacecraft the Thing traveled in to Earth in a scene reminiscent of the excavation of the alien craft in the original film. In another scene, MacReady sets a fellow team member Palmer ablaze after the blood test reveals he (Palmer) has been tainted. The blazing Palmer runs through a wall, falling down in the snow outside. Again this echoes Hawks' film.[22] Actor Richard Mauser felt that the burning sequence in Carpenter's film "was probably the biggest effect we all worked. . . . the guy who did the burn. . . a specialist at doing these full body burns. . . . He can't breathe once he's ready to go because if he does, he'll sear his lungs. He has to do the whole thing holding his breath, and it's all a matter of timing. And then the minute he came off, he had to be put out, and immediately freed so he could draw breath."[23]

What was regarded as a disgusting film, upon its release, has become, in Carpenter's words, "a kind of straightforward, tough, hard-hitting action picture with a monster in it."[24] John Kenneth Muir goes even further: *John Carpenter's The Thing* may not only be regarded as the best science fiction film of 1982, but the best, most influential sci-fi and horror film of the 1980s.[25]

Where Carpenter's film reflected the concern over AIDS during the Reagan years, *Independence Day* (1996) mirrored America's obsession with the paranormal in the 1990s. A *Newsweek* poll at the time of the film's release revealed that 48% of Americans believed that UFOs were real and 29% felt that we had contacted aliens. Another 48% believed that the government was suppressing evidence of

---

18 Muir 105, 107-108.

19 Carpenter, *John Carpenter's The Thing*, "John Carpenter's The Thing: Terror Takes Shape."

20 Muir 109-110.

21 Carpenter, *John Carpenter's The Thing*, "Feature Commentary with Director John Carpenter and Kurt Russell."

22 Muir 110.

23 Carpenter, *John Carpenter's The Thing*, "John Carpenter's The Thing: Terror Takes Shape."

24 "Feature Commentary with Director John Carpenter and Kurt Russell," Carpenter.

25 Muir 28-29.

this. Nevada's governor officially renamed State Route 375 the Extraterrestrial Highway because there were so many UFO "sightings" reported there. Three men were arrested on New York's Long Island for planning the assassination of local officials whom the would-be assassins believed had covered up a UFO landing. The American Astronomical Society announced the discovery, in deep space, of a building block for amino acids, the basis of life on Earth. "Less reputable stargazers claim to have seen Elvis eating fried chicken on Uranus." All of this prompted *Newsweek* to observe: "We're in a major alien moment."[26]

The White House explodes in *Independence Day* (1996). Photo copyright: 20th Century Fox.

The reasons for this, *Newsweek* continued, cut across generational lines: "Boomers approaching their golden years are still searching for Meaning in their lives, something more transcendent than an old Grateful Dead record. Disillusioned Gen-Xers, prone to conspiracy theorizing, are convinced they have a better chance of encountering an alien than they do of collecting Social Security. It's a substitute religion for people who haven't got one and a supplemental one for those who already do."[27]

The film opened with the arrival of an alien mother ship in Earth orbit on 2 July; it releases fifteen-mile wide alien ships that enter the Earth's atmosphere, appearing over northern Iraq, the Persian Gulf, off California, the Russian Republic, and over the Atlantic — the latter moving toward New York and Washington. President Whitmore (Bill Pullman), a Gulf War veteran, whose popularity is declining, stays in Washington, so as not to start a panic of the sort that occurred in Russia when the aliens appeared there. David Levinson (Jeff Goldblum), a cable TV technician, discovers that the aliens are using our own satellites against us to coordinate their attacks, prompting the President to order an evacuation. The aliens subsequently destroy a high-rise in Los Angeles, and then obliterate New

---

26 Rick Marin, Adam Rogers, and T. Trent Gegax, "Alien Invasion!" *Newsweek* 8 July 1996: 50.

27 Marin 52.

York, the White House, and the Capitol Building. Air Force One escapes as the ensuing fire engulfs Washington, while LA and New York are also destroyed.

3 July: Jet fighters attack the alien ship over Los Angeles but are unable to penetrate the vessel's defensive shield. The aliens then launch raiding vessels that shatter the jets, then attack the fighters' home base, Pearl Harbor style. After leaving Washington, Air Force One flies the presidential party to Area 51 in Nevada, where an alien attacker ship, similar to the one used by the aliens in their attack on Earth, has been stored for study since it landed on Earth in the 1950s. Captain Steven Hiller (Will Smith), one of the Marine Corps pilots involved in the ill-fated attack on the aliens, arrives at the base with the alien he captured after the battle. While being examined, the alien comes to life, attacking the President, probing the latter's mind. From the probe, the President learns the aliens move from planet to planet "like locust," and Earth is next on their list. They use up a planet's natural resources, then move on to another world. Based on this, the President orders nuclear weapons deployed against the aliens. In a scene reminiscent of the Flying Wing's attack on the Martians in George Pal's *The War of the Worlds*, nuclear missiles are fired at an alien ship over Houston, Texas, but fail to destroy it.

4 July: David discovers a way to beat the aliens: infect their mother ship in space with a computer virus that will, in turn, infect the alien ships on Earth, lowering their shields, enabling the military to destroy them. Using Morse code, word is sent to military forces worldwide to prepare for a counter-offensive, while the President orders all available pilots and planes to assemble for the attack. Before they take off, the President addresses them:

> "In less than an hour, aircraft from here will join others from around the world, and you will be launching the largest aerial battle in the history of mankind. Mankind — that word should have new meaning for all of us today. We can't be consumed by our petty differences anymore. [This last sentence is reminiscent of Klaatu's disdain about Earth's "petty quarrels" in *The Day the Earth Stood Still*] We will be united in our common interests. Perhaps it's fate that today is the 4th of July, and you will once again be fighting for our freedom — not from tyranny, oppression or persecution — but from annihilation. We're fighting for our right to live. To exist. And should we win the day, the 4th of July will no longer be known as an American holiday, but as the day when the world declared in one voice, we will not go quietly into the night! We will not vanish without a fight! We're going to live on! We're going to survive! Today we celebrate our independence day!"

The President then suits up with the rest of the pilots for the battle. Hiller and David, meanwhile, fly to the mother ship in the captured attacker, upload the computer virus, which causes the aliens' defensive shield to drop, allowing the attacking jets' missiles to hit their target. When the alien ship appears over the installation, Russell Casse (Randy Quaid), a crop duster who claims he was kidnapped years earlier by aliens who sexually molested him, flies into the alien ship and destroys it kamikaze style when his missile fails to fire. Before that, the alien ship attacks the installation, forcing those on the ground to flee to shelter,

September 11 style. Hiller and David barely escape the mother ship before destroying it, ending the aliens' threat to Earth.[28]

Independence Day's sole aim was to provide post-Cold War viewers with a new enemy to hate and destroy. "The US is desperately in search of an enemy," said director Paul Verhoeven. "The communists were the enemy, and the Nazis before them, but now that wonderful enemy everyone can fight has been lost. Alien sci-fi films give us a terrifying enemy that's politically correct. They're bad. They're evil. And they're not even human."[29]

One can only speculate what this means in terms of today's media depictions of other cultures.

Independence Day was the creation of 40-year-old Roland Emmerich and 35-year-old Dean Devlin. Growing up in Germany, Emmerich fell in love with sci-fi from watching American films and local science fiction television shows. "For me," he said, "going on a science-fiction movie set is like visiting toyland. You see, my brother trashed all my toys when I was a kid. It's very Freudian. For my movies you can blame my brother Andy." Devlin had movies in his blood: His father was a producer, his mother an actress.

Emmerich's first films were shot in Germany — and in English, so they could be marketed internationally. In 1989, he directed *Moon 44*, described as "an outer-space *Dirty Dozen*," the plot of which closely paralleled *ID4*: to do battle in the heavens, a former combat pilot must recruit an assortment of flyers, one of whom is "a loser with heroically suicidal tendencies."[30] *Moon 44* marked the beginning of the Emmerich-Devlin collaboration, after Devlin rewrote some of the script for Emmerich. Devlin was impressed with the way Emmerich was able to film a scene when their funds literally dried up.[31]

Universal Soldier, the duo's initial American film, starred Jan-Claude Van Damme. This was followed by *Stargate*, about a clandestine government agency searching for evidence of alien life and discovering that aliens were responsible for constructing the pyramids.[32] As Emmerich explained it, *ID4* had its origins during his promotion of *Stargate*, when a Swiss journalist asked him if he (Emmerich) believed in extraterrestrials. Emmerich's negative answer enraged the reporter, who demanded to know how he could make a film like *Stargate* if he didn't believe in aliens.

"I believe in fantasy," Emmerich supposedly answered. "I believe in the great 'What if?' What if aliens showed up? What if tomorrow morning you walked out of your door and these enormous spaceships were hovering over every single city in the world? Wouldn't *that* be exciting?" He told Devlin, "I think we've got our next movie."

28 *Independence Day: Five Star Collection*, dir Roland Emmerich, 20th Century Fox Home Entertainment, 2000.

29 Richard Corliss, "The Invasion Has Begun!" *Time* 8 July 1996: 60.

30 Corliss, "The Invasion" 64.

31 Fischer 171.

32 Corliss, "The Invasion" 64.

"We discovered some time ago that we both loved Irwin Allen disaster movies," recalled Emmerich. He added:

> "And we always said that there were no more natural disasters left to portray until this idea came up and we thought, 'What a great idea to portray an alien invasion as a natural disaster.' . . . Because the story is so simple, we had the opportunity to interject more character, more story, and more fleshed-out relationships. Because we were the aliens as a natural disaster, we were able to focus on the people, how they react and how they unite to overcome their petty problems."[33]

Devlin seconded this view: "This is why we always said that this movie was really much more patterned after the disaster films of the '70s than the alien invasion films of the '50s because a classic disaster film had many different characters who would come together in the face of some type of disaster and, in this case, that disaster was a worldwide alien invasion."[34]

Another catalyst for *ID4* was the 1994 Northridge earthquake — Emmerich's first one in Los Angeles, which brought him and his neighbors together. To keep their cinematic spectacle within its $70 million budget, Emmerich and Devlin created their own in-house special effects department at 20th Century Fox instead of employing the services of other, established effects companies.[35]

In characterizing *ID4*'s aliens, Devlin said, "They're not good guys, they're not bad guys. They don't like us, they're don't hate us. They're simply the new tenants, and we're the cockroaches. And they want the bugs cleaned out."[36] Vivica Fox, who plays Jasmine, Will Smith's wife in the film, says, "It's a feel good about America-type of movie. It makes you believe in land of the free, home of the brave."[37] Emmerich struck a similar theme: "It was very patriotic. The message was very universal: 'We get attacked. We fight back.'"[38] And, as Devlin said, it was a film about people uniting on a global level, "disparate people from disparate backgrounds coming together in an unlikely way."[39]

Released the same year as *Independence Day*, Tim Burton's *Mars Attacks!* is the comic flip side of *ID4*. When the Martian ships surround Earth, General Decker (Rod Steiger) advises immediate action to the President (Jack Nicholson). Professor Donald Kessler (Pierce Brosnan) demurs, believing that, owing to their technological advancement, "they're peaceful. An advanced civilization is, by definition, not barbaric. . . this is a great day. I and all my colleagues are extremely excited." The President decides to go public with the news. When the aliens land in the Nevada desert, they're greeted by the Army, the press, and thousands of

---

33 Fischer 179.

34 Emmerich, *Independence Day*.

35 Fischer 179.

36 Emmerich, *Independence Day*.

37 Emmerich, *Independence Day*.

38 *Action!*, American Movie Classics, Prometheus Entertainment and Foxstar Productions in Association with Fox Television Studios and AMC, 1 Feb. 2003.

39 "The Making of Independence Day," Emmerich, *Independence Day: Five Star*.

spectators. When the Martian ambassador announces "We come in peace," one of the onlookers releases a dove in celebration. The Martians mistake it as a hostile act, opening fire on the assembled gathering. Professor Kessler believes the incident to be "a cultural misunderstanding," nothing more. The Martians issue a formal apology and land on Earth to address Congress. In a scene reminiscent of Klaatu's landing in *The Day the Earth Stood Still*, the Martians' ship lands on the Capitol grounds. Once inside the Capitol building, the Martians drop all pretense of friendliness, shooting up Congress with their ray guns to the delight of one television viewer, Florence Norris (Sylvia Sidney). The President wants the people to know "that they still have two out of three branches of the government working for them, and that ain't bad," schools will still be open, "the garbage will still be carried out," and there will be a cop on every corner, "which, incidentally, we would already have if they had listened to me in the last election."

Flying saucer over the Capitol Dome in *Mars Attacks!* (1996). Photo copyright: Warner Bros.

The Martians send one of their own, disguised as a curvaceous woman (Lisa Marie — looking very computer-generated, herself), into the White House itself, where she tries to kidnap the President but is gunned down by the Secret Service. The aliens then launch a full-scale attack on Washington, toppling the Washington Monument in a scene reminiscent of *Earth vs. the Flying Saucers* (the alien ship crashing into the monument in the latter film and the alien ships, in that film and *Mars Attacks!*, firing lethal disintegrator rays from weapons projected from the underside of the ships in both films), and invading the White House, killing the First Lady (Glenn Close) by toppling a chandelier on her. The Martians ultimately kill the President himself, despite his plea for cooperation between Earth and Mars. The Martians then attack Las Vegas, then the rest of the world. When a nuclear missile is launched against the Martians, the latter deploy a device that "sucks up" the nuclear detonation, which the Martian ambassador breaths in like nitrous oxide for a laugh.

Richard Norris (Lukas Hass), the brother of a soldier killed by the Martians earlier, goes to rescue his grandmother Florence, chased by a gigantic Martian robot. The grandmother holds the key to the Martians' defeat: their heads burst apart when they hear her Slim Whitman record! Hearing his music, the Martians are defeated and Richie and Florence receive the Congressional Medal of Honor from the President's daughter (Natalie Portman).[40]

Flying saucers over Washington in *Earth vs. the Flying Saucers* (1956). Photo copyright: Columbia Pictures.

After directing *Ed Wood*, Tim Burton drew inspiration for his next project from the science fiction of the 1950s he grew up with. "I wanted to do something fun, the kind of movies I grew up watching," he said. "I've always loved the science-fiction movies of the '50s. Growing up on all those movies about Martians with big brains sort of stays with you forever."

While discussing the project with Warner Bros., Burton remembered *Mars Attacks!*, a trading-card series depicting a Martian invasion of Earth, originally created by the Topps Company in 1962. Because "of the nature of some the images," however, the series never received national distribution and was withdrawn shortly thereafter. Since then, the cards had attained cult status and became collectors' items.

"Because the cards had come out and gone so quickly, I didn't know if it was a dream or something I made up," Burton explained. "After rediscovering them, however, I couldn't get them out of my head." Once the studio acquired the rights for the series from Topps, Burton collaborated with screenwriter Jonathan Gems

40 *Mars Attacks!*, dir. Tim Burton, Warner Home Video, 2004.

to develop a storyline based on the original *Mars Attacks!* cards and "classic alien invasion films of the '50s and '60s."[41]

However different they are in format—one a drama, the other a comedy — both *Independence Day* and *Mars Attacks!* presented stories of people of different backgrounds and locations coming together against an alien invasion. Both depicted the destruction of Washington five years before September 11.

THE MIND CONTROLLERS

In addition to John Carpenter's remake of *The Thing*, two other classic '50s sci-fi films, both dealing with alien possession of humans, were given updated treatments in the '70s and '80s.

Directed by Philip Kaufman, 1978's remake of *Invasion of the Body Snatchers* featured big-name stars — Donald Sutherland, Jeff Goldblum, and Leonard Nimoy — and was set, not in a small town but San Francisco, reflecting big city life in the '70s. The film opens with the alien life forms migrating to Earth, descending in a rainstorm upon the City by the Bay, growing into flowers. The film's protagonist, Matthew Bennell (Sutherland), works for the Department of Health. His colleague, Elizabeth Driscoll (Brooke Adams), tells him her husband is different. Matthew directs her to a psychiatrist, saying, "You talk to him, he would put things in perspective. . . He would eliminate a lot of things. It would eliminate whether Geoffrey (Elizabeth's husband) was having an affair, whether he'd become gay, whether he had a social disease, whether he'd become a Republican — all the alternatives, all the things that could have happened to him to have made you feel that he had changed, something that he was doing."

Elizabeth Driscoll isn't the only one to notice that people aren't themselves. The owner of a Chinese laundry says his wife isn't his wife. Elizabeth then says her husband is involved in a conspiracy with "strange people." She also feels the whole city has changed. As she and Matthew talk while he drives, Matthew's car almost hits none other than Kevin McCarthy (in a cameo appearance reminiscent of his final scene in the original film). "Help, help!" McCarthy cries hysterically and yells: "They're coming, they're coming! Listen to me! Listen, help me! You're next . . . you're next. We're in danger . . . Here they are! They're already here! . . . They're coming! They're coming!" He runs off, chased by a throng of people, and winds up being struck and killed by another car.

At a book party for a psychiatrist, Dr. David Kibner (Nimoy), a woman tells the doctor her husband isn't her husband. The people looking on seem to be silently communicating among themselves, the implication being they're aliens themselves. Later, Kibner tells Matthew and Elizabeth he's heard the same story from his patients that same week. His diagnosis: "People are stepping in and out of relationships too fast because they don't want the responsibility. That's why marriages are going to hell. The whole family unit is shot to hell." This latter comment can be viewed as a statement on the state of human relationships in the '70s. Kibner tells Elizabeth that she feels her husband has changed because she's looking for a way out of her relationship. Kibner further tells Matthew, "It's like

---

41 Burton, "Production Notes."

there's some kind of hallucinatory flu going around. People seem to get over it in a day or two. . ."

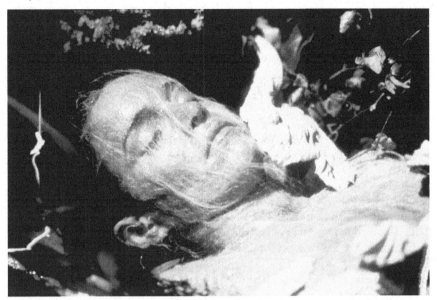

Brooke Adams in Invasion of the *Body Snatchers* (1978). Photo copyright: United Artists.

At a mud bath spa, Nancy Bellicec (Veronica Cartwright) tells a patron who complains about the music being played, "It's for the plants . . . It's wonderful for my plants. They just love it. Plants have feelings . . . just like people . . . This type of music stimulates the growth of the plants." Later, at the spa, Jack Bellicec (Jeff Goldblum) and Nancy discover a "dead body" and call Matthew to look at it. Matthew rushes off to check on Elizabeth's safety. He then lies down to sleep while the "corpse" begins to duplicate him. In the original, the pod people emerged in a sudsy form; the aliens this time emerge in embryo-like form from the plants.

Eventually, Matthew and Elizabeth are cornered by Jack, Kibner, and the others. Kibner explains:

> "Don't be trapped by old concepts . . . You're evolving into a new life form . . . We came here from a dying world. We drift through the universe, from planet to planet, pushed on by the solar winds. We adapt, and we survive. The function of life is survival."

Nancy Bellicec discovers that the aliens can be fooled by hiding one's emotions. When the aliens discover a human among them, they emit a shrill scream, alerting their brethren. The stakes are greater than in the original film: set in a big city this time, the pods are seen being loaded aboard a ship in port, presumably to spread the alien invasion beyond America's shores.

Unlike the original, the remake ends on a pessimistic note. After discovering that Elizabeth has become one of them, Matthew destroys the warehouse breeding ground and is pursued by the aliens. In the final scene, he meets Nancy on the street, then, to the latter's horror, shrieks the aliens' cry of discovery of a human.[42] This is more in line with the original ending the producers of the first film had in mind: showing Miles Bennell running, shouting among the cars on the highway, "You're next!"

Kaufman's film transports the alien menace from a small town to the big city. Ultimately the film is a commentary on '70s cynicism and despair. The world had grown more impersonal and dehumanized since 1956. The downbeat climax of the remake was more plausible in 1978. The '70s was also an age of cults. Reviewing the film at the time of its release, *Newsweek*'s David Ansen felt it was "sufficiently abstract" to comment on the issues of any era. Where Don Siegel's version examined '50s conformity, communist concerns, and McCarthyism, Philip Kaufman's remake, coming as it did in the wake of the Jonestown horror and the murders of San Francisco's Mayor George Moscone and Councilman Harvey Milk, assumed "a new layer of creepiness: it becomes a parable for an age of paranoia, conspiracy theories, psycho-babble and the invasion of the will perpetrated by cult leaders."[43] Moreover, the film reflected another '70s anxiety: ecological calamity. This issue, arising in part from a popular suspicion of science, had once been focused on physics, as was the case with Siegel's film, which presented radiation contamination as the source of the pod people's invasion. By 1978 that fear had refocused: Kaufman's version emphasized biological concerns, the hazards of genetic manipulation, and cloning, the latter portrayed in a scene where a dog has a human face![44]

Released eight years after Kaufman's film, Tobe Hooper's remake of *Invaders from Mars* came during the Reagan era when the Soviet-American conflict had chilled once again, though by the time the film was released, Reagan and Gorbachev *were* talking to each other and the "evil empire" was in its waning days. Unlike the 1953 original, seen as a Cold War parable of communist enslavement, Hooper's version made no commentary on the '80s or carried any ideological message. It was merely a remake that showed the evolution of movie special effects since the '50s. As in the original film, the child hero, this time named David Gardner (Hunter Carson), sees a spaceship land behind a hill during a storm. David's father (Timothy Bottoms), a NASA employee, goes to investigate, returns with a scar on the back of his neck, missing a slipper. Mrs. Gardner (Lorraine Newman) summons the police to find her spouse. The police chief is played by Jimmy Hunt (David Maclean in the original film). As he and his partner walk up the hill, Hunt remarks, "Gee, I haven't been up here since I was a kid" — a reference to his role in the first film. Like the police in that version, they're taken over.

42 *Invasion of the Body Snatchers*, dir. Philip Kaufman, MGM/UA Home Video, 1990.

43 David Ansen, "Flower Power," *Newsweek* 18 Dec. 1978: 85.

44 Peter M. Carroll, *It Seemed Like Nothing Happened: The Tragedy and Promise of America in the 1970s* (New York: Holt, Rinehart and Winston, 1984) 304-305.

Once they've gone over to the other side, the Martians' victims begin exhibiting odd dining habits: David's parents begin eating burnt bacon and raw hamburger, and David's teacher (Louise Fletcher) eats a frog whole. David finds an ally in the school nurse (Karen Black). He hides out in Fletcher's van, which she drives to Copper's Hill. David follows her into a cave to the Martian ship, where she speaks to the Martian leader. Compared with the 1953 version, where the Martians limited their invasion to a sand pit, the remake has them burrowing under the town, including David's school (Menzies Elementary School — a reference to William Cameron Menzies, director of the first film), making them more threatening as their "conspiracy" is more far-reaching.

In both films, the Martians come to Earth to sabotage the American space program. Whereas in 1953 they felt threatened by man's intention to send rockets into space (reflecting Cold War attitudes of the time), the Martians in Hooper's remake don't want humans visiting their planet; hence, they destroy the space probe. Moreover, the Martians in the second film aren't very sociable. When a scientist tries to communicate with them in a scene reminiscent of Dr. Carrington's attempt to communicate with James Arness's *Thing*, the Martians destroy him.

The remake digresses from the original in its depiction of the younger generation's attitude toward authority. In the '50s, children trusted and obeyed their parents and teachers. When David Gardner's teacher (Fletcher) is devoured by one of the Martian mutants, David is overjoyed to see this happen. Furthermore, compared with the more circumspect '50s, the remake graphically shows the Martian mind control probe being inserted into the necks of their victims. As with the original, Hooper's version has David waking up to discover that the Martian invasion was a dream, and that his dream may be real.[45]

What ultimately makes the remakes of *Invasion of the Body Snatchers* and *Invaders from Mars* significant is that two '50s films, considered low-grade fare in their day, were subsequently considered worthy enough to be remade as A-level productions; *Invasion of the Body Snatchers* showcases social commentary on the '70s; and *Invaders from Mars* is a high-tech '80s version of an old-fashioned space invasion story.

Friendly Alien Visitors: E.T. the Extraterrestrial

Sandwiched in between the remakes of *Invasion of the Body Snatchers* and *Invaders from Mars* was a 1982 release featuring an alien visitor far different in temperament from any hostile alien. Considering the sense of insecurity that pervades America today, struggling with domestic divisions and perceived threats from foreigners in the post-September 11 world, it may seem incredible that, in another time, the world came together under the magical influence of a movie alien. That era seems more secure, yet it must be remembered that 1982 was an age of international tensions, economic recession and high unemployment, social division, and the dawning of the AIDS epidemic. The movie that burst forth as a shining light in this dark time introduced the most beloved alien of all time: *E.T.:*

---

45 *Invaders from Mars*, dir. Tobe Hooper, Media Home Entertainment Inc., 1986.

The Extraterrestrial, directed by one of the most successful directors in film history, Steven Spielberg.

E.T. the Extraterrestrial (1982). Photo copyright: Universal Pictures.

E.T.'s odyssey began in 1978, when *Variety* announced that Spielberg was preparing what was originally conceived as a low-budget quickie film bearing the tentative title *Growing Up*. The projected film, Spielberg said, would be "a personal story of [my] own growing up." At the time he was already planning another project, *1941*. The latter film eventually came to occupy Spielberg's time, so the other concept had to be shelved for the time being. In the interim, it went through changes and different titles — *A Boy's Life* and *E.T. and Me*.

While filming *Raiders of the Lost Ark*, Spielberg became lonely due to separation from his family and friends. He compensated for this by devising an imaginary friend, one akin to one of the friendly space visitors in Spielberg's earlier film, *Close Encounters of the Third Kind*. Instead of filming a sequel to the latter, he considered doing a film similar to *Close Encounters*, only this time it would show things from the alien's perspective. "It's a 'personal movie' for me," Spielberg said, "and closer to my heart than any movie I've ever made before." *E.T.* would feature elements both of fantasy (the alien left behind on Earth by his companions) and reality. The main focus of the film would be a ten-year-old child whose parents ponder divorce — something Spielberg experienced in *his* life as a child. This notwithstanding, the child would experience life as children lived it in the 1980s.

When initially asked if she would be interested in writing the script for the film, Melissa Mathison declined the offer but, when asked a second time, she took on the assignment, ultimately preparing three drafts.[46]

To keep the child actors' performances natural, Spielberg discarded his storyboarding for this film. He decided he worked best when he worked faster: it took only 59 shooting days to wrap up *E.T.*

"*E.T.* is. . .a film about winning and losing best friends," Spielberg said. He continued:

> "What inspired me to do *E.T.* more than anything else was that my father was a computer expert, and he kept getting better jobs. And we would go from town to town. And it would just so happen I would find a best friend, and I would finally become an insider in school — in an elementary school, with a group of people, and usually a best friend, and at the moment of my greatest comfort and tranquility we'd move somewhere else. And it would always be that inevitable good-bye scene, in the train station or at the carport packing up the car to drive somewhere, or at the airport, where all my friends would be there, and we'd say goodbye to each other and I would leave. And this happened to me four major times in my life. And the older I got the harder it got. And *E.T.* reflects a lot of that. When Elliott finds E.T., he hangs on to E.T., and he announces in no uncertain terms, 'I'm keeping him,' and he means it.

> "Friendship has become much more important to me than anything else. Having friends, and having good friends, is more important to me than making movies or anything else. Because when everything else is gone. . . . Because movies are a dream. They're a fantasy. It's a cloud over your head, a lovely blue and pink cloud, the kind of thing you see on ceilings and in children's bedrooms. But that's *all* it is."

46 Douglas Brode, *The Films of Steven Spielberg* (Secaucus: The Citadel Press, 1995) 114-116.

To Spielberg's mind, *E.T.* was a children's film. There were only two significant adult figures in it: Keys, the scientist who tries to save E.T. at the end of the film (Peter Coyote) and Mary, Elliott's mother (Dee Wallace). The two principal children's roles, Elliott and Gertie, were filled by, respectively, Henry Thomas and Drew Barrymore. The film, for the most part, unfolded through Elliott's eyes. Spielberg insisted that, save for Mary, no other adult characters appear until near E.T.'s conclusion. Thus when Keys's scientific team enters the picture they seem frightening to Elliott. In reality they, like Elliott, desire to save E.T. and are just as much dreamers as Elliott is. (What truly saves E.T. is the return of his own species. It is the captain of the alien ship who left E.T. stranded on Earth who is the real villain of the story.)[47]

Essentially, *E.T.* unfolds in three acts. Act I has him left behind on Earth when scientists surprise his traveling companions, causing them to leave without him. E.T. then meets Elliott and later his teenage brother, Michael (Robert MacNaughton), and sister Gertie, all of whom join to hide E.T. In Act II, the alien rigs up a radar system to enable him to "phone home." During this, the government is watching and then enters the home they believe E.T. is hiding in. In Act III, the dying E.T. is captured by the government scientists who try to revive him. Elliott, Michael, Gertie, and other kids join forces to rescue E.T. and return him to his fellow aliens. The film then ends with "the bittersweet parting of E.T. and Elliott."[48]

E.T. received its initial public viewing at the 1982 Cannes Film Festival, where it received rave reviews. The favorable reception continued at a sneak preview in Houston in May. The film's official release to the rest of the movie-going public occurred on June 11, 1982. It became the all-time box-office hit until toppled from that spot by Spielberg's *Jurassic Park*. "During its first year of release, *E.T.* grossed a record-breaking $359,687,000 in the United States and Canada alone; before long, the film had been seen by more than 200 million people worldwide."[49] The film went on to earn an Academy Award nomination for Best Picture.[50]

The impact of *E.T.* was tremendous. The kindly alien visitor was a runner-up as *Time*'s "Man of the Year" for 1982. The film had a unifying effect on people. "I remember having the thought then that the '80s was a turbulent time. . ." recalled actor Peter Coyote, who added:

> "And . . . I always thought that one of the things that made people love this film was if two people or three people as far apart as E.T. and these children could bridge a gap and fall in love with one another and communicate, then . . . there were no two people on Earth that were that far apart. And it just seems pressing it to me that in a time, like today, that's fraught with cultural misunderstandings and danger and enmity and hatred, that this message is being replayed. . .it happens before your eyes. It's not pretended. The feelings of these child actors were not pretended. They were palpably real. That's why they moved people. And I think it's a great thing to remember, that if E.T. and these

---

47 Fischer 560, 561.

48 Brode, *The Films of Steve Spielberg* 121-122.

49 Brode, *The Films of Steve Spielberg* 120-121.

50 Fischer 562.

humans can make an understanding, there's nothing preventing any two people or two nations on Earth from doing it."

Spielberg concurred: "And that's pretty much I think what happened in the year of 1982, when the world kind of came together for *E.T.* . . . All the lines between cultures and class systems and racial barriers . . . came down in a kind of shared experience."[51]

One reason for the film's phenomenal success may have been due to the time it was released in: 1982 was a time of severe economic distress in the United States; the American economy was in its worst condition since the Great Depression of the 1930s. Hence, *E.T.*'s success could be viewed as a form of escapism during a difficult time. Moreover, *E.T.* opened the door to various interpretations of its meaning. One commentator felt, "E.T. is the teddy bear we crush forever to our bleeding hearts. E.T. is every childish fantasy we never outgrew. E.T. is the eternal child in all of us." To the editor of a national magazine, E.T. was a father figure to Elliott and his siblings, whose own father had forsaken them. ABC News correspondent Ted Koppel went even further than that: "It's essentially the Christ story. Christ was the ultimate extraterrestrial" — a view many theologians concurred in, as did other, secular, observers. "At a time when many people had grown to feel disassociated from their society, unable to return to the old religious truths and the spirituality they so desperately needed," wrote film historian Douglas Brode, "E.T. provided an alternative to conventional religion, conveying the same hopeful message one would experience at a traditional synagogue or church."[52] Another film historian, Dennis Fischer, took the Christ analogy even further:

> "Both E.T. and Christ are extraterrestrials in the sense of coming from outside the world. Both begin their adventures on Earth in less than auspicious circumstances — E.T. in a shed behind Elliott's home, and Christ in a manager in an animal shelter behind an inn. Neither is much to look at — E.T. looks something like a shell-less turtle while according to Isaiah's prophecy, Christ lacked any comeliness or beauty. Both have miraculous healing powers, and other powers over nature. Both are hunted down by ideological authorities. Both are resurrected from the dead, appearing at first only to their most trusted companions and being whisked from their 'tombs.' E.T. is even given a shroud and his 'last resting place' is thrown open and revealed to be empty. E.T., like Christ, ascends to the heavens while being watched by the people who have become his figurative disciples. He tells Elliott, 'I'll be right here,' indicating Elliott's heart and echoing Christ's 'I am with you always' (Matthew 28: 20). There is also Spielberg's use of the image of the Sacred Heart.

> "If that were not enough, only the children with their child-like faith initially are able to relate to E.T., echoing Christ's admonition, 'Unless you turn around and become like children, you will never enter the kingdom of heaven' (Matthew 18: 3). Is it surprising then that the sign on Elliott's door reads, 'Enter'? Both Christ and E.T. arrive at night, symbolically bringing light to a place of darkness. E.T.'s repeated notion of phoning home has a special meaning for people who

---

51 "E.T.: The Reunion," dir. Steven Spielberg, *E. T.: The Extraterrestrial. Two-Disc Limited Collector's Edition*, Universal Studios, Inc., 2002

52 Brode, *The Films of Steven Spielberg* 127.

consider themselves children of God and can be interpreted as representing the need for prayer. E.T.'s apparent death causes Elliott to gain strength, echoing the ideas of atonement and of God dying for man's sins."[53]

A clergyman himself, Dr. Phil Lineberger of the Metropolitan Baptist Church in Wichita, Kansas, sounded the same theme:

> "I went to see the movie with my kids. As I sat watching it, I noticed E.T.'s telepathic sympathy and I thought, That's an interesting sort of parallel to the gospel. But it wasn't until E.T. was dying, when the little boy gains strength as E.T. comes closer to death, that I thought, My goodness, that sounds like the atonement. In the gospel, Christ died for our sins so that we might live, just as E.T. was doing. When E.T. was resurrected, and then at the end when he was ascending, being watched by all the kids who had become his disciples, it all started lining up for me."

As to whether or not any of this was deliberately inserted into the film, Spielberg said:

> "I've been too busy making movies to stop and analyze how or why I make 'em. Lucas was the most surprised kid on the block when *Star Wars* became a megabit. He had tapped a nerve that not only went deep but global. George has theories now, about five years later, but at the time there was no explaining. I think George realized the meaning of what he had done as much from the critiques he read, and the psychological analysis they pinned to *Star Wars*, as from his own introspection. I'm the same way."

> "In other words," Brode writes, "it's all there, whether Spielberg consciously intended it or not."[54]

E.T. wasn't the first science fiction film to draw a parallel with Christ. One has only to recall Klaatu in *The Day the Earth Stood Still*. Whatever its meaning, E.T. is possibly the most beloved friendly space visitor in science fiction film history. It's also clear that he came along at a time when people needed a boost in a difficult time, providing lessons in love, friendship, and unity among different kinds of individuals — alien and human. This message clearly resonates with the September 11 world, a clear indication of the timelessness of this movie character.

THE END OF THE WORLD

In the 1950s end of the world disaster films depicted humanity's demise as a result of either an atomic war (*Five, Day the World Ended*) or a cosmic calamity (*When Worlds Collide*). The latter scenario was revived by Hollywood in the latter 1990s. By then, with the twenty-first century fast approaching, there was again unease concerning humanity's future, only this time the threat stemmed, not from a nuclear holocaust but from what was known as Y2K. The fear was that when the clocks struck midnight on January 1, 2000, the computers of the world, most of which were originally set to read years in only two digits, would read it not as 2000 but as 1900, shutting down essential systems worldwide. Computers were

---

53 Fischer 561.

54 Brode, *The Films of Steven Spielberg* 127.

reprogrammed and such an occurrence failed to materialize, but government and the media had succeeded in stirring up a deep and pervasive sense that some mysterious breakdown might be lurking in the near future that would throw our lives into chaos in unpredictable ways.

Two years before the turn of the century, two films, both depicting a cosmic disaster imperiling humanity, were released. *Deep Impact* presents its story with a dose of political intrigue. As the film begins, Leo Beiderman (Elijah Wood), a member of an astronomy club stargazing in Richmond, Virginia, discovers an un-identified star in the night sky. They photograph the discovery and send the pho-to to an observatory in Tucson, Arizona, where the scientist there makes another, more unsettling, discovery. Unable to e-mail his findings, he drives off to dispatch the information by regular mail, only to die in a traffic accident en route.

Fast forward one year later: MSNBC reporter Jenny Lerner (Tea Leoni) is as-signed to cover the resignation of the Secretary of the Treasury because of his wife's health. It may be a cover story. The real reason for his resignation may be that he's having an affair with a woman named "Ellie." Confronted by Lerner, the secretary tells her she has "the biggest story in history," then adds apologetically: "What difference does anything make anymore?" Lerner suspects the secretary's resignation may indeed be a cover story for presidential misconduct. This proved to be a timely plot device: that same year the American people learned that their real-life president had been involved with a White House intern. Just as Lerner has her brainstorm, she's pulled over by the FBI and taken to a secret meeting with the President himself (Morgan Freeman). In exchange for giving her the op-portunity to ask the first question at a White House press conference, she keeps quiet for now; the President will reveal the full story in 48 hours. Doing an Inter-net search, Lerner discovers that "Ellie" actually means E.L.E.: Extinction Level Event. At the press conference, the President reveals that a comet, about seven miles long, larger than Mount Everest, is on a collision course with Earth. To avoid the impact, the United States and Russia have been constructing a space-ship in Earth's orbit, the crew of which will fly to the comet and destroy it. The President directs his listeners to carry on with their lives as normal.

The space shuttle transports the astronauts to *Messiah*, the ship that will carry them and eight nuclear devices to the comet, where the nuclear devices will be used to destroy it. The joint Russian-American venture emphasizes how the world has changed since the '50s, when the Cold War prevailed. Once the crew lands on their target, christened Wolf-Beiderman after its discoverers, they implant the explosives, losing one of their men in the process. After leaving the comet, the astronauts detonate the bombs. Instead of destroying the comet, the explosion merely breaks off a piece of it, creating two. The President then ad-dresses the nation, telling the people that a joint American-Russian Titan mis-sile launch will be made to deflect the comets just before they hit Earth. Should that fail, a national lottery will choose people to relocate to a shelter, in the soft limestone caves in Missouri, where the inhabitants will remain for two years while the air clears from the comets' impact. For now, martial law has been de-clared. This recalls Cold War-era civil defense efforts, when school children were taught that ducking and covering under their desks would protect them during a nuclear attack, while their parents built fallout shelters against the same threat. Similarly, the authorities in *Them!* place Los Angeles under martial law in the face of the mutant ants' threat.

A comet hits Earth in *Deep Impact* (1998). Photo copyright: Paramount Pictures.

The titans fail to deflect the comets. Beiderman, the section of the comet that broke off from the nuclear blast, impacts the Atlantic Ocean off Virginia, engulfing New York City, toppling the Statue of Liberty and hitting the World Trade Center. *Messiah's* crew sacrifices itself by flying into Wolf, the remaining comet, destroying it with the remaining nuclear weapons, averting further catastrophe and making possible the rebuilding of life on Earth.[55]

Like *Independence Day* and *Mars Attacks!*, *Deep Impact* shows a cross-section of humanity confronting a doomsday scenario.[56] By contrast, *Armageddon*, released just weeks after *Deep Impact*, eschewed the first film's "touchy-feely" seriousness in favor of what *Newsweek* called "slap-happy adventurism. It's *The Dirty Dozen* save the world," accompanied by dazzling special effects.[57] Fade in to the space shuttle *Atlantis* being hit and destroyed by meteorites. This cinematic disaster occurred twelve years after the real-life *Challenger* disaster and five years before the shuttle *Columbia* broke up upon returning from space. A meteor shower then begins impacting Earth, causing severe damage in New York City, pummeling buildings, including a skyscraper and cars. "This is New York City," says a cab driver to his passengers. "Anything could've happened . . . It could've been terrorist bombs, a dead body . . . its probably pay day, too. Somebody probably jumped — didn't get

55 *Deep Impact*, dir. Mimi Leder, Paramount Home Video, DreamWorks SKG, 1998.

56 Richard Schickel, "A Sober Start to Summer Fun," *Time* 11 May 1998: 75.

57 David Ansen and Corrie Brown, "Demolition Man," *Newsweek* 6 July 1998: 65.

their pay check." As the meteor shower continues, the cabbie utters words that, three years before September 11 and the Iraq War that followed it, sound eerily prescient: "We're at war. Saddam Hussein is bombing us." The cause of the galactic bombardment is an asteroid, "the size of Texas," designated a "global killer" — one that will destroy all life on Earth. It will hit in 18 days.

A meteor strikes the Chrysler Building in *Armageddon* (1998). Photo copyright: None provided.

To avert calamity, the US government sends for Harry Stamper (Bruce Willis), the head of an oil drilling team. The plan is to launch a team of astronauts to land on the asteroid, drill a hole in it, implant a nuclear device to destroy it. Stamper agrees to do the job — provided his oil drilling team gets the contract to do the job.[58] The team, characterized by *Time*'s Richard Schickel as "overgrown boys," inevitably clash with "the fly-right NASA nerds" whose task is to beat the clock in training and sending Stamper's crew on their way — injecting an element of class conflict in the film.[59]

As in *Deep Impact*, détente is in play. The shuttles bearing the oil drillers-turned-astronauts send them aloft, then stop by a Russian space station for refueling. However, a mechanical error forces a quick exit from the station, with its cosmonaut accompanying the Americans as the station is destroyed. When the shuttles approach the asteroid, a collision destroys one of them; the other lands on the target. When the drilling appears to be unsuccessful, civil defense sirens sound and people enter fallout shelters. Pieces of the asteroid hit Paris like a nuclear detonation. On the asteroid, the "armadillo" drill vehicle from the downed shuttle arrives to resume drilling after the first "armadillo" is lost, which precipitated the alert. A rock storm on the asteroid damages the remote detona-

58 *Armageddon*, dir. Michael Bay, Touchstone Home Video, 1998.

59 Richard Schickel, "Insubstantial Impact," *Time* 6 July 1998: 88.

tor on the bomb, requiring someone to remain behind and detonate it manually. Ben Affleck, a member of Stamper's drilling crew, draws the "winning" straw to do the job but Stamper takes his place. The shuttle takes off as Stamper pushes the button that detonates the bomb and destroys the asteroid.[60]

Both *Armageddon* and *Deep Impact* played into people's fears — always latent and perhaps especially present the end of a century or millennium — that were given a name this time around by the Y2K phenomenon of the late 1990s. Both were '90s remakes of *When Worlds Collide*. Finally, both show how far we've come since the days of the Cold War in the fact that they show Russian-American co-operation in banishing the galactic threat confronting Earth.

MUTANTS

In the '50s, Hollywood ascribed the responsibility for mutations to the Bomb and atomic radiation. As the years passed that focus shifted to other causes such as environmental pollution. The catalyst for the latter was *The Hellstrom Chronicle* (1971), a nature documentary which postulated the idea that the very adaptability of insects would allow them to ultimately rule the world. Much as nuclear radiation inspired the marauding monsters of the Eisenhower era, *The Hellstrom Chronicle* sired a wave of ecological nightmares (*Squirm, Frogs, Bug*) at a time when environmentalism was entering the public consciousness.[61] As the 1980s dawned, consumerism became the whipping boy in Universal's *The Incredible Shrinking Woman*, a 1981 remake of the same studio's *The Incredible Shrinking Man*, which had elevated Grant Williams to stardom, and, like Williams's film, was suggested by Richard Matheson's *The Shrinking Man*.

Shrinking Woman's protagonist is Pat Kramer (Lily Tomlin). Her story begins when her husband (Charles Grodin) accidentally spills a new perfume on her blouse. She takes it off and, unbeknownst to her, it starts dissolving. This is followed by other changes: Pat notices that her fingernails seem shorter. Her bracelet falls off while she serves her husband breakfast. He, in turn, has to bend over to kiss her, and she notices that her clothes no longer fit her. "I'm getting smaller everyday," she says. Ultimately, her condition is diagnosed as resulting from her use of consumer products.

A newscaster refers to Pat as perhaps "a metaphor for the modern woman. It is no secret that the role of the modern housewife has become increasingly less significant." This observation occurs as Pat attracts public and media attention because of her plight. Her husband's boss (Ned Beatty) is anxious about the impact Pat will have on public confidence in American consumer items if she reveals the truth when she appears on *The Mike Douglas Show*. Those fears are alleviated when, during her appearance, she says the cause of her shrinking hasn't been determined.

Beatty isn't the only one interested in Pat's condition. The Organization for World Management plans to dominate the world. To accomplish this objec-

---

60 Bay.

61 Ron Hogan, *The Stewardess Is Flying the Plane! American Films of the 1970s* (New York: Bulfinch Press, 2005) 53.

tive, the group intends to develop a serum from Pat's blood to shrink people and nations, "fluoridating" water with their evil concoction. The organization kidnaps Pat, imprisoning her in a laboratory. Ultimately, she escapes with the aid of a friendly gorilla she's bonded with in captivity, and a lab technician (Mark Blankfield).

Unlike the original *Shrinking Man*, whose hero Scott Carey continues shrinking into nothingness, Pat Kramer is delivered from her plight: falling into a puddle, she returns to her normal height. But her joy is short-lived: celebrating with her family, her husband tries to put her wedding ring back on her finger, only to find it won't fit. Pat then discovers the reason: she's becoming the Amazing Colossal Woman.[62]

Compared with *The Incredible Shrinking Man*, *The Incredible Shrinking Woman* takes a lighthearted, satirical look at the plight of its shrinking protagonist. If the film's premise — that Pat Kramer's condition arose from using consumer products is accurate — then no one is immune to the threat of shrinking.

Scene from *Matinee* (1993). Photo copyright: Universal Pictures.

Universal, the studio behind *The Incredible Shrinking Woman*, returned to the mutant theme twelve years later with *Matinee*, which directly confronted both the atomic mutant theme and the fears of nuclear war in general. Directed by Joe Dante, *Matinee* is set in Key West, Florida in 1962. The local theater there is

---

62 *The Incredible Shrinking Woman*, dir. Eisha Marjara, Universal Pictures, 1981.

preparing for the arrival of horror film producer Lawrence Woolsey (John Goodman), who is coming to premiere his latest film, *Mant!* in which a man, owing to radiation exposure, mutates into an ant-like creature. The film is "Presented in Atomo Vision. With RUMBLE RAMA. The New Audience Participation Thrill That Actually Makes YOU Part of the Show!"

Woolsey's impending arrival excites one of his fans, 15-year-old Gene Loomis (Simon Fenton). Against this backdrop, reality intrudes: the Cuban missile crisis breaks, and Gene's father is called to duty on the one of the blockade ships surrounding Cuba. Gene gets to meet the great man Woolsey himself, who hires Gene to work on the film. Woolsey wires the theater seats to scare the audience during the film. His wife, who also appears in *Mant!*, dresses as a nurse in the theater lobby, having audience members sign release forms absolving the producer of responsibility if the patrons are scared to death while watching *Mant!*.

Throughout *Matinee*, the threat of war looms in the background. Gene's mother tearfully watches home movies of her husband — a reminder of the separation of servicemen and their families during the real-life Iraq War a decade after *Matinee*'s release. In the film, the jittery theater manager (Robert Picardo) constantly listens to the radio for war news and has a fallout shelter at the theater. Thinking the Russians have attacked, he runs to his shelter when, in reality, it's the special effects for Woolsey's film. Gene and his date get locked in the shelter where they ponder the possibility that they will be the sole survivors of the war. They realize that they will be responsible for repopulating the world as "Adam and Eve." Later, when an atomic blast occurs at the end of *Mant!*, the audience panics, thinking a real attack has occurred, rushing out of the theater into bright daylight, discovering the world hasn't ended.[63]

Matinee tapped into a pair of related themes: first, the real-life Cold War anxieties of the early '60s, symbolized by the Cuban missile crisis. Not only is there the fallout shelter at the theater showing *Mant!*, there's the "duck-and-cover" drill at school (a common occurrence of the time) where a girl, much to the displeasure of school officials, refuses to participate. This act of defiance was a preview of the coming student protests of the latter '60s. Years later, educator Robert K. Musil credited the "duck-and-cover" drills as the cradle of the coming '60s eruptions: "In many ways, the styles and explosions of the 1960s were born in those subterranean high-school corridors, where we decided that our elders were indeed unreliable, perhaps even insane."*[64] At the opening of *Mant!*, Woolsey appears in a radiation suit at an atomic test site, saying that "Atomo Vision" will put the audience at ground zero. "Not a safe place to be," he says, "but today there is no safe place to be" — a warning that applies to all the threats these movies represent, from radiation to terrorism to Y2K-induced havoc or the advent of an unstoppable disease. Just as life went on during the missile crisis, signified by the

---

63 *Matinee*, dir. Joe Dante, MCA Universal Home Video, 1993.

64 Skal, *The Monster Show* 278. *Matinee* presents another scene of '60s rebellion: Gene Loomis and a friend are shown secretly listening to a Lenny Bruce comedy record; their clandestine fun is interrupted when Gene's friend's mother comes home, forcing them to hurriedly stash the forbidden record away.

theater audience rushing out into the daylight at the end of *Mant!* to find all is well with the world, so, too, did life continue for Americans during the September 11-Iraq War era.

Matinee's second theme, also related to the Cold War, was what film historian David J. Skal described as Monster Culture, a phenomenon paralleling the Cold War era from the late 1950s to the mid-'60s — one characterized by TV horror hosts, horror film fan magazines, movie monster model kits, and monster sitcoms (*The Munsters, The Addams Family*) on television.[65] A monster song was even a hit on the music charts during this period: "Monster Mash," by Bobby "Boris" Pickett and the Crypt-Kickers, was the top song in America during the missile crisis.[66]

Reviewing *Matinee* for *Time*, Richard Schickel described the film's "movie within the movie" *Mant!* as derived from genuine '50s sci-fi hits *The Fly* and *Them!*[67] *Matinee*'s principle character, Lawrence Woolsey, was also inspired by a real-life '50s horror showman, William Castle. As a boy, Castle (real name William Schloss) had voided himself while watching Crane Wilbur's *The Monster* on Broadway. At age thirteen in 1927, Castle used some money he took from his sister's purse to gain admission to the stage version of *Dracula* with Bela Lugosi, and watched it nearly every night for two weeks. Presently, he began to find the audience reaction to the play more interesting than the play itself. In 1938, while working in summer stock in Stony Creek, Connecticut, Castle earned national notoriety, as well as a job offer from Columbia Pictures, by fabricating a "Nazi" vandalism of the theater to promote a member of the company, a German actress who'd refused Hitler's invitation to attend a Munich art festival. After toiling away in films for years, Castle established his style as a showman with *Macabre* (1958), described as "a morbid beat-the-clock thriller about a man trying to save his daughter whom he believes has been buried alive." For the film, Castle persuaded Lloyd's of London to insure every person in the world for $1,000 against death by shock while viewing *Macabre*. To Castle's mind, this was nothing more than a publicity gimmick; Lloyd's, on the other hand, took it very seriously, demanding that some people with preexisting ailments and any mid-film audience suicides be excluded from coverage.

The gimmick was a smashing success: *Macabre* scored. The door was opened for other Castle gimmicks. *House on Haunted Hill* (1958) featured "Emergo," in which a glowing skeleton sailed out over the audience during an on-screen blackout. Viewers of *The Tingler* (1959) were treated to "Percepto": electric vibrators placed under theater seats "tingled" those sitting in them. All of this transformed audience members from passive spectators into active participants in a kind of live theater experience. "Castle's ultimate gimmick, he once said, would be a total

---

65 Skal, *The Monster Show* 266-267, 281.

66 Skal, *The Monster Show* 279.

67 Richard Schickel, "It Came from Inner Space," *Time* 8 Feb. 1993: 78.

sensory immersion: 'The audience would taste the fog drifting through a cemetery. They'd smell the freshly dug grave. They'd feel the touch of ghastly fingers.'"[68]

Another aspect of Monster Culture displayed in *Matinee* is the fact that Gene Loomis is an avid reader of *Famous Monsters of Filmland* magazine, a real-life publication first issued in 1958, published by James Warren and edited by Forrest J. Ackerman, the latter a collector of all things sci-fi, fantasy, and horror. *Famous Monsters* was a major influence on the lives of such budding talents as Stephen King, Steven Spielberg, and *Matinee*'s own director, Joe Dante. Gene Loomis's younger brother is also obsessed with monsters: he sleeps with a Mummy figure next to his bed. This, too, is based in reality. In the fall of 1962, at the time citizens were quaking under the US-Russian showdown over missile deployment, Aurora Plastics of Hempstead, Long Island, introduced a new kind of plastic model kit, one light-years from the traditional fighter plane and ship models that had been around before then: model kits of Universal's classic monsters — The Wolf Man, Frankenstein's creation, and Dracula. Coming as they did in the midst of history's worst nuclear crisis, the Aurora monster figures offered a sense of continuity to the youngsters who purchased them — the hope that life would go on in some form. "They were," writes Skal, "transcendent resurrection figures, beings who couldn't die. The traditional monsters were perversely Christlike . . . , offering an image of survival, however distorted or grotesque." The same held true for the atomic-age mutations like Woolsey's *Mant!* and Godzilla, who both survived the Bomb and were the offspring of it.[69]

Godzilla, the granddaddy of nuclear age monsters, was himself revived and given a new look for the 1990s and a new stomping ground (New York City) in an American-made version, released in 1998, by the same team behind *Independence Day* — Dean Devlin and Roland Emmerich. "For me, it was always very simple," Emmerich explained. "Godzilla was one of the last concepts of the '50s that had never been done in modern form — that idea of the giant monster as in *Tarantula* or *The Beast from 20,000 Fathoms*. Why not do them again? But," he continued, "we were really concerned about the cheese factor."[70]

By the time Devlin and Emmerich got around to filming their version of *Godzilla*, the glory days of Japan's leading movie monster were far behind. In the '60s, Godzilla began assuming a comic bent. Toho, Godzilla's home studio, also faced competition from rival studios cashing in with their own giant monsters. Of these, the most successful was Gamera, a flying, fire-breathing turtle, produced by Daiei. Gamera sharply differed from Godzilla in that he was geared toward children. Toho followed suit. By the early '70s, Godzilla had been nearly recast as a children's monster. Escalating production costs and dwindling Japanese theater audiences — the latter mainly the result of commercial television's popularity — also took their toll. Consequently, Toho began collaborating with American companies on film projects — only the American participants weren't

68 Skal, *The Monster Show* 256-259.

69 Skal, *The Monster Show* 268-272, 274, 277-278.

70 Howard Chua-Eon, "What in the Name of Godzilla. . .?" *Time* 25 May 1998: 75.

big-name Hollywood distributors but the likes of United Productions of America (UPA), Rankin-Bass, and Allied Artists. To attract American audiences, the latter firms furnished such American "stars" as Nick Adams and Richard Jaeckel.

Drive-ins, those bastions of the glory days of '50s monster films, were also past their prime — they were casualties of the suburban boom. Consequently, Japanese monster films began turning up on television, where they won fans among children — as well as some adults. Japanese special effects maestro Eiji Tsuburaya died in 1970 just as the "Golden Age" of Japanese filmmaking expired as well. Gamera's creator Daiei went bankrupt, another studio began making "Roman porno" (soft-core porno) films. The majority of Toho's contract players were dropped and budgets greatly diminished. Godzilla director Ishiro Honda began working in television, while Haruo Nakajima, who had worn the Godzilla suit from the very first film, took off that suit for the last time.

The Godzilla films of the '70s were a far cry from their predecessors. Moreover, they had to vie with reissued '60s Japanese monster films. The combination of these reissued classics, the release of a new Godzilla film each year, and giant monster shows on television flooded the market beyond what it could handle. Added to all this was the growing volume of imported American productions and the rise of Anime.

Beginning in the 1980s with *Godzilla 1985* (*Gojira* in Japan), a new wave of Godzilla films issued forth. Still they borrowed elements from American films; by the mid-1990s they began imitating themselves.[71]

In some respects, Devlin and Emmerich's take on Godzilla is faithful to the original story. As the film opens, we see preparations for a nuclear test. Interwoven with this are scenes of iguanas and their eggs. When the Bomb detonates, the camera zooms in on one egg in particular — the egg from which Godzilla will emerge. We later learn that it was a French nuclear test that created Godzilla. In the film, the French Secret Service sends agents to New York to destroy him. Moreover, even though the Cold War was over when Devlin and Emmerich's *Godzilla* was released, the nuclear threat wasn't entirely past: at the time, India and Pakistan were making nuclear threats to one another.[72]

Ultimately, the new Godzilla storms into New York City, causing the residents to flee. TV news reporter Charles Caiman (Harry Shearer) reports that city officials are calling Godzilla's rampage "the worst act of destruction since the World Trade Center bombing" — a reference to the 1993 attack there, and words that sound chilling given the fact that the film was released three years before 9/11. (In the featurette accompanying the DVD release of the film, Roland Emmerich jokingly refers to the fact that Godzilla never comes out of his trailer. This is followed by a shot of a giant van, its door marked with a yellow star and "MR. G" under it, backing into the New York skyline — right in front of the World Trade Center!) New York's mayor, Rudolph Giuliani (at the time of September 11), earned widespread acclaim for his handling of the crisis; *Godzilla's* mayor Ebert (a play on real-life movie critic Roger Ebert), more crudely exploits Godzilla's

71 Galbraith, *Monsters* 30-32.

72 Chua-Eon 76.

rampage for political gain. (In reality, the 9/11 attacks occurred the very day of a New York mayoral election which, due to the attacks, had to be postponed).

Godzilla 1998. Photo copyright: Sony Pictures.

The military's efforts to halt Godzilla are met with frustration. When Army helicopters fire Sidewinder missiles at him, he ducks out of their way. Instead of hitting their intended target, the missiles topple the Chrysler Building. (Because Godzilla is cold-blooded, the heat-seeking Sidewinders can't lock onto him.) Indeed, the military's efforts to destroy Godzilla cause more damage than the monster does. Godzilla has come to New York to nest. Godzilla reproduces asexually, laying eggs. The nest is built in Madison Square Garden, which is destroyed by missiles. And, even though Godzilla himself is destroyed, the film ends with a shot of an egg hatching a new Godzilla.[73]

Unlike the fat, lumbering Godzilla of old, the Devlin-Emmerich creature was a lean, sprinting beast, a product of modern motion picture computer special effects. "We realized that the reason behind the whole lumbering Godzilla was that they had to shoot a guy in a heavy-rubber monster suit and film in slow motion to give him some sense of scale," Devlin explained. At 20 stories tall, he continued, "if you do the math, even if it walked at a gingerly pace, it's covering a lot of territory quickly." Devlin's partner Emmerich also noted, "Godzilla can outrun any taxi, and that was the core idea for the movie. No one can catch it. Dean and I realized we could make a different Godzilla, a movie about a hunt, about hide-and-seek."[74]

The new *Godzilla* was a box-office and critical failure upon its release. Despite that and the differences in the old and new Godzilla's design, both incarnations of this venerable character carried the same concern about nuclear war. Godzilla remained a monster with a message. The new Godzilla was a monster for the post-Cold War era. Given the possibility that terrorists could acquire radioactive "dirty" bombs for use against innocent targets, it's conceivable that there will be a Godzilla for the Age of Terrorism.

THE CULTURE WAR: *PLEASANTVILLE*

The year that saw the release of the Devlin-Emmerich *Godzilla*, *Deep Impact*, and *Armageddon*, 1998, also witnessed the release of a film that sharply delineated the differences between the America of the 1990s and the America of the 1950s. *Pleasantville*, directed by Gary Ross, juxtaposes the world of a traditional nuclear family, depicted in a '50s TV sit-com, with the divorced, single-parent world of the '90s. The film is a study of the "values war" (née "culture war)" — the clash between the past and the present. Director Ross advocated a third alternative: "an open society, an open culture, an open mind."[75]

Pleasantville, in addition to being the film's title, is the name of a black-and-white '50s sit-com airing on "TV Time," a channel devoted to airing old black-and-white shows. ("TV Time" is based on the real-life cable channel Nick-at-Nite.) David (Tobey Maguire) is a fan of the show. He and his sister Jennifer (Reese Witherspoon) are '90s teenagers, and she is more provocative than he is. Their

73 *Godzilla*, dir. Roland Emmerich, Columbia TriStar Home Video, 2006.

74 Chua-Eon 75, 76.

75 *Pleasantville*, dir. Gary Ross, New Line Home Video, 1999, "Director Commentary with Gary Ross."

divorced mother is driving off to see her boyfriend for the weekend. They get into an argument over the TV remote and destroy it just before a *Pleasantville* marathon begins and Jennifer's date is about to arrive. Miraculously, a repairman (Don Knotts) shows up. He and David trade *Pleasantville* trivia. Impressed, Knotts hands over a remote that, he says, has "a little more oomph in it," one "that'll put you right in the show." David and Jennifer immediately begin arguing again over the remote and she pushes a button on it, zapping them into the TV set just as the *Pleasantville* marathon begins; they enter the *Pleasantville* series itself. This "repair-man" had been looking for the right people to zap into the series.

Joan Allen and Tobey Maguire in *Pleasantville* (1998). Photo copyright: New Line Cinema.

Once in *Pleasantville*'s universe, David and Jennifer find their actions could upset this world, especially when Jennifer is reluctant to date the high school basketball captain. He misses hooking a basket, evidently the first time this has happened. When Jennifer asks what lies beyond Pleasantville's main street, the query astonishes her teacher. Library books have nothing printed on the inside pages, and nothing burns when a flame is applied to it.

Jennifer and David soon begin disrupting the ordered world of Pleasantville: Jennifer introduces Skip, the basketball team captain, to sex, something he knew nothing about. When David tells Jennifer she can't make love to a nonexistent person, he leaves Bill Johnson (Jeff Daniels), the soda jerk, to do things by him-self, something he's never done before without Bud (David), as if he depends on David for guidance. When Skip tells his teammates about what he and Jennifer did the night before, they fail to sink basketballs! Whenever something different happens to the residents of Pleasantville, shades of color enter their black-and-white world. The changes begin affecting the town elders as well: Bill becomes aware of a secret longing for Betty (Joan Allen), David and Jennifer's "mother" in the *Pleasantville* universe, as well as secret artistic ambitions he indulges in only once a year when he paints the soda shop for Christmas. Betty knows nothing about sex until Jennifer tells her. When her passion ignites a tree on their lawn, David rouses the fire department, showing them how to use their fire hoses to ex-tinguish the flames. When he becomes a town hero as a result of putting the fire out, the kids at the soda shop ask him how he knew how to do that. He replies that the firemen do that in his world. This leads to other questions: Where are you from? Why are the heretofore blank books filling up? Soon the new colored kids, repressed all their lives, are lining up at the library for books. The appear-ance of the "colored" people in Pleasantville displeases their elders. "Going up to that lake all the time is one thing," says one. "But now they're going to a library? What's next?" "You're right," observes another. "Somebody oughta do something about that." The final straw comes when real rain starts falling on the town. George (William H. Macy), Betty's husband, comes home to find her gone, and his dinner unprepared (Betty's with Bill, who is exploring his artistic yearnings, ultimately painting a nude picture of her). Another man wears a shirt with a burn mark from his wife's iron (she was standing there, thinking).

The Mayor of Pleasantville (J. T. Walsh) says it's "a question of values . . . that made this place great." A town meeting is called "to separate out the things that are pleasant from the things that are unpleasant." Soon signs reading "NO COL-OREDS" appear. An enraged mob smashes the picture of Betty's nude painting on the soda shop window, demolishes the soda shop, and burns library books in a bonfire reminiscent of book burnings by the Nazis and by overseas American libraries after two of Joseph McCarthy's aides, Roy Cohn and G. David Schine, toured the libraries in 1953 in search of subversive literature. (To curb the vandal-ism, a "code of conduct" is drawn up, Lovers Lane and the library are closed, and rock'n'roll music is prohibited.) When David and Bill paint a colored mural on a wall, they go on trial. Speaking in self defense, David points out that something inside you has to come out. When David asks the mayor if he really wants to punish him for disobeying the code of conduct, that is, doing what he really feels inside, the mayor turns color himself and rushes out of the "courtroom." (The "coloreds" are segregated in the top row of the courtroom). All the citizens of Pleasantville change color, as does the whole town itself. Jennifer decides to stay in Pleasantville for a time and go to college, while David returns to 1998. The film ends with George and Betty wondering what will happen next. Their safe and secure black-and-white world no longer exists. Then Bill replaces George next to Betty — implying that George may no longer be Betty's true love — another sign of the new world they now inhabit.[76]

David and Jennifer both introduce elements that radically change Pleasant-ville from an ordered, utopian society to one with knowledge and free choice and the consequences that come with that. It could be viewed as equivalent to Adam and Eve's expulsion from the Garden of Eden for acquiring forbidden knowledge. It can also be seen as a comment on feminism and gender-role reversal, as epito-

76 Ross.

mized by Betty's revolt against George, as opposed to '50s notions of men and women's roles. Pleasantville is also a microcosm of '50s America, and the changes that come to the town represent the turmoil and disruptions that followed in the '60s and ultimately culminated in the "culture war" raging in 1990s America when the film was released. The message of *Pleasantville* is that we should accept change; that the uncertainty, unpredictability, and disorder of life make it interesting; and that to resist it lowers one's humanity — a view similar to Don Siegel's notion of "pod humanity" expressed in *Invasion of the Body Snatchers*.

THE SEPTEMBER 11 ERA: RETURN OF THE B-MOVIES

The 1950s were the "golden age" of the B-movie–films that exploited the primal fears of their audience with sensational — and inexpensive — filmmaking. In the aftermath of this "golden age," the B-movie tradition continued, if less visibly. As we have seen, such '50s classics as *The Thing*, *Invasion of the Body Snatchers*, and *Invaders from Mars* were given A-level adaptations in the '70s and '80s. The immediate pre-9/11 era witnessed a revival of doomsday epics (*Deep Impact*, *Armageddon*) and the updating of the classic '50s monster Godzilla. What this signified was that what was once considered low-grade fare for baby-boomers, was now regarded by filmmakers — who matured watching such films — as classics. It could also be argued that such films provided an anchor of reassurance for the baby boom generation as it grew older in a more complex world — a link to what seemed a less complicated, more secure time.

That sense of security seemed even more urgent in the post-9/11 world. In the immediate aftermath of the 9/11 attacks, the B-movie genre received a new lease on life — this time with the finances and resources of major Hollywood studios backing them. Part of this is explained by the success of the *Lord of the Rings* films; the other by the fact that, for the first time since the Cold War, the notion of an attack on the United States itself was a very real possibility. Finally, there's an element of escape from the terrors of the time. "I think escapism is part of it," said Gregg Chabot, who, with Kevin Peterka, penned one of the films contributing to the B-movie revival, *Reign of Fire*. "Going back to our forebears who gathered round in times of drought and pestilence and told fantastical stories. Mankind has always been fascinated by death and rebirth and *Reign of Fire* is ultimately a reclamation movie."[77]

A 2002 release, *Reign of Fire* is set in the early twenty-first century, when a young boy named Quinn survives the reawakening of a race of dragons that had long slumbered and killed his mother. By AD 2020, the dragons, despite humanity's modern weapons, have decimated the world, leaving the now adult Quinn (Christian Bale) and a handful of survivors in a small community in England. The dragons now rule the world but are starving, and this makes them even more dangerous. They feed on the ash left over from the fires they start. When the crisis began, there were echoes of the Cold War: a national civil defense alert for those who could hear it; the use of nuclear weapons, only this time, instead of

---

77 Ian Nathan, "Invasion of the B-movies," www.timesonline.co.uk/article/0,,585-377799, 00.html, Accessed November 25, 2002.

the United States and Russia confronting each other, it's the whole world united against the dragon threat.

One day, a convoy of tanks arrives at the survivors' sanctuary bringing, as one of the characters says, the "only ... thing worse than a dragon — Americans." Their leader is Van Zan (Matthew McConaughey), who flew to England with his men in a National Guard plane and temporarily needs shelter. Initially, Quinn is reluctant to allow them in but relents. Van Zan is a dragon slayer, equipped with hi-tech weapons and a helicopter gunship. The two sides form an uneasy alliance. They down a female dragon. They theorize that female dragons produce eggs and perhaps only *one* male dragon has been fertilizing them. Van Zan's mission is to destroy the male dragon, hence destroying the entire species. He intends to go to London to do this. Quinn refuses his request for more men for this task. After a fight between Van Zan and Quinn, the former leaves with some of the latter's men. Van Zan's convoy is attacked and destroyed by the male dragon, which then decimates Quinn's castle sanctuary. The presence of children in Quinn's castle and their hiding during a dragon raid reminds one of civil defense-"duck-and-cover" days. After the dragon's final attack on the castle, the children recite a verse:

> "What do we do when we wake?/Keep both eyes on the sky. What do we do when we sleep?/Keep one eye on the sky. What do we do when we see him?/Dig hard, dig deep, run for shelter, and never ever look back/"

Taking place in the twenty-first century, as this film does, the dragons now signify the new terrorist threat — a long slumbering danger reawakened with greater force in the new century.

After Quinn's sanctuary is destroyed, Van Zan, his helicopter pilot, Alex, and Quinn fly to London, the dragons' lair, where they destroy the male dragon and lose Van Zan in the process. Alex and Quinn then set about creating a new sanctuary, presumably a new world.[78]

Reign of Fire is a "B" movie with "A" movie qualities. "It was the recipe of *Reign of Fire* that attracted me," recalls the film's director, Rob Bowman. "Tanks and castles, soldiers and dragons. That's kinda interesting, timeless. It's medieval and it's futuristic."[79] The dragons could be seen as the latter-day equivalent of Godzilla, a B-movie for the twenty-first century, with a gritty, dark tone and atmosphere.

Far closer in spirit to the films of the '50s, specifically the big bug films, was another Summer 2002 release, *Eight Legged Freaks*, produced by Dean Devlin and directed by Elloy Elkayem. The genesis of the film went back to 1988, when Elkayem made a short film in New Zealand, *Larger Than Life*, that was then spotted by a talent agent at the Telluride Film Festival. The agent arranged for Devlin and Roland Emmerich to see the film. "And that," Elkayem said, "was really the thing that sort of kicked it all off . . . I was just lucky enough that Roland and

---

78 *Reign of Fire*, dir. Rob Bowman, Buena Vista Home Entertainment Incorporated and Spyglass Entertainment, 2005.

79 Bowman, "Conversations with Rob Bowman."

Dean were big fans of these old '50s movies and had long dreamed of reviving that genre . . . "[80]

Reign of Fire (2002). Photo copyright: Buena Vista Pictures.

The film's star, David Arquette, was credited with providing the film's final title, *Eight Legged Freaks*, by accident. Originally, it was to be called "Arach-Attack," but was changed as the studio felt it sounded like "the name of a country under attack."[81] Set in the economically stricken community of Prosperity, Arizona, *Eight Legged Freaks* begins as the driver of a truck carrying barrels of toxic waste swerves to avoid hitting a rabbit. One of the barrels falls off the truck, landing in a river, leaking its contents into the water. The contaminated water then begins affecting crickets in the area. The crickets, in turn, are fed to the inhabitants of a local spider farm by the farm's owner, causing the spiders there to grow at an accelerated rate. One of the spiders escapes from its cage in a scene reminiscent of the tarantula's escape from Leo G. Carroll's lab in *Tarantula*. The newly freed spider kills the farm's owner. As the farmer tries to shake the spider loose, he knocks over the containers, breaking them open, and releases the other spiders. After killing the owner, the spiders leave webs all over the building. The spiders grow to a gigantic size, and escape into the

---

80 *Eight Legged Freaks*, dir. Ellory Elkayem, Warner Home Video, 2002, "Commentary."

81 Elkayem.

mine shafts under Prosperity. A small boy, Mike, the son of the town sheriff, Sam Parker (Kari Wurherer), discovers the truth but no one believes him. The spiders burrow under the town, devouring cats, dogs, and the mayor's ostriches.

Spiders in *Eight Legged Freaks* (2002). Photo copyright: Warner Bros./Village Roadshow.

From animals, the murderous arachnids begin preying on humans, beginning with the members of a motorcycle gang. When the spiders nab Chris McCormick's (David Arquette) Aunt Gladys, Chris rushes to the sheriff's residence to show Mike the remains of a giant spider's leg. While he's there, a spider attacks Sam's daughter in her bedroom. They all flee in Sam's deputy's car with the spiders in hot pursuit. A giant tarantula tries to topple a radio station that Sam uses to broadcast a warning message to the town. The spiders invade the town as the occupants of a local diner watch (similar to the cloud "blob" in *9-11*). The town's residents take shelter in the mall. The spiders eventually break into the mall, forcing everyone down into the mines, which are filled with methane gas; this makes it impossible for them to use guns, as they will ignite the gas. They also discover townspeople who've been wrapped up in "cocoons" by the spiders, presumably as food. Chris finds his Aunt Gladys in one such "cocoon" and frees her. The two of them hop on a motorcycle and ride out, but are chased by the spiders. David lights a match to ignite the gas in the mine. The cyclists manage to escape the mine as the fire engulfs the spiders, destroying the mall in the process. At the film's end, Chris discovers a mother lode of gold in the mines, which enables Prosperity's residents to return to work.[82]

According to Dean Devlin, *Eight Legged Freaks* was targeted for a specific audience and filmed quite rapidly, which he credited Elkayem with. This, Devlin says,

---

82 Elkayem.

"allowed the film to really be pure to what it is . . . a love-letter to the movies of the late '50s, early '60s."[83] This is clearly evidenced in one scene where footage of *Them!* is playing on the television in Mike's bedroom. When Mike tries once more to convince his mother of the giant spider menace, she marches over to the TV, points to it with *Them!* playing, and says, "This is exactly your problem . . . I don't want to hear any more of your media-induced, paranoid, delusional nightmares." Mike isn't the only one in the film having trouble getting people to believe him. When Chris climbs atop the mall tower to make a cell phone call for help, the 9-1-1 operator refuses to believe his story about giant spiders. Chris screams into the phone: "It's an invasion! They're here! They're here!" — a scene reminiscent of Kevin McCarthy's "You're next! You're next!" cry in the added-on finale of *Invasion of the Body Snatchers*.[84] Of all Devlin and Emmerich's films, *Eight Legged Freaks* is the closest in spirit to a '50s film, one that updates the big bug-mutation theme to the twenty-first century, replacing radiation with an ecological source as the cause of the monster threat.

Where *Reign of Fire* and *Eight Legged Freaks* directly showed audiences their monsters, *Signs*, also released that same summer, took a far subtler approach to its terror. Director M. Night Shyamalan learned an important rule of filmmaking, lost on the majority of his peers, observed *Newsweek*'s David Ansen: "It's what you *don't* see that makes a scary movie scary." Moreover, Shyamalan eschewed the splashy, overpowering filmmaking style, the standard of the day, in favor of character development to draw the audience into the film.[85] The basis for the film was Shyamalan's fascination with crop circles. From there, the style of the film was influenced by three cinema classics: Alfred Hitchcock's *The Birds* (a supernatural event occurs without explanation); *Night of the Living Dead* (the event then moves to a house, where people hold off against the threat); and *Invasion of the Body Snatchers* ("subtle but powerful suspense").[86]

The filming of *Signs* commenced under dramatic circumstances. "The day before we started filming was the day after September 11 (2001)," Shyamalan recalled. "And so we and the world were all dealing with (the) repercussions of that event, and also that we were starting with something important." Shyamalan hadn't worked with *Signs*'s star Mel Gibson before and wanted to film the scene where Graham (Gibson's character) sees his wife for the final time before she dies "to break the ice right away"; he also wanted to film an important scene the first day. When the scene was filmed on location in a forest, the film crew held a candle-light vigil prior to shooting. He said:

> "We were all crying . . . before we even started rolling, on a scene where we were doing basically a man and woman's last conversation to each other before she dies. So it was charged. The air was super-charged. And then Mel Gibson

83 Elkayem, "Commentary."

84 Elkayem.

85 David Ansen, "Families, Fear and Faith," *Newsweek* 5 August 2002: 53.

86 *Signs*, dir. M. Night Shyamalan, Touchstone Home Entertainment, 2003, "Looking for Signs."

comes to the set, and he's in his priest outfit for the first time. And when I'm an old man, I'll probably remember that day as a big day."[87]

Like one of its influences, *Invasion of the Body Snatchers*, *Signs* deals with ordinary people in an ordinary setting, in this instance, the Hess family who reside in a Pennsylvania farmhouse. In the words of the film's production designer, Larry Fulton, it was "an American farmhouse . . . a Victorian one that would be as comfortable here (Bucks County, Pennsylvania) as it would be in the Midwest. It's sort of an iconic American farmhouse . . . when you look at it very long, you see its shades of red, white, and blue. The metaphor there is that this house, standing here, is America, and it's standing alone in the middle of this field. It's strongest protection is what that family shares with each other."[88]

The film's central character, Graham Hess (Gibson), a former clergyman, awakens one morning with his brother Merrill (Joaquin Phoenix) to find his children in the crop on his farm. The children have made a discovery of their own — crop circles in the field. Later, when the children try to give their pet dog water, the canine snarls, refusing to drink it. Graham's daughter earlier believed the water was contaminated. Her brother says she's had a thing about contaminated water all her life. Graham renounced the clergy after his wife died in a car crash, an event that caused him to lose his faith. The Hess family dog isn't the only animal acting up. Other animals in the area have been acting edgy, as if they sense a predator. The Hess children's dog attacks daughter Bo (Abigail Breslin), forcing her brother Morgan (Rory Culkin) to kill the animal.

The crop circles begin appearing elsewhere — in India, in England. Morgan uses his sister's baby monitor to pick up signals (he says comes from space) of the aliens talking to each other. Later, while checking a disturbance in the cornfield, Graham catches a fleeting glimpse of what appears to be a green leg! Then the news reports that strange lights have appeared over Mexico City. The children begin wearing tin foil caps over their heads to prevent the aliens from reading their minds. Graham then gets a call from a neighbor, Ray Reddy (director Shyamalan appearing in his film à la Alfred Hitchcock), who is moving out of his house to the lake — his theory being that the aliens don't like water. Before Reddy moves, he tells Graham he was the one who killed his (Graham's) wife when he fell asleep at the wheel that night. He also tells Graham he's locked one of the aliens in his pantry at home. Back at the Hess residence, Merrill is shocked to see footage of a thin, green-skinned alien, taken at a children's birthday party in Brazil; this image prompts him to start wearing the same tin foil head cover the Hess children wear. At Reddy's place, Graham discovers a strange hand coming out of the pantry and cuts its fingers with a kitchen knife; the creature, whose fingers have been severed, screams.

The lights appear elsewhere around the world, using the crop circles as a means of navigation. "It's like *War of the Worlds*," says Merrill. Military forces have been assembled to meet the potential invaders, while houses of worship are

---

87 Shyamalan, "Making *Signs*: A Commentary by M. Night Shyamalan."

88 Shyamalan, "Building *Signs*."

crowded. The Hess family turns their home into a sanctuary and boards up doors and windows. When the invaders arrive, they take refuge in the basement. The scene is reminiscent of a family hiding in a basement or fallout shelter awaiting a nuclear attack. Ultimately, the family emerges when Morgan's asthma worsens — they need to give him medicine. Television news reports that the aliens were defeated in the Middle East. Not every alien though. The one Graham severed the fingers of is in the Hess's residence holding Morgan in his arms and threatens to release poison gas. Merrill slugs the invader with a baseball bat, spilling water on him, and confirms the theory that the aliens are afraid of water. Graham, meanwhile, rushes Morgan outside to give him his asthma medicine. He suddenly realizes the alien gas couldn't reach Morgan's lungs as they were closed, due to the asthma. Morgan lives, and Graham regains his lost faith in God. *[89]

The post-9/11 era also witnessed the updating of another '50s sci-fi classic: Steven Spielberg's 2005 remake of *War of the Worlds*. The new version shifts the action to the Eastern Seaboard, more in line with Orson Welles' legendary 1938 radio adaptation that persuaded many listeners that the Martian "invasion" they were hearing was real — a result of the recent war scare in Europe. Unlike George Pal's Martians, who came to Earth because their home planet was dying, the origin of Spielberg's invaders is never mentioned; nor are their motivations for conquering Earth made clear, only that their objective is humanity's annihilation. Spielberg merely speculates that they originated as far away as E.T. did, but, compared with E.T., they're from "a darker part of the universe." The film's star, Tom Cruise, characterizes them as E.T. "gone bad ... rogue."[90]

The film opens much the same as the 1953 version did: human beings routinely conduct their daily affairs, unaware that disaster looms. The film's central character Ray (Cruise), a blue-collar laborer, is looking after his son and daughter while his ex-wife and her boyfriend go off to her parents' residence in Boston for the weekend. In the background, news reports tell of unusual and catastrophic lightning storms at home and abroad, followed by seismic activity measuring 6.5 on the Richter scale.

The freak occurrences reach Ray's neighborhood, accompanied by the malfunctioning of all electrical appliances. Added to all this, the lightning accompanying the storm has burned a hole in the street. The latter then begins splitting apart, disgorging the aliens' three-legged machine — a walking tripod tank that proceeds to decimate all those in its path. (We subsequently learn that the tripods were already buried underground, symbolizing the terrorist threat among

---

89 Shyamalan. Recalling the final scene, Shyamalan said, "I saw this kind of Norman Rockwell opening and closing of the perfect backyard with the swing and the crops in the corner. Everything's perfect — the American ideal. And, at the end of the movie, the American ideal has changed a little because it's shattered glass (the shattered glass the camera focuses through, showing the Hess family after both Morgan is saved and the alien crisis has passed) but it's still beautiful." Shyamalan's altered American ideal could also symbolize America in the post-September 11 world. Shyamalan, "Making *Signs*: A Commentary by M. Night Shyamalan."

90 "Designing the Enemy: Tripods and Aliens," *War of the Worlds*, dir. Steven Spielberg, DreamWorks Home Entertainment, 2005.

us; the lightening bolts deposited capsules bearing the aliens into the subterranean machines.) The concept of the aliens emerging from underground originated with Spielberg as it deviated from the usual alien habit of descending from space.[91]

Ray returns home from the assault covered by dust, reminiscent of the people fleeing the dust cloud from the collapsing World Trade Center on September 11. He and his children abandon Ray's house just as the alien onslaught resumes.

"Is it the terrorists?" his daughter Rachel asks.
"No," Ray replies, "this came from someplace else."

Tom Cruise in *War of the Worlds* (2005). Photo copyright: Paramount Pictures Photographer: Frank Masi.

The trio takes refuge in Ray's wife's house, ultimately seeking shelter in the basement; while there, a plane crashes into the residence. From there, the trio sets out for Boston, along the way encountering dead bodies floating in a river, desperate mobs, and fellow refugees. Linking up with the latter, they find themselves in the midst of a battle between the military and the invaders. Ray's son, Robbie, rushes off to join the battle and is presumably killed in action.

Commenting on the "refugee scenes," Spielberg, who says that, pre-9/11, he would have made this film as a traditional Hollywood "rock 'em, sock 'em" film, explains: "My movie is more about the American refugee experience — something that you never hear — American and refugee — in the same sentence because my movie is what happens when Americans are put on the run and we all are mi-

---

91 Spielberg, *War of the Worlds*.

grating away from the danger zones where the aliens are attacking — heading away from the Eastern Seaboard. That's an image that is evocative for me and my generation post 9/11." In this, Spielberg was influenced by documentaries about World War II: "It's very evocative watching those black-and-white documentaries showing Parisians, who lived a good life, heading out of Paris with ox carts and all their worldly possessions .... long queues, miles long, on both sides of the road .... I really feel that I've tried to bring a little of that to *War of the Worlds*.[92]

Ray and Rachel are taken in by a survivalist whose mental condition progressively deteriorates. In a scene reminiscent of the farmhouse sequence in George Pal's film, the aliens dispatch a probe into the cellar, winding, snake-like, searching for humans. This is followed by the aliens themselves, no doubt curious about who dwells here. (Spielberg's aliens somewhat resemble the invaders of *Independence Day*.) Upon seeing the aliens draw blood from their human victims, the survivalist completely snaps. He begins digging a tunnel to the subway, talking of establishing a resistance force there. Ray is forced to overcome him to protect Rachel.

When the alien scanner returns, a frightened Rachel flees from the house. Chasing after her, Ray discovers the invaders have terra-formed the countryside to resemble their home world — taking a cue from H.G. Wells' book.[93] The aliens, who have already captured Rachel, ultimately seize her father, depositing him with her and the other imprisoned humans in their tripod. The humans, once they're inside the alien vessel, are digested by it. The humans free a man about to be consumed, causing the tripod to crash, freeing Ray, Rachel, and their fellow captives.

Reaching Boston, Ray and Rachel discover the aliens are dying and their machines are crashing. Emblematic of the attempted alien takeover of Earth (and, by implication, the Islamic terrorist threat to America) is the scene of the Minuteman statue in Boston, symbolic of America's own struggle for independence, entwined by the alien vegetation, only by now dying along with the aliens themselves.[94] The scenes of street fighting in Boston bring to mind the street battles then being waged in Iraq. Ray and Rachel reach the latter's mother at their grandparents' residence — the grandparents being played by Gene Barry and Ann Robinson in cameo appearances. Moreover, they find Robbie there — alive and well. Once more, an alien invasion has been thwarted by the "tiny things that God, in His wisdom, had placed on Earth."[95]

As we come to the end of this book, the War on Terrorism is still being waged, with the final outcome unforeseeable. The Cold War, which inspired the science fiction films of the 1950s, is over, with the United States declared triumphant over Soviet communism. At the time they were made, these films no doubt made

92 *Watch the Skies! Science Fiction, the 1950s and U.S.*, dir. Richard Schickel, Turner Classic Movies, 2005.

93 Schickel, *Watch the Skies*.

94 Spielberg, *War of the Worlds*, "Designing the Enemy: Tripods and Aliens."

95 Spielberg, *War of the Worlds*.

moviegoers cringe in fright. With the passage of time, what used to look frighten-ing has come to seem reassuring, even comforting. Fifties sci-fi found a new out-let on home video and DVD, and the pictures are being remade as major motion pictures by major movie studios. Beverly Garland feels that films made during a frightening era can later become treasured mementoes because "People long to see again the things that brought them comfort, joy, and entertainment from a simpler time in their lives."[96]

Half a century afterward, the terrors of the '50s look less frightening than today's troubles. Monster films and fallout shelters have taken on a nostalgic air. One reason for '50s nostalgia is that, compared with the '60s and '70s, the '50s looked calmer. Moreover, compared with the "culture war" of today, the '50s was an age of consensus, when Americans seemed to universally believe in and trust their government. Faced with an apparent communist threat, it was natural to feel a sense of national unity.

Movies as entertainment were already well established by the time the Cold War rolled around. They had already seen Americans through other, immediate crises — the Great Depression and World War II. Another entertainment me-dium, television, arrived on the scene during the Cold War. Now, as the twenty-first century dawns and wars are being waged in many parts of the globe, an-other medium, the Internet, is in its early stages. Whatever the time, or the crisis, people turn to their popular culture for relief. Beverly Garland notes:

> "In troubled times … more people look for escapist entertainment. It can be a form of therapy, really, or so I'm told. September 11th was a terrible tragedy, but we don't need terrible tragedies to need or desire an escape. For many people, just getting home after a long day at work sends them searching for anything that will take their minds off of the stresses of the day. There are audiences for all kinds of movies now. They don't all have to be good movies, they just have to be marketed effectively to their target audiences. Thankfully, there is a lot of great work being done today at all levels, including the low budget, independent route."

Garland further says:

> "The world doesn't change, only people do. There will always be events to fear, but there are also the great accomplishments that we should celebrate. It's about having and maintaining a realistic and balanced view of the world from our own individual perspectives."[97]

In some respects, the world has changed in the last 50 years. In addition to the advent of the Internet, movies have evolved to computer-generated special effects, allowing images undreamed of half a century ago. Television, too, has grown from a mere three broadcasting networks to numerous, 24-hour cable channels, offering more choices and programming to viewers. America no longer sees Communism as its primary enemy; now it is Islamic terrorism. What hasn't changed is people's need to be entertained. Whatever the era, movies do just that.

---

96 Matthews, e-mail.

97 Matthews, e-mail.

The monsters of the '50s — be they The Thing, the Martians, the emotionless "pod people," the giant ants of *Them!*, Godzilla — were icons of that age. Their influence on films today continues to be felt. Doubtless, the Age of Terrorism will produce its own distinctive brand of monsters. Whatever the age, whatever the "outside menace" that drives disparate (and desperate) Americans to circle the wagon train and join together — there will always be monsters to face, as well.

Bibliography

Films

Action! American Movie Classics, Prometheus Entertainment and Foxstar Productions in association with Fox Television Studios and AMC, 2003.

America 911: We Will Never Forget, Michael Rosenbaum, Prod. Spectrum Films, Camera Planet.com, 2004.

Armageddon. Dir. Michael Bay. Touchstone Home Video, 1998.

Day the World Ended. Dir. Roger Corman. Columbia TriStar Home Video, 1993.

Deep Impact. Dir. Mimi Leder. Paramount Home Video, Dream Works, SKG, 1998.

Eight Legged Freaks. Dir. Ellory Elkayem. Warner Home Video, 2002.

E.T.: The Extraterrestrial Two-Disc Limited. Dir. Steven Spielberg. Universal Studios, Inc., 2002.

Godzilla. [Gojira,] Original Japanese version. Dir. Ishiro Honda. Toho Video, 1954.

Godzilla. Dir. Roland Emmerich. Columbia Tri-Star Home Video, 2006.

Independence Day: Five Star Collection. Dir. Roland Emmerich. 20th Century Fox Home Entertainment, 2000.

It Came from Outer Space. Dir. Jack Arnold. Universal Studios, 2002.

It Conquered the World. Dir. Roger Corman. RCA/Columbia Pictures Home Video, 1991.

Invaders from Mars. Dir. Tobe Hooper. Media Home Entertainment, Inc., 1986.

Invaders from Mars. Dir. William Cameron Menzies. Image Entertainment, 2002.

Invasion of the Body Snatchers. Dir. Don Siegel. Republic Entertainment, 1955.

Invasion of the Body Snatchers. Dir. Philip Kaufman. MGM/UA Home Video, 1990.

Mars Attacks! Dir. Tim Burton. Warner Home Video, 2004.

Matinee. Dir. Joe Dante. MCA Universal Home Video, 1993.

Pleasantville. Dir. Gary Ross. New Line Home Video, 1999.

Reign of Fire. Dir. Rob Bowman. Buena Vista Home Entertainment Incorporated and Spyglass Entertainment, 2002.

Signs. Dir. M. Night Shyamalan. Touchstone Home Entertainment, 2003.

The Amazing Colossal Man. Dir. Bert I. Gordon. Columbia TriStar Home Video, 1992.

The Beast from 20,000 Fathoms. Dir. Eugene Lourie. Warner Home Video, 1991.

The Day the Earth Stood Still. Dir. Robert Wise. Twentieth Century Fox Home Entertainment, Inc., Fox Video, 1998.

The Fantasy Film Worlds of George Pal. Dir. Arnold Leibovit. Arnold Leibovit Productions, Ltd., 1985.

The Incredible Shrinking Man. Dir. Jack Arnold. MCA Home Video, Inc., 1988.

The Incredible Shrinking Woman. Dir. Eisha Marjara. Universal Pictures, 1981.

The Thing. Dir. John Carpenter. Universal Home Video, 1998.

The Thing from Another World. Dir. Christian Nyby. Warner Home Video, 2003.

The War of the Worlds. Dir. Byron Haskin. Paramount Pictures, 1999.

The War of the Worlds (Special Collector's Edition). Dir. Byron Haskin. Paramount Pictures, 2005.

Them! Dir. Gordon Douglas. Warner Home Video, 2002.

This Island Earth. Dir. Joseph F. Newman. MCA Home Video, Inc., 1993.

War of the Worlds. Dir. Steven Spielberg. DreamWorks Home Entertainment, 2005).

Watch the Skies! Science Fiction, the 1950s and Us. Dir. Richard Schickel. Turner Classic Movies, 2005.

When Worlds Collide. Dir. Rudolph Mate. Paramount Pictures, 2001.

Articles

Ansen, David, Corie Brown. "Demolition Man," *Newsweek* 6 July 1998: 65.

——, "Families, Fear and Faith," *Newsweek* 5 Aug. 2002: 53.

——, "Flower Power." *Newsweek* 18 Dec. 1978: 85.

——, "Frozen Slime." *Newsweek* 28 June 1982: 73.

Brown, Patricia Leigh. "Armageddon Again: Fear in the 50's and Now." *The New York Times* 23 Dec. 2001: 10.

Cloud, John, "Meet the Prophet." *Time* 1 July 2002: 50-51.

Corliss, Richard. "The Invasion Has Begun!" *Time* 8 July 1996: 60, 64.

Chua-Eon, Howard. "What in the Name of Godzilla. . . ?" *Time* 25 May 1998: 75-76.

Gabler, Neil. "This Time, the Scene Was Real." *The New York Times* 16 Sept. 2001: 4-2.

Gibbs, Nancy, "Apocalypse Now." *Time* 1 July 2002: 42, 44-47.

Marin, Rick, Adam Rogers and T. Trent Gegax. "Alien Invasion!" *Newsweek* 8 July1996: 50, 52.

Mintz, Steven, "Addressing Tragedy in the Classroom," Hnet, *www.2.h-* net.msu.edu/teaching/journals/septll/mintz/teaching.html. 20 Oct. 2002

Nathan, Ian, "Invasion of the B-movies," *The Times Online.* http://www.timesonline.co.uk 25 Nov. 2002.

Pipes, Daniel, "Distinguishing between Islam and Islamism." www.danielpipes.org. 27 July 2003.

Schickel, Richard. "Armageddon: Insubstantial Impact." *Time* 6 July 1988: 88.

———, "A Sober Start to Summer Fun." *Time* 11 May 1998: 75.

———, "It Came from Inner Space." *Time* 8 Feb. 1993: 78.

BOOKS

Arness, James with James E. Wise, Jr. *James Arness: An Autobiography.* Jefferson: McFarland & Company, Inc., 2001.

Barnet, Richard J. *The Rockets' Red Glare: When America Goes to War. The Presidents and the People.* New York: Simon and Schuster, 1990.

Biskind, Peter. *Seeing Is Believing: How Hollywood Taught Us to Stop Worrying and Love the Fifties.* New York: Pantheon Books, 1983.

Blair, Clay. *The Forgotten War: America in Korea 1950-1953.* New York: Times Books, 1987.

Brode, Douglas. *The Films of the Fifties.* Secaucus: The Citadel Press, 1976.

———, *Lost Films of the Fifties.* Secaucus: Citadel Press, 1988.

———, *The Films of Steven Spielberg.* Secaucus: The Citadel Press, 1995.

Brosnan, John. *Future Tense: The Cinema of Science Fiction.* New York: St. Martin's, 1978.

Carroll, Peter M. *It Seemed Like Nothing Happened: The Tragedy and Promise of America in the 1970s.* New York: Holt, Rinehart and Winston, 1984.

Caufield, Catherine. *Multiple Exposures: Chronicles of the Radiation Age.* New York: Harper & Row, 1989.

Clarens, Carlos. *An Illustrated History of the Horror Film.* New York: Capricorn Books, 1968.

Fischer, Dennis. *Science Fiction Film Directors, 1895-1998.* Jefferson: McFarland & Company, Inc., 2000.

Fried, Richard M. *Nightmare in Red: The McCarthy Era in Perspective.* New York: Oxford UP, 1990.

Galbraith IV, Stuart. *Japanese Science Fiction, Fantasy and Horror Films: A Critical Analysis of 103 Features Released in the United States, 1950-1992.* Jefferson: McFarland & Company, Inc., 1994.

———, *Monsters Are Attacking Tokyo! The Incredible World of Japanese Fantasy Films*. Venice: Feral House, 1998.

Halberstam, David. *The Fifties*. New York: Villard Books, 1993.

Hastings, Max. *The Korean War*. New York: Simon and Schuster, 1987.

Hine, Thomas. *Populuxe*. New York: Alfred A. Knopf, 1986.

Hogan, Ron. *The Stewardess Is Flying the Plane! American Films of the 1970s*. New York: Bulfinch Press, 2005.

Johnson, John J. J. *Cheap Tricks and Class Acts: Special Effects, Makeup and Stunts from the Films of the Fantastic Fifties*. Jefferson: McFarland & Company, Inc., 1996.

Kalat, David. *A Critical History and Filmography of Toho's Godzilla Series*. Jefferson: McFarland & Company, Inc., 1997.

Lees, J. D. and Marc Cerasini. *The Official Godzilla Compendium*. New York: Random House, 1998.

Miller, Douglas T. and Marion Nowak. *The Fifties: The Way We Really Were*. Garden City: Doubleday & Company, 1977.

Muir, John Kenneth. *The Films of John Carpenter*. Jefferson: McFarland & Company, Inc., 2000.

Newman, Kim. *Apocalypse Movies: End of the World Cinema*. New York: St. Martin's, 2000.

Oakley, J. Ronald. *God's Country: America in the Fifties*. New York: Dembner Books, 1986.

O'Connor, John E. and Martin A. Johnson, eds. *American History/American Film: Interpreting the Hollywood Image*. New York: Frederick Ungar, 1979.

Panshin, Alexei and Cory. *The World Beyond the Hill: Science Fiction and the Quest for Transcendence*. Los Angeles: Jeremy P. Tarcher, Inc., 1989.

Parla, Paul and Charles P. Mitchell. *Screen Sirens Scream! Interviews with 20 Actresses from Science Fiction, Horror, Film Noir and Mystery Movies, 1930s to 1960s*. Jefferson: McFarland & Company, Inc, 2000.

Patterson, James T. *Grand Expectations: The United States, 1945-1974*. New York: Oxford UP, 1996.

Perret, Geoffrey. *A Dream of Greatness: The American People, 1945-1963*. New York: Coward, McCann & Geoghegan, 1979.

Ryfle, Steve. *Japan's Favorite Mon-star: The Unauthorized Biography of "The Big G."* Toronto ECW Press, 1998.

Sayre, Nora. *Running Time: Films of the Cold War*. New York: The Dial Press, 1982.

Skal, David J. *The Monster Show: A Cultural History of Horror*. New York: W. W. Norton & Company, 1993.

———, *Screams of Reason: Mad Science and Modern Culture*. New York: W. W. Norton & Company, 1998.

Steinbrunner, Chris and Burt Goldblatt. *Cinema of the Fantastic*. New York: Galahad Books, 1972.

The Editors of Time-Life Books. *This Fabulous Century. Volume VI: 1950-1960.* New York: Time-Life Books, 1970.

———, *Mysteries of the Unknown: The UFO Phenomenon.* Alexandria: Time-Life Books, 1987.

Vance, Malcolm. *The Movie Ad Book.* Minneapolis: Control Data Publishing, 1981.

Vieira, Mark A. *Hollywood Horror: From Gothic to Cosmic.* New York: Harry N. Abrams, Inc., 2003.

Von Gunden, Kenneth and Stuart H. Stock. *Twenty All-Time Great Science Fiction Films.* New York: Arlington House, 1982.

Warren, Bill. *Keep Watching the Skies! American Science Fiction Movies of the Fifties.* Volume I: 1950-1957. Jefferson: McFarland & Company, Inc., 1982.

Weaver, Tom. *Attack of the Monster Movie Makers: Interviews with 20 Genre Giants.* Jefferson: McFarland & Company, Inc., 1994.

———, *I Was a Monster Movie Maker: Conversations with 22 SF and Horror Filmmakers.* Jefferson: McFarland & Company, Inc., 2001.

———, *Interviews with B Science Fiction and Horror Movie Makers.* Jefferson: McFarland & Company, Inc., 1988.

———, *It Came from Weaver Five.* Jefferson: McFarland & Company, Inc., 1996.

———, *Monsters, Mutants and Heavenly Creatures: Confessions of 14 Classic Sci-Fi/Horrormeisters!* Baltimore: Midnight Marquee, 1996.

Zinman, David. *50 from the 50s: Vintage Films from America's Mid-Century.* New Rochelle: Arlington House, 1979.

INDEX